Other books by the Author:

Harry Reunited (novel)
A Walk Through Fire (novel)
The Hermit King and New Stories (Novel & stories)
Coming of Age at the Y (novel)
A Spring of Souls (novel)
Wings of Morning (novel)
Somewhere in All This Green (stories)
The Last Queen of the Gypsies (novel)
A Time To Reap (novel)
Captain Billy's Troopers (memoir)
Sweet Home: Stories of Alabama (stories)

POMP

AND

CIRCUMSTANCE

William Cobb

Livingston Press

at

The University of West Alabama

UWA
The UNIVERSITY of
WEST ALABAMA

ISBN 13: 978-1-60489-202-4, trade paper
ISBN 13: 978-1-60489-203-1, hardcover
ISBN: 1-60489-202-1, trade paper
ISBN: 1-60489-203-X hardcover
Library of Congress Control Number: 2018931299
Printed on acid-free paper
by Publishers Graphics
Printed in the United States of America
Published in Livingston, Alabama

Hardcover binding by: HF Group
Typesetting and page layout: Sarah Coffey
Proofreading: Shelby Parrish, Erin Watt, Tricia Taylor,
Daniel Butler, Nick Noland
Cover design and layout: Amanda Nolin
Cover photo: Amanda Nolin

Livingston Press is part of The University of West Alabama,
and thereby has non-profit status.
Donations are tax-deductible:
brothers and sisters, we need 'em.

POMP AND CIRCUMSTANCE

SAPIENTIA:
Latin,
Wisdom, expertise, intellectual accomplishment

For Norman and Joan McMillan

A sense of humor is a glorious thing.

ONE

The first time Lily Putnam had seen the campus of Lakewood College with its old red brick buildings and captivating brick sidewalks was when she had come for her interview. It was like something out of another time, like a staged setting for a movie about college life, with its stately oak and elm trees and well-tended sward. It was exactly the place that Lily had dreamed of spending her academic life, quiet and contemplative, teeming with the beauty of years of intellectual pursuits, a symbol of the best that life had to offer.

Her roommate Sylvia Birch had expressed surprise that Lily had even applied to Lakewood. "It's Podunk U," she'd said, "stuck off down there in the sandy Florida panhandle, miles from anywhere."

"It's forty miles from Tallahassee," Lily had said.

"Well, whoop de do! That ain't Atlanta," Sylvia had said.

Lily had completed her course work for a PhD in American Literature at Emory University and had begun her dissertation on Toni Morrison. She was weary of the routine of classes and bored with her fellow graduate students and anxious to begin her teaching career. There was an opening in the English department at Lakewood, and Lily had applied.

"I've never heard of it," her major professor, Ralph Davidson Swanzy, said. He had edited a widely used anthology of American short stories. "But I'll certainly write you a glowing recommendation. Maybe, when you get down there, you can get them to adopt my textbook."

"I surely will," Lily said.

Her roommate Sylvia was skeptical. "I don't see why you're so anxious to run off and start teaching," she said, "you can get a teaching fellowship here while you write. And it's Hotlanta!"

"I'm tired of Atlanta," Lily said. "I'm tired of all the slobbering graduate students and young faculty members trying to get in my pants."

"I've told you before. It's the way you dress."

"It's the way I *look*," Lily said. "I don't want to be a sex object."

"Oh, I should be so lucky," Sylvia said.

"Besides, I dress the way I want to dress, the way that pleases me," Lily said. "Why should I have to pay because men can't handle it?" Lily was fond of miniskirts, the more micro the better, and tight blouses. She was proud of her figure, which she had been told since she was thirteen years old was perfect.

Lily came from a little hick town called Gilbertown, in the red clay hills of south Alabama. She had spent her high school years fending off eager boys and yearning to get away for good. She had done her undergraduate work at Birmingham-Southern College and had gone on to graduate study at Emory. Now she was ready to begin her life in earnest.

Lily had spent the night in the guest house on campus, and she was now walking over to Comer Hall for her interview with Rufus Doublet, the chairman of the English department. She had met Dr. Doublet the day before, when he had picked her up at the airport in Tallahassee after her short flight from Atlanta. He had rambled on and on during the drive out to Lakewood, and Lily remembered very little of what he had said. She was so excited and nervous. Rufus Doublet—he pronounced his name Doob-lay—was handsome, in an aging frat boy kind of way, probably in his late forties, and spoke in a soft, almost affected Southern accent. He wore a gray tweed sport jacket with a meticulously knotted knit tie and a button down, oxford cloth shirt. Lily recognized it as the uniform of the male college professor. He dressed exactly as her professors at Emory had dressed.

He told her all about the school, but she retained very little. If she got the job, she would have time for all that. She walked across the enchanting campus, pausing at the corner of the quad. Doublet had driven her around, giving her a quick tour of the campus before dropping her off at the guest house, a curiously antiquated brick cottage square in the middle of the campus, across from the library. She was careful on the brick sidewalk, because of her high heels; Dr. Doublet had warned her about that. "Don't turn one of those beautiful ankles," he had said, with a syrupy smile. She stood looking out across the quad; it could not have been more perfect. Across the way was Peterson Hall, a small, two story building with a charming cupola. Dr. Doublet had told her it housed the president's office and his staff. "It used to be the music building," he had said, "until we built the new music building. When I first came here, as a young instructor, back during the Punic Wars, ha ha ha, I would walk on the quad at night and hear piano students practicing. Their delightful music would roll, from the open windows, gracefully across the quad. It was lovely and beguiling." Lily was impressed.

She sat in Dr. Doublet's office, nervously twisting a tissue in her fingers, as he rattled on about the details of the job. She would teach twelve hours each semester, three freshmen sections and a sophomore world lit survey.

"I had hoped to teach more literature," Lily said.

"Well, upper division courses are taught exclusively by senior professors," he said. "Eleanor Bufkin, our American lit scholar, has been here since ... since ..."

"The Punic Wars?" Lily asked.

"Oh?" He chortled. Then he whispered, "Don't let *her* hear you say that!" He smiled his winsome antebellum smile.

"Yes sir," she said.

"Of course the world lit survey gives you a chance to spread your wings. There is some substantive literature there. The best of the west, as they say." He chuckled.

Was he as jittery as she was? She realized, of course, that it was her countenance, her looks. Her *image*. She had chosen a skirt that was not quite so micro, but she had still noticed him focusing on her legs. When he looked her in the face his eyes lingered for just a fraction of a second on her breasts. Had she expected that department chairmen would not, after all, be male?

"Yes, that'll be nice. I'll enjoy that," she said.

"The starting salary for an instructor," he continued, "will be $12,000 a year. It will be a one-year appointment, renewable each year, until such time as you're placed in the tenure track and become eligible for promotion. That is, should you be offered the job. And should you take it." The smile again. "I certainly hope you will give it serious consideration, Miss Putnam. You are the type of young person I want to work for me. Your recommendations are excellent, and you are a winsome young woman." Winsome? "I must tell you—and I will deny it if you ever repeat it—ha ha ha, that your interviews with Dean Wallace and President Steagall will be mostly mere formalities. They are very busy men."

"Yes, sir," Lily said.

It turned out that Dean Wallace was in a meeting and Dr. Steagall was out of town, so those interviews were canceled. Lily was horrified. She almost cried.

"Don't worry about it, Miss Putnam," Dr. Doublet said as he drove her back to the airport. "These things happen. I can assure you, though, that my recommendation carries the day, and I want to offer you the job. Does that make you feel better?"

"Do you mean you're offering me the job?" Lily asked tremulously.

"No. Actually, *I* can't offer you the job. That'll have to come from higher up. But I can tell you, confidentially, of course, that you are one of only two applicants for the job. So ..."

"You mean only two people applied?"

"Well, no. And this is off the record, you understand. We got a bunch of letters and resumes, which were so awful we threw them in the waste can."

"You didn't reply to them?" Lily asked, shocked.

"You wouldn't believe how crude and illiterate most of them were, Miss Putnam. They didn't get beyond the first glance. But yours stood out. Yours jumped up and grabbed me by the throat."

"You're shitting me—I mean," Lily caught herself, "I mean you're kidding me."

"No," he said, "I'm not ... kidding you, Miss Putnam."

He dropped her off at the airport and two weeks later the letter came offering her the job of Instructor in the English Department of Lakewood College. The letter came from the president on college letterhead, on lavender paper, with the college seal: a lamp of learning with the college motto. *Sapientia.*

TWO

Willow Behn watched the younger woman walk down the hall to her office. The walls of the hallway, painted a pale institutional green, were over-lighted by the harsh fluorescent bulbs overhead, giving the space an eerie, noxious brightness. The younger woman, Lily Putnam, wore a black mini skirt and boots—a micro mini, Willow thought, the very definition of one—her blonde hair cropped close in a style of which Willow did not wholly disapprove. It was radical, almost masculine, but Lily Putnam was anything but masculine; she was curvaceous and kittenish—her hips undulated sensually beneath the tight black cloth as she walked away— one year out of graduate school, an ABD from Emory, with a half-finished dissertation on Toni Morrison that Willow predicted to herself would never be finished, varied excuses piling up spring after spring as Lily Putnam vainly came up for promotion and tenure, assuming Lily made it past her initial one year appointment. Willow had been the lone dissenting vote in the younger woman's hiring. A vote she had found difficult to defend. She had realized she couldn't come right out and say she mistrusted the girl because she was pretty and attractive, but nonetheless, that's how she felt. She didn't trust her. The girl was lying when she insisted she'd finish her degree by the end of the academic year. Willow could tell.

Willow had been at Lakewood College for twenty-two years, since just before it went coed. Up until the mid-fifties it had been Florida College for Women; with the advent of men students it became Lakewood College, The State College of the Liberal Arts. (It was located in the small panhandle town of Lakewood, the highest point in the notoriously flat state. The hill was little more than a bump. The school, begun as Florida Industrial Institute for Women, had been founded in 1881, teaching such courses as sewing, butter making, cooking, and inscribing, a quaintly odd way of describing the handwriting arts.) As a girls' school the enrollment had shrunk to nearly 500 students, so the legislature had made it coed, with the first male students living in a hideous new dorm directly across the quad from Main Hall, the huge women's dorm that was actually three buildings tied together, three buildings that had been built in different decades and different styles, so that Corinthian columns stood side by side with Doric and Italian. The facade of Main Hall was covered in wisteria and smilax and formed a cool and somewhat private front stone porch complete with overlarge rocking chairs. The porch was called "The Loafing Porch."

The new men's dorm, Woodfin Hall, named for a turn-of-the-century professor of history who had been the first male instructor at the school, was a square brick box with narrow windows and a front door that opened directly onto the sidewalk, which was laid concrete and not the red brick streets elsewhere on campus. The college was famous for its brick streets and sidewalks, which gave the heavily shaded campus a distinctly nineteenth century look and led to turned ankles for unsuspecting female visitors and students and faculty who were foolish enough to wear high heels, which often broke clean off in the cracks.

Lily Putnam had stopped by Willow's office to ask her advice on the term paper that all freshmen students were required to write during the fall semester. Lily was teaching three sections of freshman English, each with about thirty students, far too many to be effective, but tell that to the administration. Willow, who last year had been promoted to full professor, taught only one section, Honors English, which did not use the standard syllabus required of all other sections of freshman English. (She did not require a term paper; she thought they were a waste of time. But that was *her* secret; it was nobody else's business.) In addition, in fall semester she was teaching a survey course in the English novel and a senior seminar in romantic poetry. There were only thirteen students in her Honors English class, twelve in the English novel, and six in the seminar. So she had a total number of students that was comparable to just one of Lily Putnam's freshman classes; the young instructor also taught a section of sophomore world lit survey with about forty students. But Willow was a full professor, Lily an instructor. Lily had to pay her dues.

Even though there had been a recent flurry of hiring, the number of faculty had not kept up with the burgeoning student body. Since the first men had arrived, the student population had grown to over two thousand students. So English classes were crowded, especially those in the first two years, which were required of all students; history, biology and basic math classes were the same.

"How am I supposed to grade over ninety term papers?" Lily had asked her, stopping by unannounced and uninvited.

Willow sat behind her desk. She had a third floor corner office, bright with afternoon sunlight. She could still smell the fresh damp pungency of the soil from when she'd watered her plants, which sat on her windowsills. "I don't understand the problem," she said.

"*Ninety* term papers," the girl said. "I mean, can you do them justice?"

"Justice is hardly what you're after," Willow said.

"I mean ..." The girl did not go on. There was a silence.

Willow sighed. "Have them make notecards. Take those up and put a check mark on them and hand them back to use in their paper."

"A check mark?" she said.

"Yes."

"I mean, you *read over* them, right?"

"Of course not. You put a check mark on them."

The girl looked at her. Her light sweater was tight over her breasts. They were perfectly formed. "But won't they think the check mark means you've read them?"

"They might. But you don't have *time* to read them, do you?"

"What about the papers?"

"What about them?"

"I mean, same thing? You don't have to read those either?"

"It's up to you, dear," Willow said, wishing the girl would go back to her own office.

"What do *you* do?"

"I have my methods," Willow said.

"You mean you don't read them?"

"Of course I read them. I mark them and grade them."

The girl eyed her suspiciously. "Okay," she said. She just stared at Willow. Willow thought she might start smacking a big chunk of gum. That's who she reminded Willow of, the girl who fixed her hair at Hair Solutions. A very pretty young girl who smacked gum in Willow's ear and breathed on her. Willow stared back. "Well ..." the girl said. Willow did not have much facility for small talk, and even less patience for it.

Willow stood up, as a signal that the conversation was over. Instead of leaving, the girl came toward her. She walked around her desk and stood looking up at Willow. Her eyes were deep blue, crinkled with smile lines, her cheekbones sharp and pronounced. She was a really stunning young woman. But, Willow suspected, bottom-line dumb as a signpost.

"Thank you, Dr. Behn," she said. "I think of you as my mentor."

"Yes, well ..."

"I've only taught one semester," the girl went on breathlessly, "when I finally got a teaching fellowship at Emory. So I'm not, well, experienced."

"We all have to begin some place, Miss Putnam," Willow said. She tried to smile but her face seemed stiff and frozen.

"So I really appreciate you," Lily said. "And please, call me Lily." The younger woman smiled, her teeth a brilliant alabaster. She reached out and put her fingers on Willow's wrist. Her touch was like an electric shock that ran up Willow's arm. Willow pulled her hand away. They just stood there for a few seconds.

"Okay, then," Lily Putnam said. She eased out the door. Willow watched her walk away, her eyes lingering on the younger woman's hips.

The phone on her desk was ringing. It was the president's secretary, Eloise Hoyle, calling for John Steagall to make a tennis date. It still annoyed Willow that John had his secretary call her, though he had been doing it since he was chairman of the music department, then dean of the college, and now president. Eloise Hoyle was in her fifties, tall—about the same height as Willow—and slim with black, dyed hair pulled together in a tight bun; she fancied that it was actually *she* who ran the college, and Willow thought there was probably a grain of truth to that. The students called her Olive Hoyle. John Steagall was a short man, small in stature, dwarfed by the overlarge desk in his office. He was not, and never had been, a suitable opponent for Willow on the tennis court. Willow was four inches taller than he was, wiry and strong, with long arms, and her forehand was sharp and forceful. Her serve sometimes still seemed to startle Steagall and he would flinch, losing any opportunity to return it.

The first time he'd had his secretary call, when he was chair of music (his secretary then was a heavy woman whose husband was manager of the local Piggly Wiggly), Willow was a fairly new assistant professor. She knew Steagall was married, but didn't know his wife, except to see her once at the reception for new faculty at Flowerhill, the president's residence. She seemed singularly mousy. Willow was under no delusion that she, herself, was a desirable woman, but still, she was single, in her forties, and out of the blue a male colleague was asking her to play tennis. She was flattered and wary at the same time. John Steagall had shown up at the courts dressed all in whites, down to new sneakers; he had the look of someone who had been "outfitted."

He waited until after the first game of their match to inform her, apologetically, that his game was rusty, which fact seemed to her an understatement. He was awkward, prancing about the court; he seemed more interested in how he looked than in his skills as a player. The next time his secretary called she pled a late afternoon committee meeting, but after that he persisted. She relented, and they had been occasionally playing ever since, always with the same result.

Willow looked out her window at the quad. Her office was in Comer Hall (She had overheard a student, female, out in the hallway refer to it as Come-er Hall), and she gazed through the gently turning leaves of the elm tree just outside; sometimes she thought of her office as a treehouse, nestled in the leaves, and it made her smile. She could see students crossing the quad under the ancient live oaks. The campus was gorgeous; to Willow, it was a deeply satisfying place to live and work. It was a crisp early autumn day, sunny and bright, the sky as blue as ... Lily Putnam's eyes came quickly to mind and she put the image away. She welcomed an excuse to get out in the weather, even if it was just for crushing John Steagall in tennis again. She riffled through the papers on her desk, making sure she had her well-worn lecture notes on Mary Shelley's *Frankenstein* for her novels class tomorrow. Spotting the sheaf of notes made Willow flash back to her days at Vanderbilt, when she had been one of the first women to run the gauntlet of the Good Ol Boys club that was the Vanderbilt English Department back then, a bunch of red faced, overweight old white men who faked being scholars and spent their time drinking their toddies in The Fugitive Room and making life miserable for graduate students, especially the few, very few, women courageous enough—or perhaps foolhardy enough—to want a Vanderbilt PhD. They had been no match for Willow, especially one particularly onerous eighteenth century scholar whose teaching methods were sarcasm and intimidation. Once, in a seminar, he had asked spitefully, looking down his nose as though there were an unpleasant odor in the room, "Does anyone here read Old French?" Willow, who had had a course in it as an undergraduate at Smith, raised her hand. In the silence that followed, Willow said to the perplexed and speechless old man, with a sneer to equal his, "Do *you*?"

When Lily Putnam got back to her office, a student from her sophomore survey was waiting for her. She'd left her office door open and he was sitting at her desk, in her chair; he had on a red baseball cap turned around backwards.

"Grade my papers while you're at it," she said, startling him so that he jerked around. He jumped up. He just stood there looking at her.

"Did you need to see me?" she asked. She was still unsure just how to talk to students, how to maintain a proper distance and at the same time appear friendly. She feared coming across as a stern school marm type, but she didn't want to invite too much familiarity.

"Yes M'am," he said, astonishing her. No matter how many times she'd heard it, when one of the students called her m'am it surprised her. She always had an impulse to say "Please don't do that," or something like that; it was a little embarrassing.

This boy—she couldn't dredge his name up from the endless list in her grade book—was a few inches taller than she was. His neck and shoulders bulged; she would guess he was a weight lifter. His thighs looked solid in his tight jeans. The skin of his face was smooth and tan. He had the look of a lifeguard still bronzed from several months of sun. His eyes were large, pale olive.

"Did you wish to see me?" she repeated, sounding overly stiff and unnaturally formal. She smiled to cover her awkwardness.

"I can't read this shit," he said.

"Pardon?" She was not sure she'd heard him right.

"This," he said, pulling from his backpack the thick red anthology they used in world lit survey and flipping it open on her desk. He pointed.

"What?" she asked.

"This. This." His forefinger tapped the page.

She saw that the book was opened to "The Death of Ivan Ilych," their assigned reading for that week. She elbowed him out of the way and sat in her own chair. It squeaked under her. She crossed her legs and saw him looking. "It can be difficult the first time you ..." she began.

"It's crap," he said. "Nobody wants to read that."

"Mr. ... uh ... what is your name, now?"

"Godby," he said, "David Godby."

"Oh, yes, Mr. Godby. Well ..." What to say? Challenge him, tell him to sit down and shut up, never to talk to her like that, and then have to look at a sulking, scowling post-adolescent wounded-ego male face for the rest of the semester? She smiled again. "Why don't you tell me what the problem is?"

"M'am?"

"What is your problem with Mr. Tolstoy's novella?"

"I got no *problem* with it. I mean, other than I hate it."

"Well, have you given it a chance? How much have you read?"

"Not much."

"I mean, how many pages?"

He looked off out the window. Her office faced the monotonous narrow windows of Harmon Hall, the science building. "I told you. I couldn't read it."

"Surely, Mr. Godby, you can read the English language?"

"You told us this guy was a Russian," he said.

She wondered if he were putting her on. He didn't laugh. He didn't even smile. While he was focused out the window (she fleetingly wondered what he was looking at; probably some coed going by on the sidewalk), she stealthily looked him over. He wore a faded purple Lakewood sweatshirt hanging out over his jeans; his shoulders were broad, but his cheeks were so smooth he looked as though he'd not even started shaving. Before she looked away she peeped at his junk. His crotch bulged. He turned back from the window and she looked quickly away. He almost caught her looking. He grinned. He *had* caught her.

"Yes, he *is* Russian, Mr. Godby, but this is an English translation. A very good one, I might add."

"Is he a communist?"

"*Was*, Mr. Godby. He is dead. And he certainly wasn't a communist." He was an old white man who was very far from that. Pompous old rich aristocratic misogynist, he was. But she didn't say that. "His politics are beside the point."

"Well, why did he write such gobble de gook, then?"

"Are you sure you even tried to read it?"

"I *tried*, Miss Putnam," he said, a slight whine in his voice. He sat down in the visitor's chair. She wished she could get rid of him. She should tell him that she was busy. He had no appointment. But her office hours were posted on her door, and this was one of them. She glanced at her watch. She was already getting a renewed empathy for those old professors in graduate school who had made themselves impossibly scarce. He was looking at her earnestly. Maybe he really *did* have trouble with the text, but she couldn't imagine a sophomore in college being unable to even *read* it.

"I suppose I could arrange a tutor for you," she said.

"I want Clarissa Simpson," he said eagerly.

"Who?"

"You know. Clarissa Simpson. She's in the class." Lily remembered her then. Of course. Of course he would want Miss Simpson. Willow had noticed her herself; she was a pretty blonde, with small, nicely formed breasts and, in her form fitting jeans, a tight, compact and shapely little ass. "Miss Simpson does not work in the English department," she said, "I don't even know what her major is, but I don't think it's English."

"You could ask her," he said.

"Mr. Godby," she said, getting exasperated, "we *pay* students, upper division English majors, to tutor students having trouble in their classes. They know what they're doing. I can't just *ask* a random student in the class to tutor you."

"It's not random. I asked for her."

She sighed. *Patience. A good teacher must have patience.* "Pick up the book," she said.

"This one?" He lifted the anthology from the desk.

"Yes, *that* one. Now, read me the opening of the novella."

"Out loud?"

No, not out loud, you moron. "Yes, of course."

He read it. Hesitant. Mumbling.

"During an interval in the Mel ... uh ... vinsk trial in the large building of the courts the members and public prosecutors met in Ivan ... uh." He stopped.

"Egorovich," she said sharply.

"Egorovich's private room, where the conversation turned to the celebrated Kra ... sov ... ski case. Fedor ... Fedor? Fedor Vas ... il ... ievich warmly maintained that it was not subject to their ju ... risdiction. Ivan whatsis maintained the contrary, which Peter Iva ... no ... vis ..."

"Ich," she said.

"What?"

"Ivano*vich*. Ivan Ivanovich."

"Peter," he said. An image of his bulge, his junk, popped into her mind.

"What?"

"Peter Ivanovich, not Ivan. That's the other dude's name."

"All right. Go ahead."

"Peter Ivanovich, not having entered the discussion at the start took no part in it but looked through the Gazette which had just been handed in. 'Gentlemen,' he said,' Ivan Ilych has died.'"

He stopped and looked at her. His face was blank, impassive. How could one so empty and dull be so alluring? His eye lashes were long and his lips plump and full. His dark brown hair was thick, hanging to his shoulders under the bill of the cap, which he still had not removed.

"You seemed to read that all right," she said.

He just stared at her. After a long minute he said, "What about the Russian?"

"Huh? What Russian?"

"You know. Ivannotshit, all that."

"The names?"

"Yeah. I can't read that shit. Whatever happened to Joe Smith, stuff like that? What's wrong with Joe Smith?"

"Mr. Godby, you can't possibly be as obtuse as you appear to be," she said. She felt herself getting angry. She was certain he was making fun of her.

"Since I don't know what that means, I don't know if I am or not."

"Are you serious?"

A hurt expression. It looked honest. Either she had hurt his feelings or he was a very good actor. Maybe he was a theater major.

"What's your major, Mr. Godby?" she asked.

"Phys-ed," he said. "I'm on a baseball scholarship."

That explained a lot. "Well ..." she said.

"We got a game tomorrow, you ought to come out and see us play," he said.

"Baseball? It's not the season for it, is it?"

"We play a fall season. A lot of junior colleges and stuff. It's like our spring training, only it's in the fall since our season is in the spring, you know?"

"I'm afraid I don't have time for baseball games, Mr. Godby," she said.

"You're too busy for baseball, then you're too busy." Now he looked smug.

"Yes, well, back to Sophomore English. I realize that reading Tolstoy is difficult for one who ... one who has not read a great deal of world literature before. I can understand that." What would Dr. Behn do or say? Probably throw him out of her office. "But that's the whole purpose of world lit survey, to broaden your perspectives, to allow you to sample cultures that may be foreign to your own."

"It's foreign all right."

"Plus to read good literature. Good stories." He just looked at her blankly. A sudden rise of anger. "Just exactly what do you want from me, Mr. Godby? I can't read the material *for* you. You're in college now, not high school."

He didn't reply. He just stared at her. He was so exquisite she was unnerved. He was a mere boy and a stupid one at that, and here she was, not even a month into her first teaching job, lusting after one of her students. She was furious with herself. She hoped her warring emotions were not showing on her face. She shook her head. There was nothing wrong with looking, was there? Even Dr. Behn probably appreciated the young males in her classes. Or maybe the young females, she thought, remembering how the older woman had looked at her. Would she, in ten or fifteen years, be exactly like Dr. Behn, single and scholarly, devoting her life almost exclusively to the academy and salivating over the girls in her classes? There were two other older women professors in the department who were nearing retirement, who had taught here for years, who had had their prime years when it was a girls' school. One was Eleanor Buffkin, who taught American Literature. The other was Katherine Klinger, who taught Chaucer; she told Lily she was the first woman to be awarded a PhD from the University of Chicago. She wore a little knitted cap she called a "fascinator." Lily wondered if the women even had lives outside the campus, outside the classroom. They had chosen not to marry, to devote themselves exclusively to teaching. They seemed content and relatively happy. It wasn't that Lily felt that being married, that having a man and children, was something she wanted and needed to be happy. It wasn't that. But she wanted a *life*. She wanted fun. She wanted to travel, and not in some super-organized group of over-the-hill teachers clutching guidebooks on their air-conditioned bus while cruising the byways of Italy or Greece. Lily loved literature, she loved teaching, and surely to lead a scholarly life did not mean to live a monastic one. Dr. Behn did not seem that narrowly focused, but then she was not as old as the other two women. And how Dr. Behn "seemed" might not be at all how she was; after all, Lily did not really know her well at all.

Lily looked back at the boy. Her mind had wandered, perhaps a subconscious technique of self-preservation. He *was* adorable. His eyes were big, his cheeks rounded and just fleshy enough to look exceedingly strong and healthy. He sat with his legs apart, his thighs aggressively spread. He was offering her his junk, openly.

"Mr. Godby, what do you think you are doing?"

"M'am?" His face was innocent, suddenly very young.

"Are you coming on to me?" she asked.

"*M'am?*"

"You heard me."

"Comin on to you? Not a chance."

Could she have been wrong? She swallowed away the beginnings of embarrassment. "Don't play the innocent with me, Mr. Godby," she said, hoping he couldn't hear the uncertainty in her voice.

"I don't know what you're talkin about," he said. He seemed genuinely baffled.

"Okay," she said, "maybe ..." She stopped. She sat there for a moment. She slammed his book shut and handed it to him. "Here. Read your assignment. Period. End of discussion."

"Well, thanks a lot," he said sarcastically. He stood up. He crammed the book back into his backpack. He looked at her out of the corners of his eyes. "Yeah," he said, as though he were about to make another statement. He let the word drift off into silence. He left her office, leaving the door open.

She could still smell him—a spicy aftershave, boy sweat—and feel his warmth after he was gone, and she sat gazing at the stiff wooden chair where he'd sat, at the smooth and polished seat, where she could almost see the indentation of his hard thighs.

Brasfield Finch noticed the boy leaving her office. He was across the hall, his booted foot propped on an open drawer in his desk. It was mid-afternoon and he had just had a healthy snort from a bottle of Chivas Regal that he kept in his filing cabinet. He had finished with his writing workshop, letting them go early after two tiresome short stories both set in the future and both with surprise endings. One, the last, even had an "it was all a dream" resolution, which elicited an audible groan from Finch when the girl read it aloud from the other end of the seminar table. The girl, a wispy skinny brunette with no breasts, blanched.

"I thought it was neat," Gerald Grimes said. *Yes, because you'd like to get into her skinny panties.*

"Thanks, Gerry," the girl, whose name was Miranda Gener,

said, sighing, cutting her eyes at Finch. *See!?* She shrugged then, and looked down at her manuscript on the table.

"What's *neat* about it, Mr. Grimes?" Finch asked. "Why don't you favor us with an elaboration?"

"I mean, the ending. Blam. I never saw that one coming."

"You didn't?"

"No, I didn't."

"Well, *I* did," Brasfield said. "I saw it coming from the very first line of the story, so it was no surprise to me. And since the story relied almost entirely on the surprise element for its effect and value, then the story was a total failure."

"Aww, now," the boy said. "I wouldn't say *total*. That's a little harsh."

"Harsh?"

"Yes sir."

"Mr. Grimes, a writer needs to know what the reader feels. She needs an honest response, not some mealy-mouthed here-you-go-dearie-you-get-a-trophy-too-just-because-you-competed response. I'm afraid writing isn't like children's soccer."

"I didn't say it was, Mr. Finch," the boy said. "You could at least cut her a little slack."

"There is no '*slack*' in fiction writing, Mr. Grimes."

The boy looked down and mumbled. "Oh, Jesus Christ," he said, "you don't have to hurt somebody's feelings."

"Feelings are not a part of the equation, Mr. Grimes," Finch said.

"Shit," the boy said under his breath.

"If you're going to write fiction, Mr. Grimes, you have to have a thick hide. Trust me on that one."

"But ..."

"Let it go, Gerry," the girl said.

"Class dismissed," Finch said.

Now he sat looking out into the empty hallway. The boy he'd seen walk away had been in the delicious little tart's office. He briefly envied him. Finch had had to labor long and hard to get the women in the department—whom he called "the nuns"—to hire Lily Putnam. They had wanted to hire the other candidate who had come for an interview, a wimpy, tweedy little guy who smoked a huge, overlarge pipe, a new PhD from the University of Tennessee. Putnam didn't have her degree. They had insisted on hiring someone with degree in hand, but he had held out and won, and the girl had immensely improved the scenery around Comer Hall. God forbid the enchanting girl would ever become a scholar; that body was not made for that. When he caressed her with his eyes he could palpably feel her softness. She stirred something in him that he didn't feel too often these days.

Brasfield Finch was writer-in-residence at the college, a permanent appointment he'd wrangled from that idiot President Homer Lovelady on the occasion of the publication of his second novel, a lengthy historical epic called *The Fox and The Pheasant*. The novel had garnered unkind reviews; it had been less well received than his first, a somewhat bawdy episodic novel called *Coming Of Age In South Beach*, which had acquired a kind of underground reputation on college campuses around the South, especially down in Miami. There was a seven-year gap between the two books, and it had been ten years since his second, during which time he had published only one short story in *The Southern Review*.

At the insistence of the dean of the college, Wallace Jefferson, an obese man whose doctorate was from the University of Georgia, Finch had to teach two other courses. Wallace Jefferson was extremely conservative; he maintained that any full time faculty had to teach at least nine hours, so Finch had to pick up a section of advanced composition and a trailer section of American Lit survey in addition to his writing workshop. Jefferson informed Finch that as long as he was dean, nobody would be promoted to full professor without a terminal degree, by which he meant a doctorate; he did not consider Finch's MFA from the University of Southern Mississippi a terminal degree. Finch did not care. He was writer-in-residence and Associate Professor, and he had tenure. Full professors at Lakewood earned only pennies more than associates, anyway. Wallace Jefferson could take his full professorship and cram it up his fat ass, as far as Finch was concerned. He flatly refused to teach the first semester of American Lit; "nothing but sermons and imitation British literature," he said. So Finch taught mostly Faulkner and Hemingway, ignoring the rest of modern American literature except an occasional Flannery O'Connor story. He thought poetry was tedious and annoying, so he omitted it all. But he was demanding, requiring massive amounts of reading, so he had very few students. He made the students in the advanced composition course read a long list of novels; he allowed them to write whatever they liked, never read the papers and gave everybody an A.

Rufus Doublet, the department chair, had called him on that one.

"You can't do that," Doublet said. "I was told that you told the class on the very first day that everyone had an A, whether they turned in anything or not, whether or not they even *attended* the class. The faculty handbook says ..."

"Fuck the faculty handbook," Finch said.

Doublet was one of those professional Southerners, soft spoken, handsome, unmarried, in his forties, who had not yet acknowledged he was queer as a dodo bird. He pronounced his name Doob-lay, giving it a French twist, which was a laugh; he was from the little town of Villa Rica, Georgia. He drank like a fish, told "darky" stories, and some of his drinking buddies were Dean Jefferson and his wife Paulette, who taught in the history department. They were a tight threesome. Finch often wondered what kind of sexual entanglements they got themselves into. They had come into Stache's one night when Finch was there. Stache's was one of the popular local watering holes; the actual complete name was *Your Mother's Mustache,* and there was an enormous horse hair mustache that an art student had sculpted over the front door. The three of them were drunk as skunks, and his own drinking buddy, Earl Flatt, another middle-aged bachelor who taught art, said, after they had observed them giggling and touching each other for awhile, "I wonder who's suckin who and who's fuckin who."

Finch had another good bolt of the Scotch. He took out a small comb and brushed his beard; it was long and bushy, just slightly touched with gray, so long that it ended over his belly with a little pig tail tied with a piece of red yarn. People—everyone, strangers—remarked on Brasfield Finch's beard. It was eye catching to say the least. He felt the Chivas Regal warming his insides, and he walked across the hall, his boots clumping on the linoleum tile. Lily Putnam was perched at her desk, which faced the wall; she sat high in her swivel chair. On the wall over her desk was a giant bookstore poster for Morrison's *The Bluest Eye.* Lest anyone forget: she was a Morrison specialist. Which mattered to Finch far less than the fact that she was an extremely juicy specimen. She was, as he had remarked to Earl Flatt, "completely concupiscent."

"Penny for your thoughts," he said. She turned around. She smiled, a room-brightening visage, the tips of her teeth like polished Chiclets, her lips plum red and plump. Jesus Christ Almighty! Her skirt barely covered her thighs. He felt that if he tilted his head only slightly he could glimpse the strip of silk that covered her goodies. He was about to do just that when she spoke.

"Oh, you startled me," she said, and laughed a quick little chuckle.

"How are you getting on?" he asked. "Classes going okay?"

"Oh, yes, thanks for asking."

He thought he could detect the smell of cologne lingering in the air. Naturally the boy would have liberally doused himself with it before he was seeing the sexy teacher. He smiled. He stroked his beard, letting his gaze fill up with her.

"I just hate these term papers, though," she said. "So many."

"What term papers are those?" he asked.

"You know, freshman English." She made a little face.

"My dear, I haven't taught any freshmen in twenty years," he said.

"Of course, I know that. I just meant ... Well, I don't know what I meant." She seemed flustered. She licked her lips. "I'm sorry," she said, "I'm just not used to being around a real writer."

He looked over his shoulder, up and down the hall. "What real writer?" he asked. "I don't see any real writer around here."

"You ..." She laughed then. "You're funnin me, Mr. Finch," she said.

"No, not at all. I *used* to be a real writer. Now I'm just an old drunk who used to be a real writer."

"You're not *old*, Mr. Finch," she said, fluttering her eyes.

"But I'm a drunk?"

"No, no, I didn't mean that. No." She seemed genuinely embarrassed. Her cheeks took on a pinkish bloom, like ripening peaches. "I only meant, well, you're not *old* old." She chuckled self-consciously. "You know what I mean," she said.

"I think I do." *You mean I'm not too old to give you a good poke.* "As a scholar of contemporary American literature, surely you know that, as syphilis is the occupational disease of the American soldier, drunkenness is the occupational disease of the American writer."

"Is drunkenness a contagious disease, Mr. Finch?" she asked with a saucy smile.

"I don't suppose so," he said. "Would you like to join me for a drink sometime?"

"Why ..." Warring emotions flittered across her face. "Why, yes. That would be very nice," she said. The smile returned, more forceful than ever.

"At the bar?" he asked, "or in my apartment?"

There was a slight pause, but she didn't lose her cool. "Perhaps the initial drink, Mr. Finch, should be in a bar. A clean, well-lighted bar."

"Then there will be others," he said, ignoring the Hemingway reference.

"Pardon?"

"Other drinks. Later ones. You said the *initial* drink."

"Yes, well, that'll be up to you, won't it?" She winked at him. As if to say, *isn't this fun, this playing around? We both know we're just afunnin.* He did not wink back. He did not smile. He watched her eyes play over his beard. He was wearing worn jeans and an old wrinkled khaki work shirt with a torn front pocket. Willow Behn called it his uniform. He leaned against her door frame, crossed his arms over his chest.

"What committee were you assigned to?" he asked.

The abrupt shift in topic seemed to throw her for a moment. "I don't ... Well ..." He knew full well what committee she was assigned to. Every faculty member had to be on at least one committee. He was chair of the Student Publications Committee, and he had requested her. The Student Publications Committee did very little, had very few issues. It was a sleepy little campus and the students were docile and dull witted. The Student Publications Committee and the Library Committee—which never did anything at all and rarely even met—were the two prize assignments. Finch had switched a couple of years before when the new librarian was hired, an obnoxious Yankee named Bob Winters; Winters, in one of the meetings, had referred to Finch as a "wise apple." Goodbye, library committee.

"Aren't you on Student Publications?" he asked.

"Oh. Yes. I got the memo yesterday."

"I'm chair*man* of that committee," Finch said. The women on the faculty insisted on simply "chair;" so Finch made a point of always saying "chair*man.*" "I'll take care of you."

"What ...?" she started to say. She just looked at him, her mouth slightly open.

"I mean, I'll make sure you get full credit, a good rating. You know, evaluations, in the spring, all that. Not that we ever *do* anything. But those interminable meetings will be far more pleasant with *you* there."

"Why, thank you, Dr. Finch," she said, all aflutter.

"Not doctor, God forbid. I've never operated on anybody in my life. Unlike you, upon whom the almighty doctorate will soon be bestowed, I am not in possession of one, as that asshole Jefferson never lets me forget. Just Brass will do."

"Pardon?"

"Brass. Call me Brass."

"All right. I'm sorry, I just sometimes think all ... all senior faculty are doctors."

"All *old* faculty, you mean."

"Now Mr. ... now *Brass*, you're just having me, aren't you?" She laughed gaily.

"I would love to have you, Miss Putnam," he said.

"Oh," she uttered. She looked down, then away. He would have given her an Academy Award. He saw completely through her. "Yes, well ..." she said.

"And I will," he said softly.

"What's that, Mr. Finch?"

"I'll *have* you," he said. He smiled then. A slight smile flitted across her lips. She cut her eyes at him. Sky-blue eyes, enormous. Her lips looked inviting and tender, her cheeks flushed and soft. In the late afternoon sun that beamed through her window, he could see tiny, minuscule white hairs on her skin. She continued to regard him from the corners of her eyes. She was pretending to be indignant, but only slightly.

"I really need to make a dent in these note cards before I leave the office," she said.

"Of course," he said, "I'll leave you to your scholarly pursuits, then."

"Thanks for stopping by," she said. "Brass," she added. She turned her back to him and picked up her red ball point.

"Cheerio, then," he said. Why had he said that? The awkwardness had deflected to him. He turned away, feeling incomplete and frustrated, wondering why he had come over here in the first place. He had accomplished nothing.

John W. Steagall, III, stopped back by his office before going home to Flowerhill. He had just been humiliated again by Willow Behn, trounced. He had never beaten her. He wondered why he kept going back for more; he was like a gambler, certain that the next deal would be the one, the royal flush that would make up for all the losing hands of the past. Sometimes he conjectured that he was some sort of pathetic masochist, getting off on defeat, thriving on abasement. Perhaps it went with the territory of being a college president.

Eloise Hoyle had gone for the day. Steagall didn't really seriously believe he was a masochist; he had no desire to have some vixen lash him, but he was sure Eloise would be eager for such activity if he should ever request it. She would probably pull a pair of thigh high black leather boots and a long thin whip from her supplies closet in the outer office and go at him. Maybe she would do it naked but for the boots. He smiled, thinking of his lanky executive secretary wearing nothing but thigh high black leather boots, towering over him, her bushy black nether hair on a level with his mouth as he crouched before her. Eloise had no tits to speak of; actually, she had floating ribs that stuck out in the front farther than her breasts. She wore clothing that was designed to hide that imperfection. John supposed that only he and her late husband Pookie Hoyle—he had been director of maintenance and grounds before his death—had ever seen the deformity up close, but of course he had no way of really knowing that.

He sat down behind his desk. He still enjoyed just sitting there, being president. Steagall had had to schmooze the board of trustees mightily to be allowed to even apply for the appointment. The immediate former president, Homer Lovelady, had died unexpectedly two years ago; they had found him sitting at this very desk, early one morning. Apparently he had been there since the day before, but nobody had missed him. His doddering old wife had not seemed to notice that he hadn't returned to Flowerhill at the usual time. A janitor had reported finding him; he was sitting so straight, in his neat blue serge suit, holding his favorite gold Cross pen in his fingers, that the janitor had vacuumed most of the office before he noted that Dr. Lovelady was not moving, had in no way acknowledged his presence, which was not especially noteworthy since the old man was notoriously taciturn and often seemed unaware of anything going on around him.

One of the trustees, Emmaline Rodgers, a butch attorney from down in Tampa who had graduated from Lakewood College for Women in 1941, had been adamantly opposed to his candidacy. She had insisted they have a national search, that it was inconsistent with modern higher education practice to "promote from within." She did not want anyone with even the remotest connection to the college to apply. He did anyway, submitting his resume as Dean of the College. He felt he had the inside track; the search committee was chaired by Willow Behn, his erstwhile tennis partner. Steagall was certain Emmaline Rodgers would have felt differently if some leftover hag from the girls' college years had been interested, but apparently nobody was. Steagall had heard rumors that Emmaline Rodgers had been on campus trying to find some woman to counter his candidacy, but there were no women in any upper administrative positions.

A national search was held, at some expense and a great deal of bother. Three candidates were to be brought to campus for interviews, and after winnowing the several hundred applications, the search committee had settled on Dr. Lumley Parker-Ortiz, Provost at Austen Peay State University in Tennessee—especially strong since she was both a woman and of Hispanic descent—Dr. Larry Post, president of Wallace State Community College in Alabama, and, of course, John W. Steagall, III. Dr. Parker-Ortiz turned out to be a dark, obese woman whose accent was so thick she was difficult to understand. Dr. Post's doctorate was an EdD from, no less, Auburn University, which caused no end of grumbling among the liberal arts faculty even before the interviews. A campus wide meeting was held—faculty, students and some townspeople—where the candidates were discussed, a dull, repetitious forum that would be memorable only for one acerbic comment, Brasfield Finch's endorsement of John Steagall: "Well, your own asshole doesn't stink as badly as other folks's."

Steagall sat looking out the tall windows of his office, his hands folded over his plump little belly, his tennis whites still damp from his exertions on the court. The dusky sky was streaked with orange clouds. The leaves on the live oaks and elms were brushed with their incipient turning. The autumn leaves here were never as dazzling as they'd been in his native north Georgia. There was a sameness to Florida, a kind of tropical consistency. He noted with some annoyance that the flag in the middle of the quad was still up; it hung listlessly on its pole in the still, twilit air. He noticed, then, a figure at the southeast corner of the quad, a person? He was struck by how brilliantly white it appeared to be. As he watched, the figure came toward him over the quad, on the diagonal sidewalk. Gradually he realized that it was a person, a person jogging, someone out for a jog, some student probably, and as she came closer he realized she was completely naked, not a stitch of clothing except for a ski-mask and some low top sneakers. His mouth fell open. He stared. She was *running*, not jogging. Her large breasts were rolling and swaying with her pounding. She progressed across the quad and disappeared out of sight around the corner of Main Hall. He did not move. For a moment he was certain he had not seen what he had seen. But ... "Holy crap," he said aloud in his quiet office.

THREE

Finch was late to the departmental meeting, and the room fell silent when he walked in. What had they been talking about? Rufus Doublet smirked at him.

"Our esteemed writer in residence has arrived," he said.

"Sorry," Finch said. He sat down next to Lily Putnam. He smiled at Lily. He winked at Willow Behn, who looked off out the window.

"We were discussing the newsletter," Doublet said. "You didn't miss much."

"*That's* a certainty," Finch said.

Finch detested departmental meetings. He hated all committee meetings, except his own, when he could look at the lovely Lily. Her presence somewhat redeemed the tediousness of the English Department meetings, but not entirely, because Finch did not preside. He enjoyed presiding. They had stuck that pretentious and wearisome Joe Valerio, who taught Latin, on his committee this year. Finch enjoyed abruptly adjourning the meeting right in the middle of one of Valerio's pompous tirades. Catching him mid-sentence.

"I was asking for volunteers to assist Katherine this year," the chairman said.

Finch looked over at Dr. Klinger, who was looking back at him. She was an apple-cheeked woman with large pale blue eyes and gray curls peeking from beneath the little hat, or bonnet, or whatever it was, that she always wore. She looked positively mediaeval. The students called her "The Chaucer Lady." Every year the department sent out a newsletter to graduates with all the news of the department—there was little of any interest to anybody, Finch was sure—and it was compiled and written by Katherine Klinger. She wrote in a florid, wordy Victorian style, and she sometimes slipped in sarcastic, even ugly, references that were often lost on the graduates. But not the members of the English Department.

"Not me," Finch said.

"Of course not," Dr. Klinger said, "not a chance you'd ever do anything."

"I'll help her," Lily Putnam piped up, and Finch elbowed her. "Hey, that hurt," she said.

"Sexual harassment," Eleanor Buffkin murmured under her breath.

"Hardly," Finch said.

"All right, we have a volunteer. Thank you, Lily," Doublet said unctuously. He smiled his winning, good old fraternity boy smile. "Now, we need to discuss the upcoming Capital Fund campaign. We'll need to tie the newsletter in to that, we want to get some donations for the department, too ..." Doublet's voice faded as Finch tuned him out. He sat admiring Lily Putnam's profile, her lips, her skin, the touch of peach fuzz in the shaft of sunlight that came through the window; it was like a delicate, tiny brushstroke on her cheek. He was remembering the other evening, when, at the end of the day he had asked her to go to Stache's and have a drink with him. She had demurred, but he was persistent. They had walked back toward campus. He had been feeling a little drunk; he'd had three drinks at Stache's and, of course, he'd been nipping most of the day. She'd had three drinks as well and had chattered gaily, her laughter bubbling. He'd walked her back to her apartment building. In the shadows outside he'd grabbed her and kissed her. She'd kissed him back, shoving her tongue into his mouth, and he'd begun to shuffle and tug her toward the door even while they were still embracing. She had pulled back from him. "Naughty boy," she'd said. "I've got papers tonight, but I'll see you soon." She had given him an air kiss and slipped inside.

Finch came quickly out of his pleasant reverie when he heard the name Lenora Hart.

"Wait. What?" he said.

Doublet sighed, annoyed that he had to repeat what he'd said. "I was *saying*," he said, "that I had a memo from the president's office. The date has been set for Ms. Hart's visit to the campus. She will address the campus community at the annual Seniors' Day convocation in the morning, then an afternoon reception with a Conversation With The Author that will be open to the public, when she'll answer questions and sign books. Dr. Steagall says it'll be an event in the capital fund drive."

President Steagall had been agitating for years to have the novelist visit the school. She lived down in south Florida and was an extremely popular writer. Twenty years before she had published a novel that had initially been marketed as a young adult title but had gone mainstream, had sold about ten million copies and had won the Pulitzer Prize. An award winning film had been released. Lenora Hart was much in demand, but she was notoriously reticent to appear in public, and rarely did. She refused to autograph books.

"Are you joking?" Finch asked.

"Of course not. Do you want to see the memo?"

"No, I don't want to see the goddam memo. Does Lenora Hart know about all this?"

"Well, I would assume she does, Brasfield, since the president has announced it. Calm down."

"I'm *calm*. If that twit has agreed to it, I'd be greatly surprised," he said.

"Which twit? The writer or the president?" Dr. Klinger asked with a bright smile.

"Either twit. But I was referring to the professional Southern lady writer."

Dr. Klinger cackled with glee.

"Now, Katherine ..." Doublet began.

"Leave her alone, you twit," Finch said. Doublet prissily feigned shock. "I'm going to get to the bottom of this," Finch said, standing up, striding toward the door.

"The meeting has not been adjourned," Doublet said.

"It has for me," Finch said as he walked out the door.

"What the fuck, John?" Finch said when he got to the president's office.

"Control yourself, Brasfield," Steagall said. "What's got you upset?"

Finch took a deep breath and relaxed back into the plush black leather visitor's chair. He eyed the president. Steagall was in his shirtsleeves, his suit coat hanging on a rack in the corner. "Okay," Finch said after a minute, "do you mean to tell me that Lenora Hart has agreed to all that?"

"All what?"

"Jesus Christ! All you put in that memo to that idiot Doublet!"

"Well, she has tentatively agreed to come. She wrote a very nice letter, all about her grandmother being a graduate of Lakewood."

Finch's lips were a thin line. "In which she agreed to give a speech, then to sit for some conversation with the author for your big shot donors? And to *sign books*?"

"Not in so many words, no."

"She won't do that."

"She mentioned you in the letter ..."

"I don't give a fuck," Finch said.

"Brasfield! Brasfield. What's gotten into you? What's wrong?"

"She hasn't agreed to all that, and she won't. Unless she's had a lobotomy."

"But if we have it all set up, all arranged, then..."

"You think she cares about that? It will *delight* her to fuck everything up as much as she can."

"I can't believe that. And stop saying that word."

"What word?"

"The F word."

"Fuck?"

"Yes, of course, *fuck*," Steagall said, stage whispering the word.

"You don't believe it because you don't know her."

"I've read her book, so I know her soul."

Finch laughed. "You actually buy into crap like that? Her soul? Her soul has been packaged and sold on the open market, John. She doesn't have it any more, if she ever did in the first place."

"You are a very cynical man, Brasfield," Steagall said.

"Maybe so. I've earned it. But mark my words, you will rue the day you ever set this in motion."

Olive Hoyle stuck her head in the door. "You have a call on line one, Dr. Steagall," she said.

"Used up my five minutes, huh?" Finch said, standing. "Good timing, Hoyle. You'll probably get a raise. Unless he's already slipped you one." Her head jerked back and her mouth fell open. "I didn't mean *that*, but I can see I hit a nerve," he said.

Willow Behn was sitting on the porch at Bostony House with two other women, friends and colleagues with whom she shared the house, a large Victorian that had been split into three spacious apartments. Willow had the ground floor front; Lucy Willard, a professor of history, lived on the ground floor rear, and Joan Hudson, a professor of art, lived on the second floor, where the rooms were more cramped but there was a large glassed-in sun room across the back that Joan used as her studio. All three women had taught at the college when it was a women's school and they had been living at Bostony House for years. They were having an early evening glass of wine on the porch before retiring to their individual apartments for their dinners.

"Okay, Willow, give us the skivvy. Is it true Lenora Hart is coming to campus?" Lucy Willard asked.

"I don't know," Willow said. "I understand she's been invited."

"I thought she never went anywhere," Joan Hudson said.

"Steagall has been trying for years to get her to come. It could just be a rumor, I don't know."

"John has always been quite celebrity conscious," Lucy said.

"Remember when he brought in that third rate actor who'd been in some movie or other to meet with the theater students?"

They all laughed. "And the playwright who got drunk with the students?" Willow said.

"Good gosh, yes," Joan Hudson said, "I heard he was gay."

"Gay as Dick's hat band," Willow said.

"What an odd choice of words," Lucy Willard said. They all chuckled again.

Lucy Willard had written a history of Florida that was used in every junior high school in the state. Joan Hudson was well known; she had paintings in the Dali museum in St. Petersburg and in the Ringling Museum in Sarasota. Her watercolors were hanging all over campus and all over the town as well. She was doing a series of Nelle Steagall's day lilies. Willow knew they'd sell like hotcakes. She envied the two women their success. She had been struggling to finish a book on Georges Sand for more years than she cared to count; Willow had published two essays on her and had given a paper at the South Atlantic Modern Language Association meeting in Savannah a couple of years ago. But she couldn't seem to get the book finished. She would work like a buzz saw for a month or two and then her interest would flag.

Joan Hudson leaned forward and topped up their wine glasses. They were drinking a delicate, citrusy white that Joan had bought in Tampa.

"Just a little more, and then I must run. I have a chicken breast in the oven," she said.

"Mine's in the crock pot," Lucy Willard said.

Willow envied her friends their industriousness with their dinners. She hated cooking for one person. She was making herself a sandwich, sliced lemon-pepper chicken breast from the deli at the Piggly Wiggly. She sometimes ate in the student cafeteria for lunch. They discouraged carry out, but Donna, the black girl who ran the desk swiping the meal tickets, would sometimes let her bring home her leftovers, which she made dinner from.

She had too many other things on her mind to worry about her book, one of which was the church. Willow was the first woman senior warden in the Episcopal Diocese of North Florida. She had been attending St. Marks in Lakewood since she'd first come to the college to teach, and they now had the first full time priest in the history of the small parish. He also served as a Chaplain for the students. He was a problem, and Willow suspected he would become an even greater problem in the future. He was wildly popular, especially with the students and the younger faculty who attended St. Marks, but he drank to excess, which accounted for both his lionization and her quandary. (He seemed to be growing thick with Rufus Doublet and the Jeffersons.) She had recently been called downtown to the police station at two in the morning to get him out of jail; he had been drunk and disorderly, refusing to leave Pasquali's Pizza, a joint frequented almost exclusively by students, and fighting with the police officers when they arrived to escort him out. The fight had spilled into the street. When she arrived at city hall he had been contrite, sitting in the little holding cell with a black eye and his clerical collar ripped and hanging loose. His name was Hamner Curbs. She suspected he was much older than he made himself out to be; his hair was dyed a wispy yellowish blonde. Half the vestry was indignant, the other half— that half made up of Rufus Doublet and the Jeffersons—fawningly forgiving. Willow sighed and sipped her white wine. At least he preached good sermons, even if his hand did shake when he placed the wafer.

"My God, look at that, will you?" Joan Hudson said, and the other two women looked where she was pointing. A naked man was running up the street. He didn't seem to be in much of a hurry; he looked as though he were out for his evening exercise. His face was covered, but that was all. The man's genitals dangled and swayed with his gait. He seemed to be exceptionally well endowed. Slim and muscular, probably a student. Of course a student. Who else would do such a thing?

"He seems to have forgotten his running shorts," Lucy Willard said.

"Well, bring it on!" Joan Hudson said.

They watched the man—or surely the boy—go by. They watched his tight buttocks disappear behind a hydrangea bush as he went down the sidewalk. They sat there in silence for a few moments. Joan Hudson fanned her face with her hand.

"Whew," she said, "I don't know if my old ticker could take much more of that."

"Me either," Lucy Willard said.

"Did you notice that he had hardly any body hair?" Joan said.

"That's the style now, I understand," Willow said.

"I don't think he even had any pubic hair," said Lucy.

"I didn't see any," Joan said, "I mean, with the shadows and all. Did you see any, Willow?"

"I didn't notice," Willow said. But she *had* noticed. He was as hairless as an infant.

Lily was pushing her cart down the aisle at the Piggly Wiggly when she ran into Paulette Jefferson, the dean's wife. She'd only met her once, at the reception for new faculty at Flowerhill.

"Why, Miss Putnam! How nice to see you," Paulette Jefferson said. She was a big woman with unruly dull brown hair tied back into a loose and messy twist. Her features were ambiguously masculine, a rough complexion, with a blunt nose and prominent jaw, a thin and humorless mouth. She was middle-aged, probably fifty.

"Hello, Dr. Jefferson," Lily replied. "How are you?" She knew the woman was in the history department and her degree was also from Georgia; Lily assumed she and the dean had met in graduate school. Paulette Jefferson spoke with a distinctly Midwestern accent, Chicago, Lily would have guessed. How on earth had she ever gotten to the University of Georgia for graduate study?

"Very well, thank you," the older woman said, "and I trust the same with you?" She was speaking "as the dean's wife." Lily wondered if she always spoke in that tone. To younger faculty, she probably did. She not so subtly inspected the contents of Lily's basket. Uh-oh. Lily had two six packs of Budweiser, twelve cartons of yogurt with fruit, a wedge of Brie, some rosemary crackers, and two bottles of liquor: a quart of Smirnoff vodka, and a pint of Chivas Regal, an impulse buy she'd added with a shrug, in case she were to invite Brasfield Finch to her place, an eventuality she had not planned but that with the purchase of the Scotch seemed to suddenly have become an inevitability. The Scotch had cost as much as the vodka.

"Yes m'am," Lily said, hearing the awful word come from her

own mouth, as if she, too, were a student. Or maybe that's the way you were supposed to address your dean's wife? Some middle aged women were sensitive about being addressed as if they were older. And there was the feminist thing, too. There was so much that Lily did not know, that she was having to get used to.

"Good, dear," the woman said.

"Doing your weekly grocery shopping," Lily said. She had intended it as a question but it had dwindled to a flat statement; she had realized halfway through, at just about the "weekly," that it sounded thoroughly inane.

"Oh, my, yes," Dr. Jefferson said, smiling. "One of the necessary chores, I'm afraid."

"Yes," Lily said, smiling back, dropping the "m'am."

"Are your classes getting on nicely, dear?" Dr. Jefferson's voice took on a slight British accent. Where the hell was this woman *from*?

"Quite," Lily said, hoping the woman didn't think she was parodying her.

"Wallace and I were very pleased to get a hire from Emory, Miss Putnam. An excellent school." So Paulette Jefferson thought of herself and the dean as a team. Of course she did. Lily made a mental note. "I hope you feel welcomed to the faculty, and to the town of Lakewood. We've found it a friendly place."

"Yes, m'am," she said, letting it slip. *What am I, a tongue-tied idiot?*

"I think there's a good relationship between Town and Gown. Altogether a pleasant place to live. We are near enough to Tallahassee to have the conveniences of a city and the amenities of a big University, yet Lakewood has a small town atmosphere where everybody knows everybody else." Lily didn't necessarily think that was a good thing. "And our campus is beautiful. You know of course that the central quad, the old section of the campus, was designed by the same landscape architects who designed Central Park in New York?"

"I read that in the catalogue," Lily said. "It's gorgeous."

"We've had some problems with the Dutch elm disease, but the day lilies have more than made up for that."

"Pardon?"

"Nelle Steagall's day lilies. Surely you've noticed."

"Oh, yes, of course," Lily said, though she had no idea what day lilies the woman could be talking about. Lily was not even sure she knew what a day lily looked like. "Exquisite," she said.

"Quite," the older woman said, and Lily cut her eyes at her, but the woman was still smiling encouragingly. "I hope you don't think I'm being forward, Miss Putnam, but I'd like to invite you to our church." Oh, shit. "Now don't get the wrong idea. I abhor the way some of the more ... well, the more *protestant* denominations worry people to get them to church. This is not a nag." Dr. Jefferson chuckled. "But St. Mark's Episcopal now has a delightful new priest, and there is a lively group of younger faculty who attend. I thought you might enjoy it. Rufus Doublet is a member. We would love to have you. No pressure," Dr. Jefferson said and winked.

"Oh, no," Lily said, "no pressure. I appreciate it."

"In fact, Rufus mentioned you to us just the other night," the woman went on. Lily had noticed a carton of Bluebell Mocha Almond ice cream in the woman's basket, and she wondered if it would melt before she stopped talking, much less before she got it home. "Rufus is a good friend of ours, and we get together often for a drink. Sometimes we have more than one," she said, and winked again, "and sit up all night playing B for Botticelli. Do you know the game, Miss Putnam?"

"Oh, yes," she said. She had heard it mentioned a time or two at graduate school.

"We are getting together this Friday night, at our house, and we'd love for you to come. Rufus will be there, and you can be our fourth." But he's *gay*, isn't he? "Nothing special, don't dress up or anything for heaven's sakes, we'll just have a drink and talk. And play B for Botticelli, of course."

"I'd love to, Dr. Jefferson," Lily said, "what can I bring?"

"Just your pretty self, dear," she said, "and please call me Paulette."

"Paulette," Lily said. She would have to double back and pick up a bottle of wine. It was the first invitation she'd had since coming to Lakewood—unless you counted Brasfield Finch's proffered drinks—and she knew enough to know she had to take *something*.

"See you Friday, then? About eight?"

"Okay. Eight o'clock."

Dr. Jefferson nodded and pushed her cart off down the aisle. A woman in baggy jeans behind them, who'd been waiting to pass, frowned at Lily as she went by. "Some people," the woman muttered.

Lily wanted to say *fuck you*, but she held her tongue.

Lily was originally from the small town of Gilbertown, Alabama. Her father was a pharmacist, and her mother an elementary teacher. She was an only child. Her childhood and adolescence were unremarkable, even–she felt when she remembered those times–boring, though she hadn't known they were at the time. Lily was well into high school before she ever thought of herself as a real person, as something more than a bag of meat and bones that she hung her face on; she realized she was a cipher, a blank; she was invisible, and her world was only what she saw and not what it saw when it looked back at her. One day she heard a man on a television talk show say, "You are what you are." It made her think. What was she? She had never really thought about that before. She was a girl; she was a cheerleader. She didn't really believe in much of anything, though of course she pretended she did. She liked to read; books were her best friends. And she liked boys. She had "developed" early, and boys wouldn't leave her alone. She had understood early on–while most of her friends were still giggling and flustering around–that the almost uncontrollable desire boys had for her gave her real power over them. She had also come to know—via a deflowering at the age of sixteen by a college boy who was visiting a next door neighbor—that she craved and enjoyed sex as much as the boys did, but she had determined that it would always be on her own terms.

She had never "gone steady" with anyone. She dated whomever she pleased, whenever she pleased. Everyone told her how attractive she was, and she had thought that maybe someday she would start to believe that herself. "Don't tell me you don't know you're beautiful, Lily," a boy had told her. "Okay, whatever," she'd said, "it's just that I never think of how I look at all." "Even when you look in the mirror?" "*Especially* then," she'd said.

"I don't see what the fuss about big boobs is," she'd said to her best friend Susan Hatfield, and Susan had replied, "You would if you didn't have them." They had been friends for years, since second grade, and in junior high they had "practiced" kissing and necking together, and sometimes it'd gotten sort of heated. When Lily's figure had blossomed, Susan had not wanted to do that kind of stuff anymore. "What do you think I am, a lesbo?" Susan had said.

Lily had actually had her first *real* lesbian experience when she was an undergraduate, with an older girl who was a tutor in the writing center, who had her own apartment in downtown Birmingham. It had seemed pretty much the same to her, except for the absence of the penis and the fact that the girl knew what Lily's clitoris was and what to do with it; sweaty, exciting, intensely pleasurable, far more tender and laid back than it ever was with a boy, but lacking something she had gradually come to realize was that same crude frenzy that a male brought to it, that anxious battle against the final cessation that intensified the turn-on even more, that kicked rather than caressed.

Lily did not think of herself as straight, or lesbian, or bi-sexual. She did not think of herself as sexual at all. She was what she was.

Willow felt she must be in some absurdist play: she was standing at the salad bar in the cafeteria, tongs full of crisp Romaine hovering over her bowl, when a girl–an exceptionally voluptuous completely naked girl in only a ski mask–sprinted down the center aisle and on out the door to the hoots and cheers of the students crowded around the tables. One young man near the front entrance jumped out of the way and his tray went flying, his plates and plastic glass clattering on the floor in the girl's wake. Willow had to blink and take a deep breath. My God. Streaking! She had seen an item in the newspaper about the phenomenon. People for no apparent reason running nude through public places. A silly and nonsensical practice. Invented and initiated, to be sure, by college students; Willow wished they'd display that much energy and verve in the classroom. Not coming to class naked, of course, but that might make things a bit more lively. She laughed to herself as she made her way to the faculty table in the corner. What will they come up with next?

"How about that?" Fred C. Dobbs said when she sat down at the table. Dobbs taught biology. His belly was huge and he had to wear suspenders to hold his pants up. "Welcome to the Playboy Club." He wore a hearing aid that buzzed continuously.

"Yeah," she said. "I saw one the other evening, too, a man. That was a more pleasant sight."

"Are you sure?" Dobbs asked.

"What the hell does that mean?"

"Nothing."

"You are a birdbrained buffoon, Dr. Dobbs," she said.

"Yeah, I am," he said, chuckling. He rammed a wedge of pizza into his mouth and began to chew.

"I think there've been some others, too," Bob Lallo, also from biology, said. He was a slight little man, prissy and colorless. He was eating only a salad. Willow wondered if he were anorexic.

She sliced into her grilled chicken breast. The Caf did a good job with grilled chicken breasts, and she looked forward to Thursdays, when they always served them. She avoided Friday lunches, though, because that was always fried chicken, and Willow could not abide fried foods. They made her gaseous.

"I hear the English department has some big doings coming up," Bob Lallo said.

"Oh, really? What?" she said, swallowing. She realized she had barked it. "What?" she said again, more softly.

He looked down at his plate. He was one of the most unassertive men she'd ever encountered. He did not reply.

"Are you referring to Lenora Hart?" she asked.

"I suppose so, yes," Lallo said, barely above a whisper.

"I hardly think it's 'big doings,'" she said, "you make it sound like a barn dance or something. We have writers here all the time."

"Yes, but she's a very famous one," Lallo said.

"What are you saying, that we are such a third rate English department that we can't get *famous* writers here?"

"No, Willow, you know that is not what I'm saying at all."

"Besides, what does a *scientist* know about fiction writers? You probably haven't read a novel since *The Swiss Family Robinson*, if you even read that one."

"Never heard of it," Dobbs said.

Willow buttered her roll. "I suppose it really is a pretty big thing. She's a great writer."

"Yes, most treasured here in the South," said Bob Lallo. He seemed to have surprised himself with his comment; he looked around anxiously, as if he might have said something outrageous.

"And everywhere," Willow said.

"And everywhere."

"Here, here," Fred C. Dobbs said, raising his water glass.

"Eat your chicken, Fred," Willow said, "and shut up."

Right after lunch, Willow was in the middle of her lecture on Keats when several students–without preamble or warning–stood up and went to the windows. The room where her class in romantic poetry met was on the second floor of Comer Hall, overlooking a brick street that ran from the corner near the science building down and around Brock Hall toward the women's dorms.

"Class!" Willow said. "What in heaven's name?" She rapped her pen on the lectern.

Several other students stood up and moved over toward the windows. "Come over here, Dr. Behn," one of them shouted.

"You will be seated immediately," she said. They laughed and motioned for her to join them. They started to chatter and look out the window. "This will not be tolerated," she said. She was aghast that they would interrupt her class in this way. She was beginning to get angry.

"Come on, come on, quick!" they said.

She went over to the window. Two of the students moved aside so she could look out. The street was deserted. "What?" She stuttered, "What ...?" Had they finally become completely unhinged?

Just then a car pulled up on the corner next to the science building. The door opened and a naked girl, followed by a naked boy, jumped out and sprinted down the brick street. The students cheered. Willow could hear similar merriment coming from the other windows on that side of the building, both above them and below them. She saw students across the way in the windows of Brock Hall also enjoying the exhibition. They watched the two students as they ran around the corner, their bare posteriors shining in the afternoon sun, and disappeared toward the Caf and the women's dorms beyond.

There was much hilarity and jabbering as the students were noisily reseated. They all looked at Willow expectantly to see what she would say. She would not let them think she was shocked. She said, calmly, "Well, that was something, wasn't it."

"I'll say. Wow," one of the girls said, and others tittered. Willow had not meant that, though the boy *had* been nicely equipped. You couldn't help but notice that. And the girl was slim and curvy. Willow had to admit that the fact there were two of them together this time—boy and girl—was provocative and titillating.

"Yeah," another girl said, "I think I recognized *him!*" The room exploded with more laughter.

"Who *were* those students?" Willow asked. They had both worn the now familiar ski masks.

"Mister and Miz anonymous," a boy said.

"Okay, stupid question," Willow said, "I suppose they *are* students, aren't they?"

"Who knows?" the same boy said.

"The shadow knows," another said.

"Okay, class, let's settle down," Willow said. "Let's get back to Mr. Keats."

"Do we *have* to?" a girl said.

The class was jovial. They seemed energized. Happy. It saddened Willow to think how little made them happy. The streaking *was* a phenomenon, she supposed, difficult to move away from without comment, absent some type of closure.

"Very well then," she said, "shall we all write a paper on streaking?"

They seemed to think that was hilarious. She was not serious, of course, but she hadn't thought it was *that* funny. "What makes people," she asked, when the chortles died down, "albeit two very beautiful people, want to expose themselves in that manner?"

"You noticed that, too," a boy in the back of the room said.

"I don't know if 'notice' is quite the right word," Willow said. "You don't 'notice' something that's in-your-face, do you?"

"I wouldn't mind that girl's fur being in my face," another boy, a baseball player, said.

"Mr. Hildebrand," Willow said, "that is going too far. A little jollity is one thing, but ..."

"Sorry," Scotty Hildebrand said.

"Just be careful what you say in this classroom," she said, "it's not the locker room."

"Yes m'am."

Later that afternoon, Willow sat on the front porch of her building, watching the sunset. It was getting darker earlier now, and this evening's display, with its streaks of yellow-gold clouds, was extraordinarily colorful and noisy. Willow was enjoying a glass of white wine; it had been a long day.

She relaxed in the rocking chair. Just then Freddie Quinn went by, going home from downtown, where she'd been shopping for groceries, Willow assumed, since she was pulling the little cart-wagon she took along to carry them. Freddie was married to Maury Quinn, who taught in the economics department. The couple was a Lakewood institution. They had no car; they walked everywhere they cared to go. Maury was a slight man who chain-smoked, holding his cigarettes with trembling fingers stained amber with tobacco. He was an excellent teacher. But he was withdrawn and eccentric. The students believed he had been a survivor of the Bataan Death March, which Willow knew not to be true.

"Good evening, Mrs. Quinn," Willow said, as the woman passed by, "how are you?"

"Well, I'm alive," Mrs. Quinn said. She continued on down the sidewalk and out of sight, the wheels of her cart making little squeaking noises that faded softly away in the gathering twilight.

Willow sat thinking about the pair of streakers of earlier in the afternoon. They really had been quite lovely. Two bodies bursting with youth. The image of the two of them leaping from the car and running down the street kept playing over and over in her head as if it were a film-loop that kept repeating itself. Every time she focused her thoughts on something else, the vision of the naked boy and girl would pop back: the jump from the car, the sprint down the street, over and again. It was not at all an unpleasant reverie.

She had witnessed two incidents of it in one day. Since the students had known that it would happen during her class hour and had positioned themselves to watch, Willow realized it had been well planned and publicized. It was a concerted and organized effort, it would appear. Did they have some sort of schedule? Willow would have loved to question the students more about it, but she had nudged them back to Keats by reminding them of an upcoming test. The rest of her class had continued without disruption.

As she had walked back to her office after class she met Brasfield Finch striding down the hall, or slouching along, his wrinkled jeans looking as though they hadn't been washed in weeks, his upper self clothed in a stained khaki Dickie's work shirt. He looked more like a construction worker than a college English professor; Willow supposed that pose was how Finch thought a "Writer" should appear, with his untrimmed beard and locks. Willow did not object to facial hair; in fact, she found well-trimmed beards rather appealing. But Finch's matted, tangled bristles were a reach for Rip Van Winkle.

When they passed in the hallway, Finch said to her, too loudly, with a big grin, (there were students going to and from class): "Titties and dicks everywhere you look!" She had hurried on into her office.

Just at first dark, she heard footsteps on the walk. She was sure

39

Lucy and Joan were in their apartments preparing their clever dinners; she cocked her ears. They were masculine footsteps. Whoever it was, was still behind the shrubbery. Then the person came into the pool of light that spilled out from the yellow porch bulb. She was surprised to see it was Rufus Doublet. He had shed his tweed sport coat and tie and wore a black polo shirt. He mounted the steps. Coming with some "urgent" departmental business, she was sure.

"Did you wish to see me?" she said from the shadows, and he jumped, startled.

"Dr. Behn! Willow. Um, no, actually." He shuffled his feet. He was awkward. "I was looking for Joan, actually. Is she in?"

"I assume so," she said.

"Well ..." He stood there.

"The front door's open. Second floor, knock on her door."

"Yes, of course. I know." He nodded. "Have a pleasant evening, Willow," he said. He disappeared into the front hallway, letting the heavy door with its frosted glass window thump closed behind him. Rufus Doublet. Here to see Joan. Of course. She rocked, sipping the last of her wine. Of course. She had observed Doublet's method of operation in the past; she saw completely through him, but she didn't think anyone else on campus did. He was extremely popular, with faculty and students alike, a bachelor from a small town who spoke with a creamy, velvety Southern accent that had to be fifty percent put on. Everyone liked him. Willow had seen thousands of men in the South just like him, approaching middle age–she guessed he was in his mid-forties, though there were small bags forming under his red-rimmed eyes, the eyes of a drinker, she was sure–unmarried, charming, handsome in an uninteresting way, likely gay but without the courage to be so. They were drawn to older women–their mothers?—in Doublet's case, sexually interested in them, Willow knew from her own experience, whether as a cover or as part of their denial, she did not know. He had come on to her, not overtly because she didn't let him get that far, at a departmental party a few years ago. He had really pumped up the charm for her. She had known what he was doing.

She had watched him with a sad, unfortunate woman in the home economics department, Ethel Barrineau, a still attractive unmarried woman in her sixties; Willow had observed him around her, saw how he ingratiated himself, got close to her. She could see him working his bewitchery on her, making her fall in love with

40

him, which she did. Apparently head over heels, which is what he wanted; he had broken it off with her and she'd been devastated, given to bursting into tears at inappropriate moments, such as the middle of a faculty meeting. Most people assumed she'd had a death in the family or some such, but Willow knew the truth. She knew there was something evil lurking beneath her department chairman's enthralling veneer.

And now here he was, calling on Joan Hudson. He had to all appearances chosen his next victim.

FOUR

Lily quietly sneaked away from her office the next afternoon and walked across campus to the baseball field. It was another glorious Autumn day, a high cerulean sky with only a few wisps of cottony clouds, a warm breeze that gently flapped the huge American flag on the pole beyond the fence in center field. There were only a few spectators, a tight group of girls behind the Falcons' dugout; Lily surmised they were the players' girlfriends. They were playing Elysian Fields Community College from over in New Orleans, a mostly black team. Lily took her seat in the bleachers down the third base line. She was the only one in that section of the stands. She put on a pair of black, wraparound sunglasses.

She had fished around on her cluttered desk and found the brochure on the baseball team that had come in the hand mail. She had paid little attention to it when it had first come in, but after the meeting with David Godby she gave it another look. He was the starting third baseman on the team, a sophomore, who batted third. The game was in the top of the third inning when she took her seat, the Falcons already leading 4 to 0. She watched the Elysian Fields players—who seemed undersized and uninspired— struggle at the plate against the Lakewood pitcher, a left hander. Mostly she watched David Godby, who crouched at ready with each pitch, like a large cat ready to pounce. He wore a purple uniform blouse with a gold script L on the front, his gray semi-baggy trousers hugging his butt provocatively. Behind the smoke-dark glasses she never took her eyes off him.

The inning ended with a weak ground ball to the second baseman. Godby trotted—jogged, his body in fluid control—diagonally away from her across the diamond. He disappeared in the shadow of the dugout. The first Falcons batter worked a base on balls and Godby came to the plate. She had observed him on deck, swinging two bats. He hit right handed, so she had a perfect view of his back, his broad shoulders, narrow waist, tight buttocks, his thick legs. As he strode to the plate he had looked right at her, a lingering glance that had jolted her and made her flush behind the glasses. He had a cocky grin on his face.

He hit the first pitch deep into the gap in left center for a triple, scoring the runner ahead of him. He slid into third ahead of the throw. He stood up, one foot on the bag, dusting himself off with his hands, his head tilted to the side, his dark shoulder length hair curling beneath his batting helmet, smiling at her.

Lily lived in Trilling Apartments on the edge of the campus. The building was owned by Morris Trilling, a professor of geology, "Dr. Rock," as he was known by the students. Trilling had his doctorate from the University of Oklahoma; he served as Academic Marshall, carrying the heavy ceremonial mace in all academic processions. He took his position quite seriously, mustering the faculty with brisk and curt orders, micro-managing the integrity of the ritual; he had been known to upbraid an instructor or assistant professor who had had the effrontery to borrow and wear a colleague's doctoral gown—to which he was not entitled—and send him to the end of the line or even suspend him from the processional entirely.

The apartment building was two story, faded red brick, six two bedroom apartments stacked three over three with a wide hallway and stairwell down the middle. It was occupied by junior faculty and some high school teachers with small children, so the hallways were always cluttered with big wheel tricycles and plastic toys. Lily had the left rear apartment, the only one with direct access to the fire escape at the back, a rickety, rusted iron structure that looked precarious but was substantial enough to hold a person leaving or entering from the privacy of the back yard, which was protected on three sides by high, bushy live oak trees and not visible from the street. The back yard was also littered with toys.

Lily lay back on a blue denim covered chaise she'd bought at the thrift store when she'd moved into her new apartment. She was naked. David Godby was standing before her, equally devoid of clothes. She was admiring his fat penis, heavy and root-like. She reached out and gripped it. Just then Godby gave a high wheeze and spurted onto her stomach.

"Jesus," she said, "I hope you got more where that came from."

"Yes, m'am," he said.

She gripped both his arms, pulling him on top of her, between her outstretched legs.

"Ain't you gonna wipe it off?" he asked.

"Why?" she said. "Just fuck me, okay?"

She gasped when she felt his hot penis slip inside her. He knew what to do. Boys are born knowing what to do, she thought. *Dogs* know what to do. He was snorting, breathing heavily through his nostrils. He fucked like a dog. Mechanically and fast, rapidly, without variation. She had the sense that he was concentrating on doing it right. It would be years—if ever—before he learned to do it right. But his body was smooth and firm, and, since it was his second time, he lasted for a long time.

Afterward, she gave him a beer. Might as well go all the way. She didn't know how old he was; she didn't ask. It didn't matter. He was a student, and she could be fired in a New York minute if anyone found out she'd even had him in her apartment. Lily had never been one who was afraid to take risks. There had been many times in the past when if she'd been found out—if it had been discovered what she was up to—she would have been in big trouble. She had early on learned that living on the edge gave her a thrill.

Lily's undergraduate degree was from Birmingham-Southern College, and all her graduate work was at Emory. She had done fairly well in her classes, she felt, compiling a solid B average, but she knew that in graduate school that was barely adequate. When she had completed her course work, the topic for her dissertation had been approved: "Magical Realism and Feminism in the Early Novels of Toni Morrison." The topic was as far as she'd gotten with the thesis; she had not written a word. She had been hired as an instructor on the basis of her ABD status; the department made it clear—especially the three older women, with Willow Behn the most outspoken—that her continued appointment would be contingent on her receiving her degree.

"We will reevaluate in the spring," Dr. Behn had told her, "at which time you are to demonstrate progress toward completion of your dissertation."

"What about for next year?" she'd asked the older woman.

"What do you mean, 'for next year?'"

"To be honest, I don't think I'll finish my dissertation in the spring." With the avalanche of papers she was required to mark, and two new preparations, she couldn't imagine when she would even find time to *start* on the goddamn thing.

"My dear Miss Putnam," Behn said, "I *know* you won't get your degree in the spring. But by the following spring, ahh, that is another matter. You will complete it then, and get your degree, or your contract will not be offered. *Progress*, Miss Putnam, what we'll look for is progress. And *I* will be the one making that evaluation."

"You?"

"Yes. If your evaluations are all in order, and I feel you're making progress, I'll make a recommendation to the department. And they will accept it. You needn't worry about that."

Lily thought there was some hidden agenda in Willow Behn's remarks, but she couldn't be sure what it was. Campus politics—especially within the department—was a confusing muddle to her. The chair, Dr. Doublet, was a cipher; her gaydar had alarmed loudly when she met him, but he'd looked at her with a stiff, lustful lasciviousness that chilled her. He seemed a passive administrator, more concerned with projecting his own charm than anything else. Lily had no doubt that the three older women, the holdovers from the women's school days—two of whom, she had observed, seemed to have something of a crush on the much younger Doublet—were the ones who really ran the department. There was Brasfield Finch, who seemed to exist in some sodden periphery all his own, two young instructors, Lisa Holland and Owen Fielder, both with MA degrees and one year appointments, and a host of adjuncts that the administration hired to parcel out the excess basic courses, which seemed to multiply with a growth pattern all their own; the adjuncts were made to work with no benefits and starvation wages, which seemed to suit the administration just fine.

So Willow Behn *was* her mentor. She had not been told that. Maybe she was being told that now, and maybe it was not official. The department seemed to have no formal policy of tenured faculty mentoring young, beginning professors, a practice common in many schools. Lily had heard talk of that back in graduate school, especially in the flurry of job seeking that went on.

"What do you mean?" Lily asked.

"What do you mean, what do I mean?" Behn said.

"*You* will decide?"

"I will make a recommendation. You demonstrate to me your progress, and I will make a recommendation, that's all I meant."

"Oh. Okay." She'd considered reaching out and touching the older woman again, just to see her nervous reaction, but she didn't.

Now she sat sipping her beer, looking at the boy across from her. He was sprawled on the chaise, his T shirt out over his jeans, his sneakers with their limp white socks on the floor. The boy *had* had plenty more, but he was monotonous and unimaginative. When she had moved to perform fellatio he had flinched away from her, staring at her with a mixture of excitement, fascination, and thinly veiled disgust. He could probably have gone six or seven more times, but four was enough. He *did* have a very large cock.

"Wow," she said, "that was really great." She knew she had to be extremely careful. Boys his age had a tendency to run and brag; she couldn't have that. On the other hand, she didn't want to have offended him with her over-aggression on the cock-sucking front. Who would have ever expected *that*? Or for any other unintended injury to his post-adolescent ego. She didn't want to do anything to upset him. Kid gloves. "You're really good."

"That's what they tell me," he said.

"We really can't tell anyone about this, David," she said, "not if we want it to happen again."

"Right. Coach would shit."

"He wouldn't be the only one."

He laughed and took a swig. They were drinking Budweiser out of the can. "Okay," he said. "I won't tell anybody. I want some more."

"I'm really serious." It was only now settling into her mind just how serious it *was*, how vulnerable she had made herself to this kid, about whom she knew next to nothing. Risking this job that she knew she'd been lucky to land. She knew people with degree in hand who were having trouble finding a position. She itched pleasurably with the danger. She sometimes wondered if she might not be totally psychotic; a counselor in student support services at Birmingham-Southern had told her that she had a "reckless disregard for her own well being." Whatever.

"I'm not gonna say anything," he reiterated. "My girlfriend would have a calf, too."

"You have a girlfriend?"

"Yeah."

"You never said you had a girlfriend," she said.

"You never asked me."

"Right," she said. "Do I know her? Is she in the class?"

"No."

All right. She did not care, of course, except that she didn't want some jealous little coed coming down on her. She could always deny everything. Students were always pulling some kind of shit or another. "Just keep it under your baseball cap, okay?"

"You got it, teach," he said.

He grinned. His teeth were white and square. He had smelled of lingering sweat and Dial soap from his hasty shower after the game. She got up and took his empty can and went over to the little alcove that served as her kitchen. She could feel his eyes on her. She had changed into a pair of white shorts, skimpy ones.

When she took the cold beer from the refrigerator she glanced back at him over her shoulder. He was still grinning, like a sated, satisfied bear.

"You got one beautiful ass, Miss Putnam," he said.

"How romantic," she blurted sarcastically, before she thought. "But thanks. Hey, in our little love nest here, just Lily will do. I'm not that much older than you."

"I like Miss Putnam,'" he said, "makes it more kinky."

"Okay." Maybe she had misjudged him.

"How old *are* you, anyhow?" he asked.

She hesitated. To share that information with him seemed too intimate, considering that they hardly knew each other, yet just minutes before they had been as close as two people can possibly get. Physically, at least. What the hell. "Twenty-six," she said.

"I'm nineteen," he said. Well. Congratulations. "Maude is twenty," he added.

"Maude?"

"My girlfriend." He nodded. He seemed proud of her age. Why? Because she was closer to Lily's age than he was?

"You have a girlfriend named *Maude*?"

"Yeah. Why? You know her?"

"No, no. Just that ... Well, Maude seems like the name of an old woman." She chuckled. He seemed to bristle. Uh-oh. "No, just kidding, Maude is a lovely name," she said.

"You better believe it," he said.

President Steagall sat at his heavy, mastodon-like desk, its broad, flat surface empty except for a green blotter with leather corners, an antique bronze inkwell that had been a gift from the board of trustees, his Cross pen, placed just so, diagonally on the blotter, and a mug of hot coffee, gold with *Lakewood College* in purple lettering, beneath that *State College of Liberal Arts*, in gold lined white, that Eloise Hoyle had just brought in to him. He wore a blue serge suit with narrow lapels, a white oxford button-down and a purple and gold striped tie. A tiny American flag adorned his left lapel.

He was recalling the startling visage of the naked woman running across the quadrangle, so incongruous on the quiet campus that he doubted he had actually seen the spectacle. His mind may have been playing tricks on him. Steagall, early in the previous summer, had been diagnosed with the onset of dementia. He had noticed an unsteadiness in his gait, a tendency to bump into things, his desk, a door frame. He had also become forgetful, and little things bothered him; sometimes, for example, after picking up the TV remote, he would have to pause to figure out not only how to use it but what it actually was. His doctor had been puzzled and had given him all manner of tests. One of the tests, a childish one involving putting together little plastic triangles into various patterns, had frustrated him. That had led to word association tests, the administering of simple math problems, and questions resembling the riddles that appeared in the Sunday comics section, all of which had been met with indignation on the part of Steagall. "This is ridiculous!" he'd said to his doctor, an idiot who seemed about ten years old. "Mild dementia," Dr. Merkle had said, and prescribed, laughingly, Namensa and walking every day.

Steagall had told absolutely no one about the diagnosis. Not even his wife Nelle. Especially not Nelle. She had not seemed to notice anything amiss; she was so wrapped up in being the "first lady" of Lakewood College that she didn't notice much of anything. Her current project was planting day lilies at Flowerhill and all over the town of Lakewood. The day lilies were to be her legacy, and she was so narrowly focused on them that she didn't even realize he was taking the new medications; anyway, he kept them hidden in his sock drawer. Like an alcoholic hiding liquor, he thought ruefully. He was worried that if word got out that he suffered from dementia he would be forced to retire, and he did not plan to retire until after at least one more year, when he had been promised by some influential members of the board that he would be given a sizable raise, which would increase his pension and retirement package tremendously. He had his eye on a new sailboat for their place over in Pensacola.

Steagall relaxed back into his plush black leather swivel chair and looked around the spacious office. Under the side windows that looked out over the quad was a low table with a few keepsakes and framed photographs. There was one of Nelle, an old one from her thirties, and one of him, from his swing band days, when he had first started teaching. He had his saxophone on a lanyard around his neck, a white dinner jacket and black bow tie, and a flat top haircut, blonde and shiny. His hair was now dull gray, and he noticed every morning when he shaved that it was thinning, his pink scalp becoming more and more visible, seemingly with each passing day. His cheeks sagged. He looked every minute of his sixty-three years.

Eloise Hoyle stuck her head in the door. "Mr. Finch is here," she said.

The tiresome Mr. Finch. But John needed him. He hoped he was sober.

Finch sat down across from Steagall. He had on boots and dungarees, a wrinkled shirt, dressed like a gardener. His absurd beard seemed to have grown longer and unrulier since Steagall had last seen him.

"What can I do for you, John?" he asked. No pleasantries, no good morning, nothing.

"I needed to talk with you, Brasfield," Steagall said.

"So talk." Finch made no effort to hide his contempt for administrators. Not only did he insist on equal footing with them, he tended to talk down to them.

"How have you been?" Steagall asked.

"Fine. You?"

"Oh, you know. Busy, too busy."

"Ha," Finch said, but he did not smile. He looked at his wristwatch. "I've got a class," he said.

"Oh yes, of course. I think I mentioned to you once before that I invited Lenora Hart to the campus."

For a moment Finch did not reply, nor react. He just gazed at Steagall. He shook his head. "Yes," he said, finally, "you did. Several times, as a matter of fact."

"Did I?"

"Get on with it, John," Finch said.

"Okay." The president just sat there. He seemed to have lost his train of thought. He picked up a pen and doodled on a little pad.

"My understanding is," Finch said, "her fee is twenty-five thousand dollars, if you can even get her to come. I think I remember telling you that before, didn't I?"

"Yes, you did." Steagall seemed to snap out of it. "But here's the thing. I've managed to wrest a few dollars from the foundation, and combined with funds from the Concert and Lecture series, I think we can swing her fee okay."

"Twenty-five thousand dollars?"

"Yes. It's not that much."

"Only half my salary, John. Jesus fucking Christ."

"You don't have to get vulgar, now, Finch."

"Twenty-five thousand dollars for that hack?"

"I hardly think she's a hack."

"Hack. That novel is shit."

"That novel is one of the most beloved novels in American literature," Steagall said. "It's a best-seller."

"Beloved, as in sappy and phony. No. We don't need her here. Besides, she won't go anywhere. She won't even answer letters. I'm surprised she even answered yours."

"But, you know her, don't you?"

"Yes, I know her. What's that got to do with it?"

"Well, it's been a while since we've heard from her. I've tried to call her, but her number is unlisted. I've written her several letters about our plans for her here when she visits. No reply."

"That's par for the course, John."

"You could personally write her a letter assuring her that she'll be welcome here. Or give her a call. You probably have her number?"

"No, I don't have her goddam number," Finch said.

"Even with the twenty-five thousand dollars I'm afraid she may be backing out."

"I thought that's where this was going. No, I won't write the bitch. Or call her, either. Forget it."

"You shouldn't call a beloved writer a bitch," Steagall said.

"Stop saying 'beloved,' John, you're wearing it out."

John crossed his hands on top of his desk. "You are hardly in a position to refuse this request, Brasfield," he said calmly. "Dean Jefferson has gotten reports that you've come to class drunk ..."

Finch snorted.

"... or at least smelling of drink. So far ..." He paused. "So far, those reports have gone no farther than this desk. I have the option to act on them, administer some discipline or something even ... harsher, which would be regrettable, or pass them on up to the board. Or ignore them." He waited.

"All right, John," Finch said, after a minute, "I'll write your little celebrity writer." The man's eyes were narrow slits over his bizarre beard. "You can get a few more feathers for your chief's bonnet, eh?"

"Wow, I heard that Lenora Hart was definitely going to be here in the spring," Lily Putnam said to him as he walked to his office door. Lily was standing in front of her own office, in a green mini dress. He had a slight little scrotum tingle when he saw her.

"What?" he said, stopping abruptly.

"Lenora Hart? The Seniors' Day convocation?"

Jesus God, what did Steagall do, send out an Extra Express Wednesday Memo? It was that fucking Olive Hoyle. She and the ladies in her book club, at which Finch had once been a guest, average age seventy plus—they served only a rancid fruit punch and hard cookies—were probably creaming their granny panties at the prospect. They had no idea how unpleasant their "beloved" writer could be.

"Unfortunately," he said.

"She can't come?"

"No, unfortunate that she probably will." He gave her his best, twisted artist's smile, more a grimace.

"But ... but she's a great writer, isn't she?"

"No. She is a drudge. A lackey."

"Oh," she said. She quickly slipped into her office. Finch unlocked his door and went in. His advanced composition class was not for another fifteen minutes, so he pulled out a yellow legal pad and began to draft a letter to Lenora Hart. Most people tried to write her at her address in Naples, but Finch had her address in Manhattan, where she spent much of her time in a penthouse apartment in the east eighties overlooking the park. He had been there. He even had her private phone numbers, and if he had to he would break down and call her. If Steagall wanted the disagreeable woman so passionately, Finch would deliver her.

He had first met Lenora Hart some fifteen years earlier, in Hattiesburg. He had gone back to graduate school in his forties to get an MFA degree in fiction writing. (The previous dean had recognized the degree as terminal; not so the moronic Jefferson.) Though he had published one moderately successful novel—a couple of decent reviews, sales figures discouraging—and had been hard at work on another—which got longer and longer as he worked—the administration at Lakewood College had decided that he had to have the MFA degree for tenure. He had applied at both Cornell and Iowa and been rejected. The University of Southern Mississippi accepted him. Lenora Hart had come there as a visiting writer for a week, and he had been assigned as her guide and host. She had made a huge splash with her first novel, *To Lynch A Wild Duck*, which Finch thought was utterly puerile, callow, and infantile, but it had sold wildly, made her a millionaire, and got her the Pulitzer. They became drinking buddies, got drunk together, and wound up in bed, an incident of which Finch could recall nothing at all. Lenora Hart must have thought it was a fine time, since she began writing him mash notes.

She was a heavy, squatty woman, thick-thighed, with a round flat face like the bottom of a pie pan, not his cup of tea at all. He had responded indifferently to her letters, barely acknowledging them. They had met next at a Modern Language Association meeting in New York, where they were both giving readings, and she had joined him for drinks and then invited him to her apartment. They got together a few years later, again in New York, this time at Book Expo America, when Finch's novel *The Fox and The Pheasant*—for which she had given him a blurb—was published. They occasionally talked on the phone. Once he had asked her to blurb one of his students' collection of short stories, and she had simply sent his letter back with "Hell No!" scrawled across the top. She would not grant interviews. She had never published anything but the novel, not even a short story, and some graduate student let out of school had published an essay in *The Southern Review* suggesting that she had not even written the novel herself but had stolen it from a blind young girl, a poet, at the University of Florida. He offered as proof a fragment of a tattered Braille manuscript that proved nothing but that a section of Hart's novel had been rendered into Braille sometime in the past, whether originally or copied it was difficult, if not impossible, to determine.

He finished the draft, copied it over on a college letterhead, addressed it, sealed it and dropped it in the out basket on his way to his class.

In the late afternoon, after his writing workshop, Finch noticed that Lily Putnam's door was cracked open. He peeked inside. She was at her desk, clutching her red ball point pen. Everybody else had gone, including the departmental secretary, Oona Faulk. The senior faculty had student assistants, but they all shared the one secretary; Oona was middle aged, gray, and cranky and sat at a desk at the end of the hall, in the middle of a cluster of offices. She attended some god-awful fundamental church and had little to say to Finch, which was fine with him. When she was introduced to him, she'd said, "Nice to meet you, Mr. Finch, I hope you are blessed today." "It seems exceedingly unlikely," he'd replied. She had glowered at him. He did not need a secretary anyway, and he declined a student assistant. They were more trouble than they were worth.

He stood in the hallway for a few moments, watching the girl. The late afternoon sunlight crossed her desk obliquely, illuminating the forest green mini dress she was wearing. She was sitting carelessly, and he could see pleasant expanses of soft inner thighs. She was gripping the pen so hard he thought she might snap it in two; she chewed on her lovely lower lip, looking fixedly at the paper on the desk in front of her. She mumbled something. It sounded like "shit." She made a slashing mark that tore the paper. "Oh, shit!" she said, more audibly.

He spied on her for a couple more minutes, then went across the hall to his office and deposited a stack of manuscripts on his cluttered desk. He had his students read them aloud in class, so he wouldn't have to read them himself, though he pretended he had as he made his workshop comments off the top of his head. He locked his office door and went back over to Putnam's. She was still perched there in her chair. Why did so many young women these days chop their hair off like a boy's? He found the look slightly unnerving. As the boys let their hair grow longer and shaggier, lots of the girls had theirs cut to look like Marine recruits. Putnam's was one of the extremes; her hair was short, parted, and brushed down on the sides in front of her ears to give her "sideburns." But she was still a ravishing creature. Perhaps her style was even more comely because of the boyish look. Were he putting her in a book, he would have called her "foxy."

He tapped his knuckles softly on her door, and her head snapped around.

"Oh," she said. The smile. "I thought I was the only one still here."

"My workshop ran over," he said. "How about I buy you a drink?"

"Bar or apartment?" she said. She laughed and winked at him.

"We've already been to a bar. How about my apartment?"

"Oh, ho, we better wait on that one."

"Bar it is, then. You like Stache's, don't you?"

"I've only been there the one time, when I went with you, but, yeah. It's nice."

Nice was not a word Finch would have used to describe Stache's. It was cool and unique; the tables and chairs were mismatched old castoffs, the walls papered with an eclectic collection of drawings and posters announcing open mic poetry readings, art openings, and college theater productions. It was in an old house, with a covered front porch. Finch found it especially comfortable, precisely because it was *not* nice. They poured a fair and decent Scotch on the rocks and made excellent Martinis. Most of the students who went there of course drank copious amounts of beer.

"Then let's go. All work and no play ... You know the routine."

She seemed to hesitate. "Could we *walk* downtown? It's a beautiful day. And I need to stop by my apartment and pick up something."

"No problem. Where do you live?"

"Trilling Apartments."

"AKA 'the roach palace.' Old Morris hasn't had a pest control company in there in forty years. It's right on the way."

She brought a green canvas book bag full of papers with her, slinging it over her shoulder. He touched her elbow as they walked down the hall.

When they'd gotten to the front of her building she had said, "Just be a second," and sprinted up the sidewalk and through the front door. Finch had stood on the street, waiting. When she'd returned she was without the book bag; instead, a plastic bag was dangling from her arm. "All set," she'd said.

It was a Thursday afternoon and Stache's was not crowded. She set the bag on the floor by her chair. They had a small wobbly table in a corner of the porch. The waiter, a pony tailed boy that Finch thought may have been in his writing workshop one time or another, took their orders. "I'll have a vodka and tonic, please," she said. Finch had been afraid she'd order a pina colada or a Tom Collins, something like that. "Chivas Regal on the rocks," he said.

"Yes sir, Mr. Finch, the usual," the boy said. Yes, he looked vaguely familiar.

"How've you been?" Finch asked him, in case he *had* been in his class.

The boy shrugged. "About the same, I guess," he said, and slouched back through the front door.

"One of your students?" she asked when the boy was gone.

"I have no idea," he said, "more to the point, how have *you* been?"

"Papers! I'm buried."

"Throw them down the stairs," he said.

She chuckled. "I wish," she said.

She looked around. "This is a neat place," she said.

"Hardly neat."

"I didn't mean ..."

"Come now, Miss Putnam. I'm not so old and decrepit that I don't know the slang meaning of neat."

"Why do you keep referring to yourself as 'not so old' or something? Methinks the gentleman doth protest too much."

"Touché," he said. "Don't you realize I'm fishing for a compliment?"

"You are?"

"Of course. I want you to tell me how young and vital I am."

"Well, you're not old. Stop saying you are."

"Okay." He looked at her. Just then the boy set their drinks before them.

"Thank you," she said.

When the boy had shuffled away, he said, "I've still got a little gas in the tank."

"I bet you do," she said, looking saucily at him over the rim of her glass. "Tell me about Lenora Hart."

"Oh, thttt," he said, making a raspberry. "It's going to be a nice sunset."

The sky looked brushed with gold, like faint watercolor strokes.

"Florida has nice sunsets," she said. "You can't see anything in Atlanta. Tell me about Lenora Hart."

"Why do you want to talk about that charlatan?"

She watched him sip his drink. Now that she'd gotten used to it, she'd decided that his beard was awesome. She'd never been with a man with a beard like that. She wondered what it would be like to kiss through it. How it would feel tickling her inner thighs. She crossed her legs and took a drink of her vodka-tonic. "Why do you call her a charlatan?"

"Why, indeed," he said.

"No, I really want to know. Lenora Hart is a well-respected, admired—"

"Don't say beloved,' please," he interrupted.

"A *great* writer. At least *I* think so. And about a million other people."

"Quite right. She has a sterling reputation, a loyal following." He stopped. She expected him to go on, but he didn't.

"Well, is she coming or not? The coffee room was all atwitter this afternoon."

"Probably," he said.

"I've always heard ..."

"Yes, that is right. The only reason she'll come is that *I* urged her to."

"Is she a friend of yours?"

"Of sorts. We are old acquaintances."

"But you don't like her? You don't like her work?"

"She is difficult. And her work, which consists only of one children's book, is pablum."

"You really think so?"

"Yes, I think so. I wouldn't say it if I didn't."

"So you are right and everybody else in America is wrong?"

"Miss Putnam, I really want to like you. Let's talk about something else." He reached out and patted her hand. Some of the long hairs from his mustache curtained his mouth and glistened with tiny droplets of Scotch.

"Okay, and I asked you to call me Lily."

"Of course. Lily."

"So," she said, relaxing back in her chair. "How are your classes going?"

"Onerous," he said, "try something else."

"Aren't you going to ask me about *my* classes?"

"No, classes are a pain in the ass, Lily. We all know that."

He certainly had a funny way of flirting. "There is one thing I'd like to ask you," she said.

"Fire away."

"Well, is Willow Behn my mentor?"

"Pardon?"

"Dr. Behn. Is she my mentor?"

"I'd think you'd know that better than me. Why? Do you consider her one?"

"Well, not in so many words. They said in graduate school that some colleges had a mentoring program, senior faculty mentoring junior, like that. I wondered if we have something like that."

"If we do, I don't know anything about it," he said. He looked shrewdly at her. The green dress melded into the shrubbery beside the porch; in contrast her skin was glowing like bleached pearls. So. That's what was going on. Willow Behn was trying to beat him into those thongs. "I'd be happy to be your mentor, Lily," he said. He patted her hand again.

"That's sweet," she said.

"In fact, why don't we start tonight? I've got a quart of vodka at my place. We could ..."

"I've got *papers*," she said. "But *soon*, though." She smiled at him. He was admiring her, pleased that she'd left the door open. He saw her eyes, which were focused on the street, widen. "What the fuck?" she said.

He swung around to look where she was looking. He blinked. A man was jogging by on the sidewalk, in nothing but a red ski mask and sneakers. He was jogging casually and slowly, as if he were out somewhere all alone. His penis flopped back and forth. They watched him in stunned silence. Other people on the porch had seen him and laughed and cheered. He gave no sign he'd heard them. He just continued—slowly, almost a parody of a jog—down the sidewalk.

"What was that?" Finch said.

"Pretty awesome stuff," Lily Putnam replied.

FIVE

Paulette Jefferson, meeting Lily at the door, startled the younger woman with her pink pedal pushers and flowered blouse. She accepted Lily's wine without comment; she glanced at the label and said, "Come get something to drink." Oh, shit, she'd brought something tacky. She followed the woman into the kitchen, where a bar had been set up on the counter. There were half-gallon bottles of bourbon, scotch, gin and vodka, a bowl of ice, mixers, a pitcher of water. Paulette set the wine on the counter next to the whiskey. "What's your poison?" she asked.

"Um, gosh, choices," Lily said. She laughed nervously.

"Well?" the woman said, not smiling.

"Vodka, please. With tonic." She looked around. "You have a really charming place here, Dr. Jefferson."

The woman snorted. It was a cramped, tiny cottage, not what Lily had expected a dean to live in at all. It was not even especially clean. Certainly not neat. "Hardly charming, dear," the dean's wife said, "and please, Paulette. We have no titles here." She poured a generous portion of vodka over ice and added tonic from a small bottle, one of a six pack sitting on the bar. She didn't bother with a lime. There were none evident.

"Thanks," Lily said, taking the drink, in a large almost iced tea size glass, "Paulette."

"We are planning to build," the older woman said. "Wallace keeps delaying it. He won't admit it, but he has his eye on the presidency of a community college in Pensacola. He doesn't want anyone to know in case he doesn't get it."

"Really? You might leave?"

"No, dear." She winked. "Masculine fantasy, you know. We must indulge them."

"Yes, m ..." She almost said "m'am."

"You almost said 'm'am,'" Paulette Jefferson said.

"Okay. You got me."

It struck Lily as a bit too familiar, this woman telling her about her husband's thwarted ambitions as soon as she walked in the door. Oh, well.

"Let's join the boys in the living room," Paulette said, and Lily followed her up the short hallway and into a parlor crammed with furniture. The dean stood, holding a tumbler of whiskey; he wore a gray sweatshirt and baggy cargo shorts. Rufus Doublet stood as well. He wore jeans and a tight black T shirt—almost, Lily thought, a muscle shirt. Both men moved toward her. She stuck out her hand. But they both wanted to hug her, as if she were a long lost relative or something. They both squeezed her tightly, flattening her breasts against their chests.

"The lovely Lily," the dean said, loud and jovial. "Welcome."

Lily didn't think she'd spoken more than two or three words to him before, at the reception for new faculty at Flowerhill. Rufus Doublet—her department chairman, the man she thought of as her boss—smiled warmly, his eyes twinkling. He, too, held a heavy glass tumbler of whiskey. "Lily, how nice," he said. He looked her over admiringly, not like a gay guy would at all. His eyes almost burned her breasts. She didn't think he'd looked at her that way before; she didn't think he'd even *noticed* her particularly, which was why she'd presumed he was gay. Maybe he was bi. Whatever was available. She'd known people like that before.

"Let's sit down," Paulette said, and they all sat. The room was dim, lit by only one small table lamp. Lily sipped and looked around. The art on the walls was imitation interior-decorator chic, the kind you can buy at Wal-Mart. There were no bookcases. She had to pause a moment to remember the dean's specialty. History, of course! She squinted. No books. Her own tiny apartment was stuffed with papers and books, literally littered with them. She could hardly move for them. Though the Jeffersons' living room was cluttered and crowded, there was no indication that anyone worked there, or even read.

"So nice of you to come," the dean boomed. "Paulette fixed you up with a drink, I see."

"Sure did," she said, feeling a bit foolish hearing herself trying to match his jocoseness. Her smile stiffened.

"Good, good," he said. "Rufus was just telling me that you're writing about some colored lady."

"I beg your pardon?" she said. She wasn't sure she'd heard him correctly.

"Oh, goatfeathers, Wally," Doublet said, chuckling, "I never said any such thing. I said her dissertation was on Toni Morrison. I would never ..."

"You said Toni Morrison was a darky."

"Please, Wallace," Paulette said.

"I said she was a Negro writer," Rufus said. He shook his head at Lily, grinning, as in Can you believe it?

"Black, Afro-American, whatever they're calling themselves these days," Dean Jefferson said.

"African-American," Lily said.

"Whatever," the dean said, waving his drink. "But let's not talk academic stuff, it's Friday night."

"Are you settled, Lily?" Paulette asked.

"Huh?"

"In your apartment? You're in Trilling's apartments, aren't you?"

"Oh, yes," Lily said. "It's ... comfortable. I feel right at h—"

The dean interrupted her with a guffaw. "Comfortable? Come now, lovely Lily."

"You should have seen my place in Atlanta," Lily said, laughing.

"You were right, Rufus," the dean said, "she's charming, and witty, too."

Lily squirmed slightly in her incommodious chair, which seemed to be a dining room chair being used as living room furniture. What had she said that could remotely be labeled *witty?*

"We're very excited about Lenora Hart's coming to campus," Paulette Jefferson said. "I've read all her books."

All? There's just one, isn't there? "Very exciting," Lily said.

"Brasfield's got his panties all in a wad about it, though," Rufus said. He crossed his legs. "A bit of professional jealousy there, wouldn't you say?"

Lily said nothing. She surprised herself by feeling oddly defensive of Finch, though she ordinarily found him exceedingly annoying. He was boorish; but he had been surprisingly moved and humbled when she'd taken his two novels out of the bag that night at Stache's and asked him to autograph them. "Where'd you find those old things?" he'd asked, almost shyly. "At a bookstore in Atlanta," she'd replied, "where'd you think?" "For Lily Putnam," he had written, "your lovely presence makes north Florida an exceptionally better place." He had signed them with a flourish.

Lily took a big slug of her drink. A heavy silence settled into the room. Dean Jefferson picked up a pipe and began to stuff it from a leather pouch.

"Must you?" Paulette asked.

"Better than those," he said, pointing, and Lily noticed that

Paulette was smoking a cigarette.

"B for Botticelli," Mrs. Jefferson said brightly. "You know how to play, don't you?"

"Oh, yes," she said. (She'd asked Finch that afternoon to refresh her memory about the game. "You must be going over to those dreadful Jeffersons," he'd said.)

"I'm going first," Wallace pronounced.

"All right, dear," Paulette said.

"I'm an A," the dean said.

"Lily?" Paulette said.

"Okay," Lily said. She wrinkled her forehead, thinking. Minutes ticked by. Her mind was blank. A. Okay, it came to her. "Are you the son of a Greek immigrant who made good?" she asked.

"Not very specific," the dean said. He closed his eyes, leaned his head back. He was sitting in an old vinyl recliner. The gray smoke drifted up around him, curling toward the ceiling. He thought and thought. "All right," he said finally, "I'm not Aristotle Onassis."

"That's an O," Paulette said.

"You're not Spiro Agnew," Lily said.

"Oh, a good one," Paulette said. " 'The nattering nabobs of negativism!' He really knows how to tell off the liberal media, doesn't he?"

"He's not Greek, is he?" the dean said. "I don't think he's Greek."

"Ask him your direct," Paulette said to Lily.

"He's not *Greek*," the dean said.

"Oh, be quiet. Lily?"

"Are you living?"

"Yes and no," Dean Jefferson said.

"Oh, good grief, here we go again," Rufus Doublet said, laughing gaily.

They went round and round. The smoke in the packed room grew thick. Poets, athletes. Other politicians, actors. On and on. It became apparent that they weren't going to guess Wallace Jefferson's person. But it was fun. There was lots of laughter. Long timeouts. Lily lost count of her drinks. She didn't even try to keep up.

"So you're from Atlanta," Paulette said to her once.

"Decatur, actually," Lily said.

"I'm originally from Chicago," (Aha!) the woman said, "but my family moved to Fort Lauderdale when I was in high school.

My father retired."

"Oh, was your family, you know, older?"

"No," she said, "just richer!" She laughed merrily.

Dean Jefferson put on a Lotte Lenya recording and turned it up. The woman's screeching drowned everything else out for a few minutes. "Turn that down!" Paulette shouted above it.

Once, in the kitchen, Lily was getting another drink and found herself in there with Rufus Doublet. Her head was swimmy. They could hear Paulette and Wallace having an argument in the living room. Suddenly, out of nowhere, he grabbed her and planted a wet, sloppy kiss on her mouth. His tongue was like a stumpy sausage.

Lily let him kiss her. She eased back from him. "Whew," she said. "I mean, wow." She didn't know what she meant. The vodka was coursing through her brain. He fixed her with a smoldering look, his eyes drooping half shut. She was not at all attracted to him, but she didn't want to offend him. After all, he was her boss. But he had an aging fraternity-boy look, a military style haircut shaved on the sides that she found unappealing. (In fact, Willow had told her one day that he actually was the advisor to a local fraternity.) "That was ... was ... a surprise," she said.

In a sexy drawl, he said, "There's more where that came from," and she had to catch herself to keep from laughing in his face. She had to be careful.

The game resumed. She kept forgetting what they were doing. When Lily looked at her watch she was astonished to see that it was after two o'clock. She was drunk. The others were as well. The three of them finally gave up the game, surrendered it to the dean.

"I am Ahura Mazda," Dean Jefferson said.

"Who?" Lily blurted. She giggled.

"Ahura Mazda."

"Who the fuck is that?" Rufus asked. Tongues had gotten looser as the evening had worn on.

"An ancient Zoroastrian deity," Jefferson said smugly. He puffed his pipe.

"No fair," Paulette said.

"Yes fair," Jefferson said.

Paulette stood up. She staggered a bit. "You are a sack of shit," she said to her husband. She did not laugh.

"Well, I guess I better be going," Lily said. She felt woozy when she stood. "It's late. I certainly had a wonderful time."

"Come back, dear," the older woman said. She made no move to show Lily out.

"All right, then," Lily said, "Goodnight. I enjoyed it, guys." She let herself out the front door. There was a faint nip in the early morning air, the singular and lonely sign of autumn in north Florida.

"I want you two to be an ad hoc committee for Lenora Hart's visit," Rufus Doublet said to Finch and Willow. They were sitting in the chairman's office.

"No way," Finch said.

"Why do you need a *committee*, for heaven's sakes?" Willow asked. "In my opinion, there are far too many committees already."

"I want this to go smoothly," Doublet said, "Steagall does, too."

"Good luck with that," Finch said.

"Just what, exactly, do you have against this woman, Brasfield?" Doublet asked.

"She's a fraud," Finch said.

"I thought you were old friends. You told me once ..."

"I *knew* her, yes," Finch said.

"Ahhh, bad blood, eh?" He was looking suspiciously at the writer.

"I'm afraid I'm not very good with punch and cookies," Willow said.

"Oh, that's all been taken care of. The caf will cater everything."

"Then what do you need a committee for?"

"To make things run smoothly."

"You said that," Willow said, "How am *I* supposed to 'make things run smoothly?'"

"You are both senior faculty," Rufus said, "and we want to make a good impression. Sometimes people tend to get giddy when there is a celebrity around. *Maturity* is important."

"Maturity? Ha," said Willow.

"You just want me on some committee so you can keep an eye on me," Finch said. "You and that moron Steagall are both afraid I'll embarrass you. You won't need *me* for that."

"Steagall wants *you* to introduce her," Doublet said to Finch.

"And you want *me* to police *him*. No thanks," Willow said.

"No. You are both impressive people. You have credentials. This is a big deal." He shook out a memo on lavender paper, the president's color. "John has filled me in on Hart's contract. The woman has requested—no, *required*—a four-star hotel, nothing less. She refuses to stay in guest housing on campus. The nearest four-star hotel is the Wynfrey, in Tallahassee. She will not allow a student or faculty member to drive her back and forth; she demands a limo and driver. She sent John a list of things she wants in her hotel suite, waiting for her: liquor—she specified Jack Daniels—chocolate covered *strawberries*, for God's sakes. She wants a *radio*! No TV allowed, a radio! The woman is impossible."

"What did I tell you?" Finch said, laughing.

"I suppose great writers are allowed some degree of eccentricity, but this is a bit much."

"You said it yourself, Rufus, she's a celebrity."

"The board and Steagall are meeting every requirement. The legislature will be in session in Tallahassee, and they've invited every big-wig in state government. The governor has accepted."

"I'm surprised the little moron didn't ask *him* to introduce her," Finch said.

"He did. The governor declined that honor, but said he'd come. John is beside himself."

"Oh, so I'm second choice? Sloppy seconds?"

"Don't be vulgar, Brasfield," Doublet said. "John is happy with that. He thinks it's appropriate for a writer to introduce a writer. Just make sure you're sober."

"You better hope that *she* is. And I didn't say I'd do it."

Willow was watching the two men, yakking about a third, thinking: with men in charge, no wonder the world is in such a cataclysmal state. There had never been a female university or college president in the state of Florida, and in Willow's opinion, it was considerably past time for that consummation to be realized. There were a couple of women chairs at Lakewood, left over from the girls' school days, but most of them had been replaced with men, usually slick, wet-behind-the-ears young men. The progress of the women's movement was slow in north Florida.

"Are we finished here?" Willow asked.

"Yes," Doublet said. "I just wanted to give you two a heads up. Brasfield, you'll get a formal request to do the introduction from the president's office."

"Not a chance in hell," Finch said.

"We'll see," said Doublet.

Willow settled into her seat, third row, on the aisle, in the recital hall of the music building. It was the annual concert given by Street and Meyer, duo pianists who were artists in residence at Lakewood College. Marilyn Street and Calvin Meyer were a married couple who played two grand pianos at the same time; they toured around the southeast in a black Cadillac, pulling a high trailer loaded with their pianos. Willow wondered why they had to carry their pianos with them; maybe some of the places they played had only one grand piano. Besides, in her opinion, Street and Meyer were getting a little long in the tooth to keep touring around like rock stars. They had been at Lakewood for years, and it was her understanding that they taught very little. She was sure that was Steagall's doing. Taking care of his own.

Marilyn was six inches taller than Calvin and must have outweighed him by forty pounds. Calvin's dark, curly hair—dyed, no doubt—was long and brushed out to the side in a sweeping wave, which gave him a fortuitously off-centered look. He wore a white tie and tails, she a long black dress. They put the pianos together, fitting them intimately like two large brown animals, and sat facing each other, pounding away, not looking at each other but staring at their hands on the keyboard like any other long married couple with little to say to one another.

They were about halfway through their first number, a piece for two pianos by Bach, when it happened. A tall nude girl, wearing only a ski mask, came running down the aisle and leapt onto the low stage. She did a quick shimmy before they stopped playing; the performance came to a standstill with an abrupt, ear-splitting and disharmonious chord as Marilyn's fingers were brought violently down on the keys. In the silence that followed, the cacophonous tones lingered in the air like an odor. Then there were titters and murmurs rolling through the audience.

The girl danced her way to center stage, then high-stepped off upstage right and was gone.

President Steagall was on his feet down front. He looked around indignantly, raising himself to his full five foot three inches. "Who was that woman?" he shouted. Nobody answered him.

Then Calvin Meyer began to laugh. Marilyn followed him, and quickly the entire crowd was roaring with laughter. Everyone laughed but President Steagall, whose face was a murderous red. Willow happily joined in. She was almost sure she knew who the girl was. There was a tall English major in her English novels seminar; something about the naked girl's demeanor was like her. And she had looked, Willow thought, exactly like the girl would look without her clothes on.

Steagall had mounted the stage. He held his hands out over his head. There was gradual quiet. "I want to sincerely apologize to everyone here tonight for what just happened." His voice was tight with tension, his eyes bulging. "I will not tolerate such offensive behavior on our campus. Believe me, the students involved in these ... these displays will suffer the consequences. This is not a silly prank. It is indecent exposure."

"Awww, Doc, cut her some slack," said a male voice from the rear of the auditorium.

"Yeah, I thought it was right decent," said another.

"Silence!" ordered President Steagall. "This is no laughing matter. This is not a *joke*!"

His little round face was bright crimson, his jaws clenched. His gray hair sat flat and thin on his head. His blue serge suit was neat and pressed, the jacket buttoned, his purple and gold striped tie knotted just right. Willow actually felt a ripple of compassion for him; he looked so like he did when she slaughtered him in tennis.

Street and Meyer were still sitting at their pianos. Steagall looked at them. "You may continue," he said, and sat down.

With neither a signal nor a look passed between them, they started the piece over from the beginning, a perfectly timed and synchronized opening burst of notes.

Willow happened to be leaving Comer one late afternoon at the same time as Lily Putnam. The two women walked down the stairs together and out onto the sidewalk. It was a brisk early winter evening, the sky beginning to color. Lily was planning to walk downtown to Lucky's Market to pick up some yogurt.

"It's a nice day," she said to the older woman, "a great day for a walk. Why don't you come along? Unless ..." She glanced down at Willow's worn leather briefcase. Lily was carrying her forest green Harvard book bag slung over her shoulder.

"Oh no," Willow said. "*Yes*, I mean. To the walk. Why not?" She was pleasantly surprised by the invitation.

They began to stroll downtown.

"I heard about what happened the other night at the recital," Lily said. "You were there weren't you?"

"Indeed," Willow said. "It was quite something. I thought John Steagall was going to have a cow." They walked along in silence for a while. "*You've* never done anything like that, have you? I mean, when you were a student?"

"No," Lily said, "why do you ask?"

"I don't know. I just wonder what goes on in the mind of someone who decides to do that. I mean, is it a form of temporary insanity, or what?"

Lily laughed. "Something like that, I'm sure," she said.

The two woman were passing Doodles, the campus bookstore, and they paused to look in the front window. "So many sweat-shirts, so few books," Willow said.

"Yes, I like that gold hoody with the Falcon on the chest," Lily said.

"It'll be basketball season before long," Willow said. "Do you like basketball? I try to get over and watch the Lady Falcons occasionally."

"Go birds," Lily said. They continued walking. "Baseball's my game these days," she said and chuckled lightheartedly. Willow wondered what was so amusing about baseball, but she didn't pursue it. The younger woman had never answered her question about liking basketball, but she didn't pursue that, either. She didn't want to come off as pushy.

They passed a bar called The Falcon's Nest, where students hung out. It was already winding up. They passed Stache's. "Maybe we can stop for a quickie on the way back," the girl said.

"Well," Willow said. "Perhaps so." It surprised her that she was so pleased at the younger woman's attention. Willow tried to be kind to the younger faculty; it gratified her that they all seemed to like her, even if they kept their own distance, which suited her just fine. She knew they talked behind their hands about the senior faculty, laughed at them, called them "old farts," but she was certain she was not included in their derision. She was still young enough not to be "the old guard," and she was not an administrator. Her relationship with younger faculty had always been cordial, so long as they respected her boundaries. She was senior faculty, but she did not think of herself as "senior." She was trim, quick and healthy. And she was growing fond of Lily Putnam, somewhat to her astonishment. Maybe the woman was more than a pretty face and a gorgeous figure.

They went into Lucky's Market. Lily pondered the yogurt section. "They have a better selection at the Pig," she said, before choosing half a dozen cartons of pineapple Greek. As an afterthought, she put a shiny plump apple into her plastic bag. After paying, she tied the handles of the bag neatly and put the parcel into her green canvas book bag. "There," she said, smiling, "now to more important things."

"Don't you need to get those in the refrigerator?" Willow asked.

"They'll be okay."

They walked back toward the college. When they got to Stache's Lily said, "Shall we?"

"Why not?" Willow answered.

Willow had not been in Stache's for some time. She avoided it because it was usually noisy and crowded, a mixture of younger faculty and students, mostly art and theater majors who seemed to be abnormally loud. For a cocktail out, she much preferred the bar at the old St. George Hotel on the edge of downtown. It was now more a bed and breakfast place, with not many rooms to let, but it still had the big, antique mahogany bar with its long, ornate mirror and its pressed tin ceilings. She went there occasionally with friends.

They went in under the gigantic sculpted moustache. "That's one hell of a sculpture," Lily said.

"Yes, quite," Willow said.

It was early and not yet crowded. They found a table for two. It was wobbly; one of the legs must have been too short. A boy in a ponytail and a soiled white apron sidled up and handed them two laminated menus.

"We don't want dinner," Lily said, "just a drink. I'll have one of your delicious pomegranate martinis."

"Oh, dear, really?" Willow said. "That's a new one on me. Do you have white wine? Of course you have white wine. What's your house-by-the-glass?"

"Sauvignon blanc," he said.

"Fine." When the waiter had gone, Willow said, "Well, this is nice. How are your classes going, Lily?"

"Great, Dr. Mentor," the girl said, smiling. She seemed to have an excess of bright, glistening, exceedingly clean teeth. Willow admired her chopped off blonde hair. The girl apparently had put a little pomade or something in the front because it stuck up sharply, almost like Dean Jefferson's flat-top.

"I like the way you wear your hair," she said.

"Well, thank you," Lily said. "That's sweet."

"Have you finished those dreadful term papers?" Willow asked.

"Ugh," the girl said. She shrugged. She looked around. She seemed to be checking out everyone in the bar.

"Are you looking for someone, dear?" Willow asked.

"Oh, no," she said. She smiled and winked. "But you never know!"

My, my, thought Willow. It was a reminder that the girl was of a different generation entirely. No girl in Willow's day would ever have admitted looking for some interesting man in a bar. The boy brought their drinks and set them on the wiggly table. Willow's was in what looked like a juice glass. Oh, well.

"So ... you've been at Lakewood ... how long?" the girl asked.

"Twenty-two years," Willow said.

"How long did it take you to make full professor?" Lily asked.

"Well, you have to make assistant, first, of course, and then associate. I came as an assistant; I had my degree in hand."

"Yeah, that," the girl said. Willow wasn't quite sure what she meant. She was still peering around the bar, squinting in the dimness. "I know," she said suddenly, "Vanderbilt and all that. Hoity, toity. Big time."

"Pardon?"

"Just joking, Dr. Mentor," she said. The teeth again, bright and straight. Her lips were plump, not overly red; Willow couldn't tell if she were wearing lipstick or not. She thought not; Lily's lips were naturally tinted. "No offense," the girl said.

"None taken."

The girl sipped the pale pink martini. Pomegranate? "So," the girl said. "So Brass is not all that pleased that Lenora Hart's coming to the campus, is he?"

"Brass?"

"Oh, I'm sorry. Mr. Finch. He told me to call him Brass."

"No, he's not," Willow said.

"I betcha they had something, way back in the past," the girl said. Way back?

"What makes you say that?"

"Well, he's so bent out of shape about it."

"You can't pay too much attention to what Brasfield Finch says, Lily. He's usually in his cups."

"His what?"

"Tipsy. Surely you've noticed he drinks."

"Oh, sure." She leaned forward, closer to Willow. Willow could smell her shampoo, faint vanilla. The girl whispered, "Does everybody know he drinks during the day? Even before he goes to class?"

"*Especially* before he goes to class." Willow clucked her tongue. "I assume everybody does know," she said, "he makes no effort to hide it." She shifted in her chair. "Let's stop talking about Brasfield Finch, okay? He ... he bores me."

"He does?"

"Yes, he does." Lily cocked her head and looked at Willow out of the corners of her eyes. "Well, he does." The girl continued to gaze at her, a sly smile in her eyes. "What?" Willow said.

"Methinks the lady doth protest too much," she said.

"Now you *are* joking. Surely. Me and ... ?" She laughed heartily. "It *is* funny," she said, "but I'd prefer you not say anything of the sort again."

"Okay." A saucy grin.

"Really."

"O*kay.*"

"Let's talk about you," Willow said.

"Not very interesting, I'm afraid."

"Tell me something about yourself, something that's not on your *curriculum vita.*"

"Oh. Okay." She thought a minute. "I can't tell you about all the felonies." Willow just stared at her, somewhat taken aback. "Hey, I'm kidding, Dr. Behn," she said, chuckling. "Okay, let's see. Okay. When I first went to graduate school I worked as a waitress at Zing's Place."

"My, my," Willow said, "you did? Topless?"

"Good grief no," she said. "Well, *practically*. Those skimpy little blouses they make you wear. And those tiny little tight black pants! They fit tighter than panties. Half my ass cheeks would hang out."

The girl downed the last of her martini. "You want to have

another?" she asked.

"No, one's my limit, I'm afraid," Willow said and immediately wondered if that made her sound like an old fart. "If you ... I mean ... go ahead if you like."

"Oh no," Lily said. "I've got reading to do. I'm trying to keep ahead of my students!"

Willow chuckled. They gathered themselves and left the bar.

It was full dark by the time they got back as far as Willow's apartment house. She paused on the sidewalk. "Well, this has been a treat, Lily," she said.

"Oh, you live here?" Lily said. "What a beautiful old house."

"Yes, it's quite nice," Willow said. "There are three apartments."

"Could I see your place?" the girl asked.

"Well," Willow said. She was taken aback by the girl's request. She had not picked up and it had been days since she'd dusted. "Well, certainly, but it's not much, I'm afraid."

"I'd just like to see where my mentor lives," Lily said.

They mounted the steps, and as they approached the front door it opened and out came Rufus Doublet. He stopped short when he saw them. It seemed to take him a few seconds to compose himself. "Well, hello Willow. Lily." He nodded, looking from one to the other and back. He arched his eyebrows, pursed his lips.

"Good evening, Rufus," Willow said.

"Dr. Doublet!" Lily said. "You live here, too? How neat!"

He glared at her. "No, I ... I was just leaving. Good evening," he said. He went down the steps and disappeared into the shadows.

"Visiting somebody, I guess," Lily said. When they were in the vestibule the girl asked, "Who else lives here?" Well, Willow thought, the girl can be forgiven for all her questions because she's so new. Maybe it's just natural curiosity. Nosy, but naive.

"Lucy Willard and Joan Hudson," Willow said.

"The painter lady?"

"Yes." Willow opened her door and they went in. She was struck anew by how small the place was. The few pieces of her mother's heavy, Victorian furniture dwarfed everything else in the room. Willow had assumed they would be lovely in the old house, but they seemed to her now gaudy and overdone.

"Which one was he visiting?" the girl asked.

"I have no idea," Willow said. Why should she protect that

pompous little ass? Or Joan, either, for that matter. "Joan Hudson, I think," she said.

"But isn't she ... you know ...?"

"Older? Yes, she is. Won't you sit down?"

"I can't stay," Lily said, but she sat down anyway and put her book bag on the floor. "I can only stay a minute," she said.

"She is, as they say, mature, of a certain age, all that." Willow laughed. "The Piggly Wiggly gives a five percent discount on Wednesdays to what they euphemistically call 'experienced shoppers,' so as not to give offense, I suppose." She realized that to call Joan "experienced" under the circumstances might give the wrong idea. Or, as she startlingly reminded herself, the *right* idea. Joan was an artist after all. "She is at least twenty years older than Rufus, perhaps more."

The girl laughed, a guttural chuckle. "He likes older women, I take it," she said.

"You might say that, yes," Willow said. Was she gossiping? She had often thought that Rufus Doublet was an agent of the devil, so it wouldn't hurt to warn the girl. "I guess that's what, as you young people say, turns him on."

Lily looked around. "This is lovely, Dr. Behn," she said.

"Why don't you, when we're not around the office or out in public, call me Willow?"

"Okay," she said. Her smile was truly incandescent. "When it's just us, I'll call you 'Wil,' how about that? And you can call me 'Lil.' It'll be our private little way of acknowledging each other."

"All right," Willow said.

The girl stood up. "Oh my gosh, I've *got* to go," she said. Willow moved with her to the door; Lily went out into the hall. "This has been absolutely wonderful," she said, "Wil." That radiance again.

"Yes, we must have a drink again, and talk," Willow said. "Lil," she added.

"Well, good night."

The girl strode to the door. Willow looked at her hips in the scant miniskirt. Panties. Ass cheeks. Lily slung the canvas book bag over her shoulder in a gesture much like Santa Clause and vanished into the night.

SIX

The Dean of Men, Billy "Big Hoss" Murphy, made the first bust. Big Hoss was the first dean of men Lakewood had ever had, coming on board in the mid-fifties when the college had gone coed. He was a former professional baseball player and a PE teacher, a big gruff man with a bristly crew cut. He was a hail-fellow-well-met, always joking around and poking people on the arms, but beneath his jocular exterior was a decidedly mean streak.

Big Hoss had made his reputation when, three or four years after the changeover from a girls' college, there had been a series of panty raids on campus. The boys would gather outside one of the girls' dorms and chant for panties, and, to Big Hoss's considerable astonishment, some of the girls would toss their underwear down and the panties would end up on the flagpole in the quad. Which would not do.

On those occasions Big Hoss would mill through the crowd of raucous boys, shoving them aside, barking at them. "Are you gentlemen? No!" he would yell. "You get your ass back to the dorm! Now!" He prevailed on Officer Puckett, the campus policeman, a portly jocund fellow much loved by the students, to make some arrests. "They ain't breakin any laws, not as I can see," Officer Puckett said. Murphy screamed, "They are breaking *rules!*" "Show me where it says they can't have one of these panty raids," Officer Puckett said, "it ain't in there." "Conduct unbecoming a Lakewood student!" Dean Murphy sputtered. "That's too vague," Puckett said, "wouldn't hold up in a court of law." "Goddamit, Earl," Big Hoss said, "this ain't no freakin TV show!"

Big Hoss took down names and threatened several of the students with disciplinary action. Either he put the fear of God in them, or they grew tired of gathering in the middle of the night, because they quit the panty raids as quickly as they'd started. The raids were senseless, frivolous things, anyway.

Not so the streaking. It was getting out of hand. It was a serious matter.

"This is an embarrassment to the college," President Steagall said at their administrative council meeting. "This must stop."

"It has to," Alberta Wingate, the Dean of Women, said.

"It *will* stop, by God," Mrs. Hoyle said. She sat perched with her stenographers' pad on her knee, ready to record the minutes of the meeting. President Steagall held up the front page of the *Tallahassee Tribune*. There was a picture—censored, thankfully, with black patches over the genitals and nipples—of a girl in a ski mask, jogging down the street. "This picture was made on campus and sent to the paper. They called to ask for a statement. No comment, I said. What could I say? And then, this," he said. He picked up the latest edition of the *Lakewood Purple and Gold*, the student newspaper. He opened it to the center section and displayed it for them. They had all seen it, of course, but they all (everyone but Brasfield Finch, who had been invited this morning as chairman of the student publications committee) clucked their tongues and sighed. Both pages of the spread were full of black and white pictures, *unretouched*, pubic hair and all, graphic demonstrations of the craze that seemed to have gripped the campus. John Steagall's lips shook; he ground his teeth. "This is pornographic," he said, "and it goes out to *every high school* in the state, the schools where we recruit ..."

"Stop it. Put your foot down. Don't let it go out," Big Hoss Murphy said.

"Too late," Steagall said. "It's already gone out."

"Shut it down!" Murphy said. "Stop the presses for good!"

"I've called Ronald Alton in—"

"This afternoon," Mrs. Hoyle interjected.

"—and I'll read him the riot act. This is unacceptable, irresponsible."

"Freedom of the press," Brasfield Finch spoke up.

"I beg your pardon?" Steagall said, unable to hide his annoyance.

"I said, this is a matter of freedom of the press," Finch said.

"This is not the 'press,' Mr. Finch. This is a student newspaper. Something we allow them to have, and they have abused the privilege. I want you there this afternoon when I meet with Alton, understood?"

"Of course," Finch said. This would be *good*! Ronnie Alton was one of his students, a mediocre poet and fiction writer, but a very intelligent and liberal minded young man. Finch had promised him when he ran for the position that if he won he wouldn't interfere with him. So far, Alton had published little more than a few diatribes against the food in the caf, and one particularly distasteful—but amusing—editorial about a professor in the biology department—Fred C. Dobbs—and his experiments with the sexual organs of frogs. Finch had been delighted with the piece, as witty and vulgar as it was. But there was grumbling around the campus.

"And this editorial," Steagall said, turning the page. "Something like this will not be tolerated."

Finch remained silent. The latest editorial was taking the university to task for charging a student with indecent exposure. Big Hoss Murphy had busted the boy crossing the quad the other day midmorning. The boy, Johnny Hargraves, was handicapped; one of his legs was about twenty inches shorter than the other, and he wore a hollow steel contraption with another shoe under his regular one. The students teased him for the way he clumped down the hall. (He had also taken Finch's creative writing course, producing appallingly awful imitations of H. P. Lovecraft.) When he had his pants on the deformity was audible but not visible; naked but for a ski mask it was painfully obvious who the streaker was. Hargraves could not run very fast, and before he could get all the way across the quad Murphy had dashed from his office and had chased the boy down and tackled him. He had had him arrested for indecent exposure, and Johnny Hargraves was in the Lakewood city jail.

"My friends," John Steagall said, "Mr. Alton proposes that we are all Nazis. Listen to this." He read, "Anyone who would chase and overpower a mobility-challenged person in that manner is a fascist bully, no two ways about it. And to charge him with a sexual crime is to label him for the rest of his life.'" Steagall looked around. "*Is* it a sexual crime? I don't ..."

"He will have to register as a sexual offender. Exposing his ... his genitals in that way," Big Hoss said.

"Don't be ridiculous," Finch said.

"Mr. Finch ..." Murphy began.

"Who else was on the quad? Who did he expose himself to?" Finch asked.

"Well, nobody. But some lady could have been looking out the window, or could have left a building at any moment. And remember, Finch, he exposed them to *me*!"

"Anything you haven't seen in the locker room, Hoss?" Finch asked. "This is absurd. It was a prank."

"It's gone beyond that," Steagall said. "It's disgusting."

"I rather enjoy watching them, myself," Finch said.

"I'll bet," Murphy said.

"Gentlemen," Steagall said.

"Why would a young man or a young woman *do* that?" Dean Wingate asked plaintively. It was clearly totally beyond her comprehension.

"The world has gone mad, Alberta," Finch said, "get out of the way or you'll be run over."

"Whose side are you on, Finch?" Murphy said.

"The side of right. And decency."

"Decency? Haw!"

"Right? I can smell the alcohol all the way over here, and its not even lunchtime yet," Dean Wingate said.

"It's dark right now somewhere in the world, Alberta," Finch said.

"Must we carry on like children?" Steagall said.

"Well!" Dean Wingate said huffily.

Before it was time to walk across campus to the president's office, Brasfield Finch went down to the seminar room where his writing workshop met and taped a note to the door. "No class today. Go play Donkey Kong. BF." Back at his office he still had a few minutes left and he noticed Lily Putnam in her office across the hall. He rapped the back of his knuckles on her door and she looked up. My God! A vision of loveliness.

"Brass! What's happening?" she said.

"Everything and nothing, dear girl," he said. "Did you see the *Purple and Gold?*"

"Yes," she smiled, "I did. There were seventeen pictures on two pages. Were some of them of the same person, do you think?"

"Probably," he said.

"That's awful about that Hargraves boy," she said, "a cripple like that."

Finch winced at the word. Do people still say that? "Yes, terrible," he said.

"Is he still in jail?"

"I think so," he said. "I think if the suits have their way he'll be in prison a long time."

"*Prison*?!" She looked alarmed.

"Not really, I don't believe, but they're making quite a big thing out of it."

"There's nothing wrong with a little nudity," she said.

"That's what I've always said," he said, locking his eyes onto hers. Was she blushing? If not she was a damn good actress. "Clothes are always getting in the way," he added.

"You might say that, yes," she said, grinning, and looked down at her desk.

Jesus Christ Almighty. He was going to get into those panties before the semester was over! Or die trying. "Lily," he said, "as the vice chairman of the publications committee, would you like to accompany me to the president's office this afternoon for a meeting with the editor of the *Purple and Gold*?"

"*I'm* vice chairman? That's the first I've heard of that."

"I hereby appoint you vice chairman. You are my associate."

"Mr. Finch," she said, "the *president's* office?"

"Yes. Bring a notebook. Pretend to take notes."

"*Pretend?*"

"Yes. Just scribble down anything. Just to make them think we're making a record of what goes on."

"Yes sir."

"And Lily, not *Mr.* Finch, please."

"Okay."

So that afternoon the two of them were seated in Dr. Steagall's office with the president, Mrs. Hoyle, and Brandon Briggs, the college attorney and member of the board of trust. Ronnie Alton was sitting in the outer office. When Finch and Lily had come through, he had given them a thumbs up.

"Technically, yes," Briggs was saying, "but ... what about the parents? They're going to raise a ruckus. They may even sue." He and Steagall had apparently been at it for awhile.

"I talked to the father," Steagall said. "He said to me, and I quote, 'Throw the goddam book at him.'"

"On the phone? And you want to do what he says? Have you ever heard of entrapment?" Briggs asked.

"He sounded like he meant it."

"Yes. *Right now* he means it. He's embarrassed. If we 'throw the book at him,' then later on, and not too much longer later on, somebody's going to get to him. Then he'll be out after blood. You've already gone pretty far, John. Maybe it can be patched up."

Lily scratched away at her ring notebook. Everybody was looking at her. When he had walked in with her, Olive Hoyle and Steagall had reacted with discourtesy, almost recoiling. "Miss ...

Miss … Putlam, I believe," Steagall had gotten out unenthusiastically.

"She is my assistant," Finch had said, "if you can have Hoyle there, I can have Lily. And it's Put*nam*."

"Yes, yes of course," Steagall had muttered. He was flustered. Finch knew that a big part of Steagall's unease was Lily's striking physical attractiveness. Finch was greatly amused; just bringing along the dazzling creature had thrown a monkey wrench into Steagall's gears. "Miss Putnam," Brandon Briggs had said, standing and taking her hand, "charmed."

"Did you get it all down, Lily?" Finch asked to break the silence.

"What?" she asked, looking up, surprised at all the eyes on her. "What?" He nodded to her notebook. "Oh, yes sir. Yes sir." She looked down and continued scribbling.

"That seems hardly necessary, Brasfield," Steagall said.

"We all have to cover our asses," Finch said.

"There is no need to be vulgar," Steagall said.

"I often say the same thing, John," Finch said, "but I suppose our individual definitions of vulgarity are vastly different."

"This is a lot of fun, guys, but I have to get back to the office sometime this afternoon," Briggs said. "Some of us actually *work* for a living."

"All right," Steagall said. "Moving along. Mrs. Hoyle, would you ask Mr. Alton to step in, please?" When the student was in the room and seated, Dr. Steagall said, without preamble, "I want you to retract your editorial and apologize. And there will be no more pornographic pictures. Do I make myself clear?"

"I won't do it," Ronnie Alton said. He scrunched down in the chair and looked around. Finch saw him look at Lily's ample display of thighs. His eyes met Finch's and he shrugged.

"I don't think you heard me correctly, Mr. Alton. This is non-negotiable."

"I heard you, Dr. Steagall, and I won't do it. I won't publish something I don't believe. And if things happen on campus, and I have a photographer to record it, those pictures will appear in the paper."

There was a heavy silence.

"We'll see about that," Steagall said. "Briggs?"

"You'd better be careful here, John," the attorney said.

"But he is a student!"

"He is a citizen, John, and a person. Then a student."

"This is insubordination, clear and simple," Steagall said. "As long as I am in charge of this institution, no student is going to tell me how to run it."

"John ..." Finch interjected.

"And no faculty member, either, by damn!"

"I think you'd better calm down, John," Briggs said.

"I *am* calm!" The president's face was flushed. "They are making a mockery of the dignity of this institution. And I will *not stand for it!*" He brought his little fist down hard on his desk. Finch saw him wince. He hoped the son of a bitch broke it.

"Make a note of that," Finch said to Lily.

"What?"

"That," Finch said, pointing at Steagall's hand resting on the blotter.

"You mean ... you mean that ... that he hit his desk?" she asked incredulously.

"Yes, of course," Finch said.

She looked wide-eyed back at him. Then she began to doodle, moving her pen erratically about the page. Her shoulders gave a slight twitch. She seemed to be concentrating hard on what she was jotting down. Finch felt sorry for putting her in this situation. She was such an innocent child. He would have to make it up to her.

"You are making sport of this, Finch," Steagall said. "I might have known."

"I'm chairman of the Student Publications Committee," Finch said, "I have a dog in this hunt."

"Why do I even try?" the president said, rolling his eyes to the ceiling. Mrs. Hoyle was also scribbling away. The only sounds were the scratching of the two pens.

Brasfield Finch lived on the top floor of a three story condominium complex outside town. It was called The Florida Arms. It was built in a kind of faux Mediterranean style, with balconies and heavy window shutters that opened out. The exterior was a color called "sand," though there was no beach within sixty miles of Lakewood. The hill on which the town of Lakewood stood—hence also the college—was sandy red clay.

Finch owned a small one bedroom with a balcony that overlooked the heavily wooded, swampy Apalachicola River delta. It was a peaceful place, and he liked to sit out on his balcony, drink Scotch, and watch for alligators and the occasional sea birds that seemed to be momentarily lost; he imagined they were frantic to get back to the Gulf. His desk faced the large, sliding glass doors to the balcony; on the desk was his typewriter (a portable Remington Selectric) and an inch-thick stack of manuscript pages: half his unfinished novel, the best thing he'd ever done. It was called *The Secret Butterfly*, about a little boy who has a butterfly collection. He had not yet discovered what, beyond that, it might be about. He worked on it intermittently, spasmodically, whenever the urge struck him, which was not too often. He was not troubled by his lack of progress; it was enough to be writing a book. He really didn't *want* to finish it; he was not eager to step out once again and get his balls kicked.

He had told Lily a little about his novel in progress and she'd asked if she could read some of it. Of course. That's why he'd told her about it in the first place; it was the perfect way to get her up to his place. He had always considered pussy a part of his royalties; the more he got, the better he was doing. It had always been that way. He had to admit that lately—in the last five or even ten years—he'd not been doing that well at all, but things were changing. Lily was the most delicious looking morsel to come along in a long while; she was ripe.

He heard the doorbell chime. He went to the door. She had on jeans that looked shrink wrapped on her body. She wore a navy blue T shirt and obviously no bra; her breasts were not large, but they seemed perfectly formed, a hint of perky nipples nudging at the cloth. He was eager to see them freed of clothes.

"Wow," she said when she came in, looking around. The condo was nice but nothing really special; there was lots of interior wood, and the sunlight played lightly over the patio furniture outside the glass doors. She went to the doors and looked out at the dense tangle of live oaks and palmettoes. "Wow," she said again.

"It's a dump," he said. "What a dump! Who said that?"

"Huh?"

"Never mind. Sit down. What'll you have?"

"Vodka? Tonic?"

"Coming right up," he said. He made her a stiff one. She was sitting in a wooden and cushiony chair that looked as if it could be on the deck of a cruise ship. He had bought the place furnished; there was nautical shit all over the place. Maybe not what he would have chosen, but bottom line it was all right with him. At least he didn't have to shop for it. He poured himself a Scotch on the rocks.

"Hey, thanks for the other day," he said, handing her her drink and sitting himself in a matching deck chair.

"What's that?" she asked.

"The president's office."

"Oh. Sure. Glad to do it." Her smile was radiant. She leaned back, crossed her legs. Every movement was graceful. Like part of a dance move. He was sure he could just sit and watch her. For hours at a time. No. That would drive him crazy. Just glancing at her made him tingly in his gonads. He gazed at her. "Lily," he said pensively, "you are one of the most ravishing women I've ever known."

"Hey, thanks," she said jauntily, bubbly, "that's sweet."

He had meant to set a sincere, earnest tone; she'd not picked up on it.

"Could I read it?" she asked.

"Eh?"

"Your novel. I've reread the other two. I like your work. You're a good writer."

"Well, thank you, that's kind of you to say."

"I'm becoming one of the experts on the fiction of Brasfield Finch," she said.

"The *only* one, I daresay." She frowned, *mugged* at him, like a nanny reassuring an upset child. This was not going at all the way he had hoped. The start of something, the beginning, was of paramount importance; he was convinced that if he could get a novel off to the right start the narrative would flow from its own energy. This was also true in life. Finding, establishing that starting point was a delicate choice, because it determined the precise outcome down the line, whether page 350 or his king sized bed.

"Well?" she asked.

"Of course," he said. "That's what we're here for, isn't it?"

She cut her eyes coyly at him and smiled. "Yes," she said.

He stood up to retrieve the first chapter from his desk. "It's only a draft, mind you."

"Sure, I understand." She took the pages and began to read. He had forgotten what it was like to be able to read without glasses. Oh, youth. Like a fresh breeze on a rare spring morning. He had smelled her when he was close to her, skin, hair, clean and bracing. She pursed her lips as she read. After a few minutes she looked up. "Are you just going to sit there and watch me read?" she asked. "It creeps me out when somebody does that."

"My pleasure," he said. She tossed her head and rolled her eyes. She refocused on the manuscript. He got up and retrieved her glass and made them both another drink. It was two o'clock on a Saturday and they had the whole day. At least *he* did. The afternoon stretched invitingly before them. Afternoon delight. This is the day the lord hath made.

It was quiet. He could hear the hum of the refrigerator in the little kitchen alcove. He picked up a *New Yorker* and flipped it open to the back to the movie reviews. He didn't go to many movies but he liked to read about them. He usually read the book reviews, too, delighting in any negative notice anyone received; better them than him. He read an occasional piece of fiction, though he found the stories they published pretentious. The only other things that drew his attention were the cartoons, which seemed less and less funny to him the older he got.

She chuckled.

"What?" he asked.

"This kid's voice. It's almost perfect."

"Really?" He was quite pleased.

"Yeah. It's funny, and touching. I'm a sucker for little boys," she said.

He almost blurted something suggestive and wicked, playing on the word "suck," but he held back. It was like writing dialogue. You had to be keenly aware of the tone, or it would be all wrong. "Thank you, dear," he said.

"Not a problem," she said, looking back at the manuscript. What did she mean by that? Probably some young person's slang. His students were always bursting out with something that he was certain he understood but that was nonetheless off-center enough to still be puzzling.

He surreptitiously watched her read; he was sure she'd soon sense him staring, since he could feel his eyes hotly caressing her. While her gaze was downcast and she was engaged with his narrative, he lingered on the parts of her beauty, her body, that he tried not to gape at when she could see him. She improved every time he saw her. Familiarity enhanced and increased her charms.

"You really are good," she said. She looked up and caught him looking at her breasts. She smiled.

"You don't know the half of it," he said, "you ought to try me."

"Naughty, naughty," she said, still smiling.

"Naughty is what makes the world go round," he said.

She fixed him with a mocking, joking look. "If you're as good as you think you are, I'll be overwhelmed."

"Prepare to be overwhelmed," he said. He stood up. His erection was straining against his jeans. She put the manuscript down, carefully marking her place.

Lily was naked, on all fours on his bed; Finch was behind her. What he was doing with his tongue was about to drive her wild. Jesus! "Oh God, oh God, oh God," she moaned. "Don't stop!" She had already reached two or three orgasms; the man was a fucking machine. It was so different from the wham-bam-thank-you-m'am of David Godby. The boy's body was better, but in the throes that didn't matter. Finch's beard took some getting used to. It was so long it kept getting in the way; it was so bushy it scratched the insides of her thighs. He seemed to be able to last forever. She wondered if he had taken Viagra; she didn't care.

Afterward they lay naked and exhausted on the black silk sheets of his king sized bed. The sheets had felt smooth and cool to the touch but were so slippery they almost slid off on the floor a couple of times.

"Wow," she said. She stretched. He was propped back against the headboard smoking a cigarette. She flicked his now flaccid penis with her finger. "You fuck as good as you write."

"It ain't braggin if you can do it," he said.

She laughed. "Was it like that with her?" she asked.

"Her? Who?"

"Lenora Hart."

"Why do you bring that ugly bitch's name into this idyll?"

"Was it?"

"No, no, no. Nothing like that. I was too young. I didn't know what I was doing."

"I know that routine," Lily said. "Tell me about your thing with Lenora Hart."

"There's nothing really to tell, Lily," he said, "we talked, we knew each other, perhaps a bit in the Biblical sense, too, but it was most unremarkable. She was so totally narcissistic even back then. She had had that big success, that was getting bigger all the time, with the movie and all, and it went straight to her head."

"Were you jealous?"

"Hell, no! Why should I be jealous? My first novel was ten times better than hers."

She leaned on her elbow and looked at him. "But she got rich. She sold a zillion copies. All that."

"And it turned her into a monster."

"Not really a monster, Brass. You just don't like her, you ..."

"How the fuck do *you* know, Lily?! You don't know her. Don't try to tell me anything about that woman. You're right, I don't like her. And I'm going to enjoy the hell out of seeing her show her ass when she comes. They're already in a snit about all her demands. Do you know how much we're paying her?"

"No. How much."

"Twenty-Five thousand dollars," he said.

"You're kidding," she said, "twenty-five thousand dollars? Whew. I don't make half that much in a year!"

"No, and you're worth more than she is, trust me on that."

"You're sweet."

"No, you are. As delicious as a ripe peach," he said. He stuck his tongue out and wagged it at her. She rolled over and climbed on top of him. "Whoa," he said. Then, "Okay, okay!"

SEVEN

Willow watched Father Hamner Curbs sway down the aisle, following the choir and the crucifer. He had an odd way of stepping obliquely, his thin shoulders slanted, little short staccato footsteps on the stone tile of the floor, barely audible above the choir as he went by. She could hear the screeching of Paulette Jefferson's annoying off-key soprano soaring over the rest of the choir; Willow supposed the woman fancied that she was "leading" the rest of them through the processional. The noisy tile floor was a contentious issue with the vestry; a large number of parishioners wanted to put down a nice, plush carpet, but the choir director and organist, Betty Lou Larkin, who taught in the music department, would not hear of it. She maintained that the acoustics in little St. Mark's were "equal to the finest European cathedrals." Willow, as senior warden, had to preside over numerous tiresome debates and heated arguments about it.

Willow still thought of Hamner Curbs as the "new priest," though he'd been at St. Mark's now for over two years. He was a slight man, slim and stooped, pale; his curly hair was white, whether grayed or bleached it was hard to tell. He had a youthful, springy, effeminate air about him which was belied when you looked into his face, which was angular and emaciated—like a Walker Evans photograph—his eyes reddened and watery, which Willow knew to be from excess drink. He was the first full time priest St. Mark's had ever had, and she had come to believe the bishop had sent him there to get him out of his hair. She knew—she was not supposed to, but she had friends—that Curbs had been removed from a parish in Dunedin at the request of their vestry. In the two years since he'd been at St. Mark's, he'd had two DUIs, two stints in the city jail—once when he was found drunk, sitting at one of the outside tables at Pasquale's at three in the morning, long after they'd closed, and the second time at Stache's, when he'd become disorderly and had attempted to pick a fight—from which Willow, as senior warden, had had to get him released after being jarred awake by a jangling phone call in the middle of the night.

Willow always sat near the back so she could count the congregation; there was a form to be filled out after each service, and Father Curbs could not be bothered, and old Lyman Wilbanks, the vestry treasurer who was responsible, could not be relied upon for anywhere near an accurate count. He usually forgot, then tried, as he put it, to "guesstimate." That would not do for Willow.

Rufus Doublet and Wallace Jefferson were sitting together near the front. The previous Sunday, Father Curbs had been "sick," and Rufus had filled in as lay reader for morning prayer. Willow had been repelled by his overly saccharine intonations and showy, self-important demeanor. It struck her as ironic that the agent of the devil was conducting morning prayer. It had not been a pleasant experience for her.

Just after the choir had settled in and Curbs had begun his opening sentences, in his stagy stentorian tones, Lily Putnam walked in. The girl stopped at the back, at the center aisle. The younger woman did not see Willow. She seemed hesitant, looking around, then sat on the end about three pews in front of Willow. She was wearing a tasteful burgundy wool suit, the skirt slightly longer and more modest than usual. Willow saw old Agnes Evans, whose breath was so fetid it permeated the entire area in which she was seated and lingered heavily in the chalice after she'd received the Eucharist, turn and offer Lily an opened prayer book. Willow always made it a point to get to the altar rail ahead of Mrs. Evans, whose deceased husband had been head of the biology department, to avoid having to sniff the malodorous air.

Willow watched the girl peruse the prayer book. She could tell by the way she examined it that she was bewildered. Willow had no idea of Lily's religious background, or even if she had one; it was probably Baptist or Methodist, which to Willow was tantamount to being nothing at all. She hoped she wasn't a Roman, and from the manner in which the girl seemed to be puzzling over the prayer book, she probably wasn't. "The Lord be with you," intoned Hamner Curbs, and the girl jumped slightly at the congregation's response, "And with thy spirit," because she was sitting in front of that Delaney family with their two little girls who shouted their responses in jubilant voices in some misguided show of enthusiasm for the Lord. They annoyed Willow, especially at the end of every service when they literally yelled, at the tops of their voices, "Thanks be to God" in response to Curbs' "Go in peace to love and serve the Lord."

Willow had a good angle from which to observe Lily. She watched the girl turning the pages of the prayer book. Her lips were pursed, as if she were concentrating all her energies on the order of service. Willow was so caught up in scrutinizing the girl that she was surprised when Curbs mounted the pulpit to begin his homily. One thing she had to admit about Curbs was that he preached a good sermon. His brain may have been addled, but his heart was in the right place. And he was careful in the composing of his remarks. This morning's sermon was "The Desert Shall Bloom Again." He was big on renewal, resurrection. She tried to focus on what he was saying.

Other than his degenerate behavior, one of the biggest things that bothered Willow about the man was his refusal to use any of the trial liturgies. In fact, Willow had not even known about them until she went to a meeting of senior wardens in Tallahassee and heard them discussed. Every other parish in the diocese—probably every other parish in the entire Episcopal Church U.S.A.—was using the trial liturgies, as the church was in the process of revising the prayer book. There was the "Zebra" book, so called because of its striped cover, and the "Red" book. When Willow had brought it up in vestry, she had been met with a stunned, stubborn silence.

"We will continue to use the 1928 Prayer Book," Hamner Curbs had said, with finality. "Exclusively."

"That's what we prefer," Wallace Jefferson had said. Rufus Doublet had nodded his assent. Lyman Wilbanks was asleep.

"It doesn't matter what we *prefer*," Willow had said. "We are not a congregational church; it is not up for our vote. We do what the Bishop and Diocesan council tell us to do. Why haven't we been even *informed* of the trial liturgies?"

"Because the 1928 Prayer Book is quite good enough," Curbs said.

"*You* decided that?"

"The *Rubrics* ... "

"To hell with the rubrics," Willow said.

Willow had placed a call to the diocesan office in Tallahassee.

"Dr. Behn, just settle down," the bishop had told her. "These things have a way of working out, with God's help."

What God needed to help them with was to send them a woman bishop! There was not even a single woman priest in the entire diocese. It was as bad as the Romans.

The organ swelled. The homily was over, the alms basin was being passed, and the choir sang an anthem, Betty Lou Larkin's own arrangement of "Raise High the Cross." Once again Paulette Jefferson's strident voice penetrated to the rafters of the church, leaving the other voices hovering below like a cloud of dust. The woman was incorrigible. Once, at coffee in the parish hall after church, she and Willow had been talking and the subject of "women's liberation" had come up. "I don't need anybody to liberate *me*," the woman had said in her harsh Midwestern accent, "I got my PhD myself, for myself. I didn't need any *amendment!*"

Willow watched to see if Lily rose to go down for communion. When the girl slid into the aisle Willow hastily skipped up next to her, ignoring the glares of the Delaney family. She took the girl's elbow, moving her ahead of Mrs. Evans, who was struggling with her coat. Lily looked at Willow and smiled. She led the girl down the aisle, guiding her with a light touch. They knelt at the altar rail, side by side, with Mrs. Evans thankfully down to their left. Willow subtly showed Lily how to steady the chalice. "The blood of Christ," the chalice bearer said, "the cup of salvation." She held her hands out, palms up, right in left, and Lily followed suit. Curbs came along with the wafers; he had a way of waving them in the air almost as if he were shaking them free of lint before he placed them in the palm, his fingers shaking. "The body of Christ," Curbs muttered, "feed on him in thy heart." Willow didn't think that was quite correct from the prayer book, or complete, but no matter. She escorted Lily back up the aisle, holding her upper arm. She saw Doublet and Jefferson looking curiously at them. Others were staring as well, gawking at the beautiful young woman like children at a new kid in school. As they passed, Willow said to the two men, "Peace." That was something else they objected to: the passing of the peace, which was a part of the new liturgies.

At coffee after the service, Willow introduced Lily to several people. The two women got coffee and a hard, stale chocolate chip cookie. Hamner Curbs made a bee-line to them. "So nice to have you, Miss Putnam," he said, shaking her hand, "did you sign the guest book in the vestibule?"

"Pardon?" Lily said.

"*I* know who she is, Hamner," Willow said.

"We need her address, so we can send her the newsletter," the priest said.

Willow wanted to say, if you want her to come back, you nit, don't be so pushy. She saw Paulette Jefferson barreling out of the sacristy, where she had shed her choir robe, and bearing down on them. She had a proprietary grin on her face. "Lily!" she said. "I'm so glad to see you!" She ignored Willow completely. "When I extended the invitation," she said, in a loud voice so she could be heard by all those standing around, "I hoped you'd come, and now here you are!" She took Lily by the arm and actually pulled her away from Willow. "I must introduce you around."

"I already have," Willow said.

The woman ignored that, too. "Helen, have you met ..." she was saying to a short, stumpy woman in a hat. Helen Anderson. Chair of the Altar Guild. Willow refused to join the women who made up the guild, who set up the altar every Sunday morning; she had always felt that the fact they were all women made them seem servile. "I'm not a nun," she had said to Helen Anderson when she'd inquired of Willow if she might not want to take her turn on the altar. "When you recruit some of the *men*, perhaps I'll reconsider." "But ... but ..." the woman had stammered, "this is the *altar guild!*" "Precisely," Willow had replied.

She watched Paulette Jefferson steer Lily all around the Parish Hall. The woman acted as if she *owned* the church. She probably believed she did. Since Wallace had been appointed dean she'd acted as if she owned the college as well. She was as bad as the president's wife. Willow was glad those awful Steagalls went to the Methodist Church; St. Mark's was not big enough for two women like that. She saw Paulette introducing Lily to her widowed mother, Mrs. Rondelay, who had recently moved up here from Fort Lauderdale and bought a little house; the old woman chain smoked and there was a yellow nicotine streak in her gray hair. (Willow had been amused one morning when she'd heard one of the little Sunday school girls ask her, "Lady, why do you put mustard in your hair?" Mrs. Rondelay had huffily turned her back on the little girl.) She was as unpleasant as her daughter.

Willow sipped her tepid coffee in its Styrofoam cup. She noticed, sitting against a wall all by himself, a man—a boy?—she'd never seen before. He was not dressed in church clothes; he wore faded jeans and a white T shirt with writing on the front. She couldn't make out what it said. He had close cropped hair. She immediately thought, 'military.' He was muscular; his biceps bulged beneath the sleeves of the tight shirt. He had a tattoo on his arm. He was old for a student. Probably a returning veteran. She approached him.

"Hello, I'm Willow Behn, senior warden." She held out her hand. "Welcome to St. Mark's."

He looked baffled. "Senior what?" he asked.

She chuckled, pumping his hand. He was clearly not an Episcopalian. "Never mind," she said, "not important. Is this your first time with us?"

"Yeah," he said. He did not stand up. This one was born in a barn. "Lavell Delahoosie," he said.

"Well, we're glad to have you," she said, "did you get coffee and cookies?"

"Yeah." She could see that the tattoo was a little cartoon skunk, with "Little Stinky" written beneath it. Charming. She leaned back to better see the front of his shirt. It said, "What Would Jesus Do?" What, indeed? Some fundamentalist Jesus freak had wandered in. She wondered what he made of it all.

"Are you Episcopalian?" she asked. She was already regretting the impulsive impetuousness of her welcome. She had felt a flash of warm dutifulness. The sensation had vanished. It had been a reflex.

"No," he said. It seemed he would not offer any further explanation, and that only sharpened her curiosity.

"Visiting?" she asked. "Family? Or friends?"

"Friend," he said. "I'm visiting Father Ham."

"Who?"

"Father Ham. You know."

"Father Curbs?"

"Yeah."

Father *Ham*? That was a new one. "How do you know Father Curbs?" she asked.

"I met him in Pensacola," he said.

"Oh? You are from Pensacola?"

"Nome, I was stationed there. Navy." That explained the tattoo. "I met him over there. In a bar, The Jolly Roger, down on the waterfront." That figures. "I got out a few weeks ago, and I been looking for some kind of work. He said I could work for him. So I came over here with him. That's some car he's got." Hamner drove a long black Pontiac Bonneville.

"Work for him? Doing what?"

"Just whatever he needs done. Drive for him, like that." Of course. Drive him home when he's drunk. The priest lived in a sparsely furnished apartment. Willow couldn't imagine what else he might "need done." He had no grass to cut. Shopping? Willow had been at his apartment once, after she had driven him home from one of his jail stays, and she'd looked in his refrigerator; there was nothing in there but two six packs of beer and a carton of cigarettes. Maybe the boy would clean. The dust had been an inch thick over everything. "He said some of the folks in the church would hire me to trim hedges and mow lawns and stuff."

"Oh?" she said. "And did you find some place to live?"

"He said I could live here."

"Here?"

"Yeah. There's plenty of room."

"Here?" she said, aghast. "In the Parish Hall? You can't *live* here!"

"There's a kitchen and a bathroom," he said.

"But ..."

"I sleep upstairs," he said.

"Up*stairs*?!" That's where the nursery was. There was a cot, where they put the babies down to sleep. "You can't sleep up there," she said.

"He said it belongs to God," Lavell Delahoosie said.

"It may belong to God, but He doesn't pay the mortgage on it," she said. "No. I'll have to speak with Hamner about this. It won't do."

"I'm homeless," Lavell said.

"That's *your* problem, isn't it?" she said. She looked around. The crowd was thinning out. She didn't see Lily anywhere. The Jeffersons were gone as well. She sought out Hamner Curbs. He was leaning against the wall talking to Patrick Annandale, who taught in the French department.

"Hamner, I need to speak with you, please," she said and both men looked annoyed at the interruption.

"So speak," the priest said.

"In your office."

"Yes *m'am*," he said officiously. He followed her into the office and she pushed the door shut.

"So you met this young man in Pensacola and just brought him home with you?" she asked.

"Lavell?"

"Of course, Lavell. Who else? When did this great act of charity occur?"

"Last weekend, Willow, if it's any of your business."

"Last *weekend*? You were sick last weekend."

"I was out of town," he said.

"Yes, yes, of course," she said sourly. "Pfffft." She fluttered her fingers. "You met this fellow in some dive ..."

"A bar in Pensacola that I happen to like. Sure it's a down and out place. I like to minister there. Like Christ, I go down among the thieves and the prostitutes." He swelled himself to his full height, which was still a couple of inches shorter than she was; he seemed to be standing on his tip-toes.

"Yes, I'll just bet you do," Willow said. She was beginning to get the picture. It was as if she'd been isolated in some quiet, peaceful room, only gradually becoming aware of a steady knocking that was almost imperceptible but was growing progressively louder and louder until she had to notice it, could no longer fail to hear it. "You ... ? All right. I give up. Whatever else you may be up to I suppose *is* your business. But this man cannot live in the Parish Hall. Get him out, or I will, do you hear me? I will call the bishop!"

"He has no place to go," the priest said.

"*You* brought him over here, Hamner. Let him stay with you."

"How do you suppose that would look?"

"Ha! It's a little late for worrying about that, isn't it? Out! Today! Out!"

Lily was not at all sure she wanted to start drinking right after church, in the middle of the day, but Paulette Jefferson insisted. "You *must* come," the dean's wife said. "It's a *tradition* with us. Rufus is coming by, too. I have a roast in the oven. You can stay for lunch."

"A tradition?" Lily asked.

"Yes. We do it every Sunday. It's the only time we drink during the day. Except football Saturdays. Wallace likes to watch the games and yell at the referees. Rufus and I stay in the kitchen, out of his way." Rufus and I. Lily could tell by the way she said it that she was not at all displeased to be isolated with Rufus. Yep. Lily might have known. But Mrs. Jefferson was not *that* much older than Rufus, was she?

When Lily was waiting in the front hallway Dean Jefferson was coming down the stairs. He had changed from his dark suit into a black polo shirt and khaki cargo pants (Lily wondered fleetingly at the size of them, as tent-like as they were; he was really quite obese). The air was saturated with the smell of garlicky roasting meat.

"Ahh, the lovely Lily," he said, clutching her into a fierce bear hug. He was actually squeezing her. At just about the moment she was going to begin to resist he released her and stepped back. "How are you, Lovely Lily? Did you enjoy the service?"

"Yes. It was ... interesting," she said. "I ..."

"I've always loved the liturgy," he boomed, interrupting her, "the way it connects us to our past. There is nothing more traditional than liturgy. The beauty of the language."

"Yes, it's ..."

"The liberal wing of the church wants to do away with that beautiful Shakespearean language," he said, "they want to replace it with 'modern' language, replace the thy and thous with you and your and such. 'And with *your* spirit!' Jesus is not my roommate! Gin and tonic, is it?" He didn't wait for her reply but began preparing her a drink. "They are the same people who are always agitating for women priests. They want to gut all that's strong and powerful from the church. And you wouldn't believe what they are doing to the hymns in the new hymnal, which thankfully we don't have at St. Mark's. 'Rise up oh *saints* of God' instead of '*men*!' God protect me!" He smiled broadly and handed her her drink. "That's not how it was originally written. They have no right to change it." He marched toward the living room and she followed him. "I'm sick to death of all this 'political correctness,' especially since it's now permeating the church." He sprawled back in his old recliner and kicked his feet up. He was wearing penny loafers without socks. How old *were* these people? Fifties? Sixties? Willow had told Lily that she was fifty-three; the Jeffersons acted older than that.

"Yahoo?" came a voice from the front doorway. It was Rufus Doublet. He, too, had changed. He was wearing jeans with a white, short sleeved button down oxford cloth shirt hanging out, that Willow thought was probably the one he'd worn with his jacket and tie earlier. Lily sat down quickly to avoid the inevitable hug. Doublet flung his arm across her shoulders and squashed her shoulder blades together anyway. His lack of a greeting struck her as too intimate, as if she'd been expected to be there and there was no need to audibly acknowledge it.

"Go get you a drink, Rufe," the dean said, "Pauldo will be down in a minute." Lily recalled then, from the B for Botticelli night, that their affectionate names for each other were "Pauldo" and "Waldo," said with a kind of cloying, exaggerated sweetness that Lily found annoying. Paulette Jefferson made her entrance, wafting down the stairs with brisk, lively little steps that belied the heaviness of her hips. She had changed to a plain, dull gray cotton house dress. Lily still wore her Sunday suit. She had not known the protocol; she felt a bit awkward. She had gone by her apartment on the way over here but had not thought to change.

Mrs. Jefferson disappeared into the kitchen. The garlic and burned meat smells were stronger now. She came back into the living room with a drink in her hand, a tumbler of dark whiskey, Rufus Doublet following behind. "What's Waldo going on about?" she asked. "I could hear him all the way upstairs."

"You know *me*," the dean said, smiling.

The doorbell rang. When Paulette came back in she had the priest and another man with him. "Lily, you met Hamner this morning, didn't you?" she said. "And this is ..."

"Lavell Dellahoosie," the man said.

"Yes," Paulette said.

Lily nodded to both of them. The priest looked even thinner and more wizened without his vestments. He wore a severe black suit that seemed about a size too big for him, a black shirt with a white clerical collar. His face was wasted and haggard, his hair shockingly white and lank. Even in the dark suit he had a pale, washed out look. The man with him was probably about Lily's age. He had a hardened, leathery look about him, as though he'd spent a great deal of time in the sun. He had on a tight T shirt that read WHAT WOULD JESUS DO? His hair was cut so short it was little more than a layer of fuzz on his head, which was as perfectly round as a bowling ball. Lily thought he looked like a wrestler. He had a tattoo on his bicep, but she was not close enough to him to tell what it was. She had noticed him in the parish hall and thought he was probably a student.

Lavell Dellahoosie took her in; his eyes strayed up and down her body, lingering on her breasts. He made no attempt to disguise his lecherous gaze. "What's happening?" he said to her.

"Hamner brought him back from Pensacola," Paulette said brightly. "He met him in a bar. Hamner likes to proselytize down there among all those sailors and seaman."

I'll bet, Lily thought.

"We worry about his safety," the woman went on.

"Oh," Lily said. She didn't know what else to say. This priest had found him a boy-toy. From the way the boy-toy looked at Lily, he probably went both ways.

"Beer, I'll have a beer," Lavell Dellahoosie said.

"Oh, dear, I'm afraid we're out of beer," Paulette said.

"Give him some whiskey," the priest said.

"Coming right up," Paulette said perkily.

"Nice sermon this morning, Hamner," the dean said.

"Why, thanks."

"Yes. Extraordinary," Rufus said.

Lily sat listening to the babble, watching them all puffing away on their cigarettes. The air in the room was becoming close; she could actually see a cumulus of smoke hovering near the ceiling. The charred garlic odor drifting from the kitchen was most unappetizing. Paulette opened a can of smoked oysters and set out a box of saltines. Lily got a whiff of them, too, and she wondered if her sense of smell was especially acute today. It was as if her nose were being assaulted.

"Did *you* enjoy the service, dear?" the priest asked.

After a minute of silence, Paulette said, "Lily?"

"Oh, you mean me. Yes, yes, I enjoyed it very much."

Lily drained her drink and set the glass on the coffee table. She was wondering how she could extricate herself from this shambles of a social occasion. The dean was holding forth again on the Prayer Book issue. Doublet was echoing him, nodding, laughing, as was Father Curbs. Lavell Dellahoosie sat morosely sipping a glass of bourbon. He kept staring at Lily. It made her uncomfortable. She was watching Doublet and Jefferson, thinking: these two incompetent boobs—her department chair and her dean—hold my future in their hands. She shivered. It didn't matter. One year here was probably enough. They would likely do her a great favor when they didn't renew her contract. Still, it depressed her. She felt a moment of panic. She had begun to feel so settled. So content. It was troubling to have to think about finding another job.

"Hey, good looking, what you got cooking," Dellahoosie said. He was looking at her with a smirk.

"Pardon?"

"Why don't me and you get out of here, leave these old people to theirselves?"

"Behave yourself, Lavell," Curbs said.

Paulette laughed gaily. "Oh, *you*," she said, "Lily is Rufus's girlfriend!"

"What?!" Lily said.

"Hey, sorry," Dellahoosie said, "didn't mean to move in on the perfessor there."

Lily sat fuming. She wanted to correct the misconception, but thought it might be better to just let it slide. At least the man had stopped ogling her. She glanced over at Rufus Doublet; he was talking excitedly to the dean and the priest as if he were unaware of what Paulette had said. Maybe he didn't hear it.

Paulette took her glass. "I really must be going," Lily said.

"Nonsense," the older woman said. "The roast will be out soon."

If it doesn't come out right away, thought Lily, it won't be edible. Which turned out to be the case. The drinking and the blather went on for at least another hour. With her second drink Lily relaxed a bit, but she still kept her eye on Lavell Dellahoosie. The Jeffersons made the drinks quite strong and the decibel level of the voices, often speaking all at once, went up exponentially as time wore on. On the way into the dining room, Dellahoosie cupped her buttock in his palm and squeezed. His fingers went right into her crack. She gave an involuntary "Whoops!" and everybody laughed. She didn't know if they'd seen what prompted her outcry or not. They gathered around the table and Paulette made everyone hold hands. Lily jumped when Father Curbs unexpectedly exclaimed, "The Lord be with thee!" and everybody bowed their heads. "Lord," the priest intoned, "bless this bounty we are about to receive, and make us servants of thy peace." Everybody mumbled an amen.

The roast was so overcooked the dean had trouble carving it. It had shriveled into a hard blob of stringy, singed meat. There were green beans cooked in cream of mushroom soup. A salad of fruit bits suspended in raspberry jello. "Ummm, ummm," several of them murmured. Lavell took a huge piece of the roast and went at it with a steak knife. Lily took a tiny bite of the meat; it was singed and caustic. Dry as sand.

EIGHT

Garcia Russo was sitting in his office in Harmon Hall. He was scribbling on a yellow legal pad. Russo was an assistant professor of mathematics at Lakewood, a small thin man with a heavy black beard; he wore severe dark suits and narrow ties. The sunlight came through the blinds on the window and made gold bars on his desk, which was neat and uncluttered.

Garcia Russo hated. He hated everyone, especially the administration of the university, especially President Steagall, who, Russo was convinced, was the man most responsible for his—Russo's—stagnation at the level of assistant professor. He had applied for tenure and had been granted it, but when, after six years as an assistant, he applied for associate, he was turned down. His colleagues in the department passed on him, but it was blocked higher up, by, Russo knew, that asshole Dean Jefferson and Steagall. Three times he had gotten above the department level, only to be rejected again because, they said, he had no publications to speak of. He was convinced that he was a victim of discrimination; his great grandparents had immigrated from Cuba many years ago, which made him of Hispanic descent. He was angry, and he hated the administration with a withering and furious passion.

He was writing a broadside, the first of many, he hoped; he had already paid one of his students twenty bucks to take the sheets around campus and put them in faculty and staff mailboxes. He would use the mimeograph machine in the departmental office to run off as many as he needed. He wasn't worried about getting observed. Dr. McPherson, the chairman, was so old and doddering he didn't know what was going on half the time, and the secretary, Siri Paul, took long, three-hour lunch breaks. Russo suspected she went downtown to Stache's or somewhere, because he smelled alcohol on her breath from time to time; he said nothing, only filed it away in case he later had to use it as leverage. He would have plenty of time to run off his broadside and send the student on his errand.

He was especially incensed this morning over the news he'd just heard that week: that that moron Steagall was spending $25,000 to bring some lady writer to campus in the spring. That was more than half his yearly salary. He was not about to let the president get away with such frivolity without a fight. He had asked to speak at the Faculty Council, but the chair, a *woman* from the business department, would not put him on the agenda. He planned to speak at length at the next faculty meeting, whenever that might be; Steagall did not like presiding at meetings that might turn hostile, so he simply didn't call many.

Russo perused his notes on the pad. He was trying to hold back; he didn't want to let them have it with both barrels right off the bat. STEAGALL IS PLAYING FAST AND LOOSE WITH OUR FUNDS would be his lead. He would accuse the president of poor stewardship and wasteful spending. THE TIME IS FAST APPROACHING WHEN WE MUST ACT. He wanted to rouse the faculty to his own level of righteous anger, but he knew that would be a difficult task. They were, for the most part, listless and uninterested in anything beyond their grade books and their withered lecture notes. They were a colorless bunch of sheep, following their leader docilely.

But Garcia Russo's plan was nothing less that to get rid of Steagall, to force him to resign. It might be a long and arduous process, but he was up to it.

"Dr. Russo?"

He turned to the door. One of his students, whose name he couldn't immediately recall, was standing there.

"Yes?" he said, harshly. He didn't like being interrupted. The girl looked startled. She was a pretty little thing, tight jeans, a form fitting T shirt. "I'm sorry," he said, "you caught me thinking of something else."

She smiled. "I just wanted you to know," she said, "that I'll be streaking today, down the street between Harmon and Comer. This afternoon at two."

"I beg your pardon?" he said.

"You know, streaking," she said.

"Yes, I know what it is. I've seen it, of course." He peered at her. Her short blonde hair was shiny in the sunlight through his window. "But I thought it was, well, anonymous. Don't you wear a ski mask?"

"Yes sir," she said.

"But you're telling me it'll be you, so I'll know it's you even if you have on a mask?"

"Yes sir."

"You'll be naked?" he asked.

"Yes sir. Naked as a jaybird."

"Well, I'll be sure and catch your, uh, performance, Miss ...?"

"Lovelady," she said. She winked.

He watched her walk away down the hall, the tight jeans hugging her ass.

Willow found the broadside in her box after lunch. She was leafing through her pile of hand mail and brochures from publishers when she discovered the amateurish sheet. At first she thought it must be some student prank. She read it quickly and grunted. She was suddenly aware that Brasfield Finch was standing near her. He glanced at the sheet in her hand.

"Illiterate," he said. "But he does make some good points."

"This is the kind of thing that should not be tolerated on a college campus," she said.

"Even if he's right?" Finch said.

"He, or she, or whoever, didn't even have the courage to sign his name," she said.

"Oh, it's a he all right," he said.

"Now how do you know that, Mr. Finch?" she asked haughtily.

"It has Russo's fingerprints all over it," he said.

"Russo?" she asked. "That little twit in the math department?"

"That's the twit," he said, "I'd bet good money on it."

She snorted. "He was the one who called Dean Jefferson a liar to his face in an Arts and Sciences meeting, wasn't he?"

"One and the same," Finch said. "He was correct then, too."

"Oh my," she said, "Lord deliver me from such as this. I have neither the time nor the inclination to indulge in such nonsense as this." She sniffed. He was standing all the way at the end of the row of mailboxes, but she could cleanly smell the whiskey on him. She was always tempted to ask him if he was going to publish another book, to embarrass him. "How's your new book coming?" she asked abruptly.

He peered curiously at her. He cleared his throat. "As a matter of fact, very well," he said. "Thank you for asking."

"And when might we be seeing it in the bookstores?"

"Oh, it's a year or two away, I would guess. I don't work fast."

"No, you don't, do you?" She gathered her mail and books. "Well, I must get to my office," she said, "good day, Mr. Finch."

"And good day to you, Willow," he said. She could hear him

chuckling behind her as she walked away. He was an incorrigible man. A terrible man.

Rufus Doublet was waiting for her at her office. "I suppose you read the broadside," he said, "everybody's talking about it." He was wearing a new tweed jacket and a red knit tie.

"Yes," she said, unlocking her door, "I read it." She pulled it out of her stack of mail and tossed it into the trash can.

"I'll bet John is having a hissy fit," he said. "Who do you suppose is behind this?"

"I have no idea."

"Well, I have a few ideas," he whispered.

"Please spare me," she said, sitting down at her desk. "I don't care to speculate. The only thing on my mind is my lecture on Keats." She knew that Rufus was dying to gossip about it. She could tell by the way he was holding his mouth. And his whispering. Whenever he whispered he had something confidential to tell you.

The telephone on her desk rang. "Excuse me," she said, "Hello?"

"Is this Miz Behn?" a woman said.

"Yes, who is calling, please?"

"This is Martha, Father Curbs's housekeeper," the woman said.

"Yes. What is it?"

"You better get over here to his apartment," she said.

Willow covered the phone. "Rufus, excuse me, please," she said, "and close the door if you would." When the chairman was gone, she said, "What is it, Martha?"

"Well, that Delaroosie fellow, he done beat up Father Curbs and stole his car and gone."

"What? Beat him up? When?"

"I don't know. Last night, I reckon. There's plenty of beer cans sittin around, so ..."

"All right. I'll be right there." *What next?* Willow thought, *what next?*

Hamner Curbs lived in a small apartment house near the campus, equidistant from Comer Hall and St. Mark's Church. He lived in a Spartan apartment; his only indulgences seemed to be his ridiculously long and pretentious car and his penchant for whiskey.

He was particularly fond of the bar at the Clara Neal Motel on the edge of town. Willow had had to fetch him from there on several occasions when he became too drunk to drive home.

Willow was initially surprised when Paulette Jefferson opened the front door, but then immediately surmised that she should not have been surprised at all.

"Where is he?" she asked, without preamble.

"He's in bed," Paulette Jefferson said. Willow looked around. There was nothing in the living room but one chair and a television set against one wall.

"Asleep, I suppose," Willow said shortly.

"No, he's awake." Paulette touched Willow's arm. "He's upset. This had been traumatic for him."

Willow felt herself softening, but she steeled herself. "I guess so," she said, "what happened?"

"They had a fight. Delaroosie left in his car."

"A fight?" Willow said. "I can imagine how that one came out."

"Yes, he's beaten up pretty badly."

"Maybe he's learned his lesson about bringing home boy toys from Pensacola," Willow said.

Paulette Jefferson swelled. "Whatever do you mean?" she asked.

"For heaven's sakes, Paulette, you know what I mean."

"Whatever you're implying ... Willow, he is our *priest*. A man of God. Please be civil."

"He may be a priest, but he's also a drunk and a closet homosexual and a hypocrite."

"Bite your tongue, Dr. Behn! You are jumping to conclusions that have no merit. I'm surprised at you. Where is your Christian compassion?"

Willow snorted. "Lead me to him."

"All right." Paulette turned toward the bedroom door. Willow noticed that she staggered slightly.

"Have you been drinking, Paulette?" she asked.

"He needed a drink. I didn't want him drinking alone, so ..."

"I see," Willow said. She had heard rumors that some students had reported that they smelled liquor on Paulette in her history classes. She followed the woman into Curbs' bedroom. "I suppose there are advantages to being married to the dean," she said to the back of her head. Paulette pretended she hadn't heard her.

"Here is the patient," Paulette said brightly.

Curbs was propped up in his bed, wearing a red and green plaid bathrobe. His right eye was black and the other side of his face was red and raw. His lips were swollen. He was holding a tumbler of whiskey.

"Good afternoon, Willow," he said, "peace be with you."

"Yes," Willow said. "I suppose I should see the other guy."

Curbs laughed weakly. "I'm afraid I didn't do much damage to him," he said, "I'm not much of a fighter."

"No, you're not, are you?" she said, remembering the time he had tried to fight the policeman outside Pasquale's. "Have you seen a doctor?"

"I don't need a doctor," he said.

"Have you called the police?"

"The police? Why?"

"Well, you've been assaulted. And your car has been stolen."

"Aren't you even going to ask how I'm feeling?" he asked.

"All right. How are you feeling?"

"Not well. And I'm not going to report the car stolen. Lavell *borrowed* it."

"*Borrowed* it? For what, to run to the store for a six-pack?"

"No."

"Where is he, then?" Curbs did not answer. He took a swig of his drink. "You don't know where he is. He's probably back in Pensacola, looking for another sucker to roll."

"Willow, you are a cynic," he said.

"No, I am a realist, Hamner. And I've about had it from you, up to here. I'm going to put in a call to the Bishop this afternoon."

"Don't do that," he said, "please."

"Willow," Paulette said, "calm down."

"I am calm. I am very calm," Willow said.

John Steagall sat behind his big desk, looking at Lillian Lallo, the chair of the Faculty Council, in one of his visitors' chairs. On the desk was a small stack of the broadsides, which seemed to come weekly with a regularity that alarmed Steagall. In addition, of course, to the contents. It was propaganda. They were all aimed at him and they had become increasingly more vicious with each new issue.

"You must find out who's behind this," Steagall said, "it has gone on long enough. It is undermining my ability to run the institution."

"And it is undermining faculty morale," Dr. Lallo said.

"This latest one calls for my resignation!" Steagall said. "Ridiculous!"

"Yes. But dangerous," she said.

"Come now. These are the ramblings of a lunatic. Surely nobody takes them seriously?"

"There are rumblings," she said.

"Rumblings?"

"Of discontent. It takes very little to stir up the kooks on the faculty."

"Are there any who aren't kooks?" he asked. "Present company excluded."

Lallo chuckled. "Of course. No. Seriously, there are always a number of radicals looking for a fight."

"Do you think these broadsides are the results of some organized conspiracy? Surely not."

"I don't know, John. Nothing official, of course. I have tried to block these people from infiltrating the council, but I hear things. Some people are upset that you're spending all that money on Lenora Hart."

"Oh for heaven's sake, she's one of the most beloved writers in America. We're lucky and fortunate to get her."

"I agree. But not everyone does."

"Have you been talking to Brasfield Finch?"

"No. Why?"

"Never mind. Well, they can just get over it. It'll be a feather in our cap. The publicity alone will more than make up for her fee, which, by the way, is coming mostly from the foundation. None of their salaries will be affected, which is all they care about, anyway."

Lallo chuckled again. "Anyway," she said after a minute, "if these people get out of hand, get too much power, it could be dangerous."

"What people, if I may ask?" Steagall asked.

"I'm not at liberty to name names at this point," she said.

"Oh come now, Lillian. You have some idea, I know."

"Perhaps. But you could guess as well as I can." She chuckled. "The usual suspects, I suppose."

"R. D. Wettermark," he said, naming a grousy member of the physics department.

Lillian Lallo remained silent.

"Alexander Daniels, in the math department." Daniels still wore his hair down to his shoulders and sported a huge handle bar mustache, which made him, in Steagall's estimation, extremely untrustworthy.

"I'm sorry, John," Dr. Lallo said.

"Where is your loyalty, Lillian?"

"I am chair of the *faculty* council," she said.

"But by virtue of your position, you are more administration than faculty."

"I don't think my salary would reflect that," Lallo said.

"There are ways, Lillian, recommendations and so forth."

"Are you trying to bribe me, John?"

"Call it what you like. We are in this together. We are allies. Surely you don't want to cast your lot with the rabble rousers. There is no future in that."

"I will try to keep you posted, John. Keep you updated. That's the most I can do at this point."

"All right," John Steagall said.

After Dr. Lallo was gone, Steagall sat at his desk, chewing on his lip and thinking. He didn't know which he found more annoying, the streakers or the broadsides. There were always dissatisfied faculty out to stir up trouble. And he was no longer terribly surprised at anything students might do, but he thought the streaking crossed the line. He could not fathom the young mind that thought that stripping naked and running through a public place was a good thing to do. What did that get them? Some kind of sexual satisfaction, he supposed, and he shuddered to think that. The plethora of galloping hormones among the student body was terrifying to him, and the sight of nubile young bodies being flaunted like that was disgusting.

He had had a heated telephone call from the governor, who was de facto chairman of the board of trust, though he never attended the meetings.

"Dr. Steagall," he'd said, "if you don't get control of your campus, then I'll have to come over there and do it myself."

"Yes sir," Steagall had said, "I'll get it under control. Don't worry."

"If another Playboy picture goes out from your place, it'll be your head, Steagall. And I hope you know I mean it."

"Yes sir."

"And somebody has been sending these little Xeroxed editorials about you to my office. Sounds like somebody is out to get you."

"I know. Disgruntled faculty members."

"You can't let the inmates run the asylum, Dr. Steagall."

"Yes sir."

Lily was walking to her apartment, loaded down with composition papers; her green book bag was bulging with them. Sometimes she thought one of her fingers might turn into a red pen. There was no way she could give her students much individual attention, she had so many of them. And most of her waking hours were spent marking papers.

She was almost across campus, strolling on the brick sidewalk, when she noticed someone walking toward her. It was dusk, and there was a slight chill in the air. As he got closer she realized it was Rufus Doublet, her department chairman and her erstwhile "boyfriend." She had been decidedly cool to Rufus since that Sunday at the Jeffersons, though she was hesitant to be downright cold. After all, he was her boss. Or one of them, anyway. She just avoided him as much as she could, and he had made no moves toward her one way or the other. Though not unattractive, Doublet was sexless. He had a limp, Old-South air about him that Lily found repulsive.

"Well, the lovely Lily," he said as he approached, echoing his friend Wallace Jefferson. She imagined them discussing her, calling her "the lovely Lily." They fancied themselves charming wits. They probably lusted after her, though she still was almost certain that Rufus was gay. Maybe he went both ways. And she wondered about Jefferson, too; his eyes lingered on Lily's breasts, but his wife Paulette was very butchy. She set off Lily's gaydar as well. Brasfield had remarked once, when they'd seen them in Stache's, "Here come the suck buddies." She hadn't asked him what he meant; she didn't really want to know.

"Hello, Dr. Doublet," she said.

He stopped in front of her, so she stopped, too. He nodded toward her book bag. "Papers?" he asked.

"Lord yes," she said, "a batch of them."

"Gets tedious sometimes, doesn't it?"

She started to agree, then stopped herself. She didn't want him to think she was complaining about her work. "Goes with the territory, I guess," she said.

"Lily, will you sit?" he asked. It was so stilted and formal she at first didn't know what he meant. There was a bench along the walkway, and he nodded toward it.

"I really should ..." she began. Then she sat down. It was getting dark, but the lamps around the campus had come on.

"I wanted to ask how your dissertation is coming," he said when he was seated.

She glanced toward her book bag. "Well, it's hard to find the time," she said.

"But one must find the time," he said.

"Yes, of course. I meant it's hard to get any periods of time when I don't have papers to grade or preparations for my classes."

"I understand," he said. "As you get more experience, you'll be able to balance your work better. One must learn to balance ... to balance."

"Yes sir," she said.

"Lily, please don't say 'sir' to me, and I am not Dr. Doublet to you, but Rufus. You do like me, don't you?"

"Well," she said. He sounded like a high school boy. "Of course. I like you fine. I mean, we're colleagues."

"I mean, more than that," he said. She could see him smiling confidently in the dimness.

"What do you mean, uh, Rufus?" she asked, though she knew very well what he meant.

"Oh, come now, Lily, surely you've noticed how I look at you," he said. *Yes*, she thought, *with that sappy molasses look on your face.*

"I really don't know what you're driving at," she said.

"Going to be coy, huh?" Even in the dark she could see that he was holding his head in a cocky, over-confident way.

"I'm not being coy," she said, smiling, deciding to flirt, "I'm not your coy kind of girl."

"No, you're not, are you?" he said. He laughed. She sensed he laughed to ease the tension. *His* tension. She realized that he was nervous as hell. She reached out and touched his hand.

"Relax," she said. "Rufus," she added.

His reaction was electric. He seemed at first stupefied, then he laughed jovially and loudly. He tossed his head. "My, my, you are something else, aren't you?" he said, his voice rising an octave. He gripped her hand. Hard.

She pulled back, but he held her tight.

"Lily," he said, "I've wanted to be alone with you for some time. You are one of the most ... the most attractive women I've ever known."

"Why thank you," she said. It was all she could do to keep from wincing from his grip. He just kept looking at her, his eyes wide. "You're ... hurting my hand," she said.

"Oh. Oh, I'm so sorry," he said, releasing her. "Please forgive me. Your nearness simply drives me crazy. You've no idea how you affect me."

"Are you sure?" she asked, rubbing her hand.

"I'm sorry?"

"Well, I just assumed ..." She stopped herself. He was her boss. He would be a major factor in deciding whether or not her contract was renewed for next year. She had to be careful. "Never mind," she said. She gave him her most winning smile.

That was a mistake, because before she knew it he had slid over on the bench and put a bear hug on her and was kissing her on the lips. His lips were dry and hard, and he shoved his fat tongue between her teeth. She struggled slightly. She pushed him away.

"Whew," she said, "you move fast, don't you?" she said.

They sat there for awhile, kissing. He gripped her buttocks with both hands. He ground his lips against hers like a horny adolescent. Maybe she had been wrong about him, but he obviously had had little experience. At least with women. She was afraid that a student or another faculty member would walk by and see them.

"I really should go," she murmured against his panting. "To get right on these papers," she added.

He leaned back and looked at her with a proprietary air. "Let me walk you to your apartment," he said. "I'll carry your Harvard book bag. At Emory, did they call these Harvard book bags? That's what we called them at Mississippi State. These green monstrosities." He threw her bag over his shoulder and grunted. "You must have some books in there, too," he said, and chuckled. He took her arm and they started down the path toward her apartment. He rattled on as they walked, about nothing, and she barely listened to him. She was thinking about what would happen when they got to her door. She knew he wouldn't let her go at the front of her building, but would insist on accompanying her to her apartment. Which he did. "Oh, you don't need to be carrying this heavy bag up these steps," he said, "delicate little thing like you." He put his free arm around her waist as they mounted the stairs. When they got to her door he stood there as solidly as if he were planted. She paused. He glanced at his wristwatch. "It's cocktail hour," he said, "I could come in for a quickie."

"Well ..." she said, "all right, but it needs to be a real quickie. I need to get on these papers."

"All work and no play makes Lily a dull lady," he said, and winked at her.

She unlocked her door and they went in. She straightened some magazines, a *Time* and a *New Yorker*, on her coffee table. He sat on the sofa and crossed his legs at the knees.

"I'll be right back," she said. "I have Vodka." She remembered the bottle she had bought in case Brasfield Finch stopped by. "And Scotch."

"Scotch," he said, "with a splash of water."

"Coming right up."

She had to struggle with the ice tray. The freezer on her refrigerator froze the cubes so hard they were difficult to get out. She ran some hot water over the bottom of the tray and that helped.

"Here you go," she said, handing him his drink. She had made herself a light Vodka and tonic. She really *did* intend to spend the evening grading papers. She had planned to eat a Lean Cuisine and get right to work.

"Here's to us," he said, holding his glass up and rattling his ice.

"To ..." she paused, " ... us." She sipped her drink.

After a minute, he said, "Lily, I'm falling in love with you."

"You ... ?" she said, and stopped. "Really, Rufus? We hardly know each other."

"How can you say that? After what we just shared."

She was astonished. As far as she was concerned, what they had just shared were some fervent, heated, and childish kisses and his determined caressing of her ass. It hardly amounted to love. "Well, I ..." She chose her words carefully. "I don't feel like I know *you* that well. You have to ... give me time, I guess I'm trying to say."

"We have world enough and time, Lily," he said, chuckling, congratulating himself on his clever Marvell quote.

"Yes ... well ..." She sipped her drink.

"You, of course, recognize the allusion, don't you?"

"Yes," she said. She thought of the title of the poem. *To His Coy Mistress*. It was a poem that every sophomore English major—

after he had discovered it in English Lit Survey—used to try to seduce his girlfriend. But this man was chairman of the English Department at Lakewood College. With a PhD from Mississippi State. Lily had not known they even *offered* a doctorate at Mississippi State. "Well," she said, after a long silence, "I really must ... I mean ... get to work."

"You work too hard, dear," Doublet said.

"That's what I get paid for," Lily said, "though not very much."

"Well, I can do something about that," he said.

Lily realized again, at that moment, that Rufus Doublet held all the cards.

When they were in the bedroom, Lily removed her clothes and stretched out on the bed. Rufus stood at the foot, gazing at her admiringly. His dark brown eyes played over her body. He stood there for a long time. She looked for a tell-tale bulge in his pants and saw none.

"Aren't you going to get undressed?" she asked.

"Of course," he said. "Just admiring the scenery."

"Thanks."

"You really are a beautiful young woman, Lily," he said.

"Flattery will get you anywhere," she said, smiling.

He made no move to remove his clothing. Was he stalling? Yes, he was stalling. She squirmed alluringly on the bed. She could see beads of sweat on his upper lip. His eyes narrowed as he stared at her. He began to unbutton his shirt. He went slowly, as if to convince her that it was sexy. Or maybe he was trying to convince himself.

"Hurry," she whispered breathlessly. He grinned at her, a forced, conscripted grin.

He quickly removed the remainder of his clothes. He stood there posing. He was slim and almost hairless. His penis, which was sizable, hung on him like a limp hosepipe. He was in no way aroused. His breath was even and steady. There was a long silence.

"Is something the matter?" she asked.

He seemed to hesitate. After a few moments he said, "I can't seem to get an erection."

"I noticed," she said.

"I'm sorry," he said.

"Don't worry about it," she said, "it happens."

"It's never happened to me before," he said.

I'll bet, she thought.

He continued to stand there, in all his impotent nakedness.

"Do you want me to ...?" she began.

"No, that's okay," he interrupted.

Slowly he put his clothing back on. He wore whitey-tighties. When he had tucked his button-down shirt into his pants, he slipped his feet into his loafers. He wore penny loafers like his friend Wallace Jefferson. After a few minutes had passed, he said, "Lily, I hope you would never say anything about this to anyone."

"My lips are sealed," she said.

He left her lying naked on the bed. She sighed, pressing her head back into the pillow.

NINE

They were sitting around in the den of R. D. Wettermark's house. They were Garcia Russo, Alexander Daniels, Wettermark and Donald Katz, a disgruntled associate professor in the biology department.

"Let's think of ourselves as the 'modern mafia,'" Russo was saying.

"That's good," Katz said. "I like that." He spoke with a clipped northern accent, though it was pronounced as a slow drawl because of his years of teaching in the Deep South. It made for a strange and unusual way of speaking, which Katz fancied was impressive for his students.

They were having drinks, light whisky and water that Wettermark called "Bourbon and Branch." Wettermark made his drinks very weak, which was annoying to the others, but none of them remarked on it. Wettermark was very proud of his Southern Heritage. He spoke deliberately with the soft 'R' of Southern aristocracy. His den was decorated with Auburn memorabilia, where he had obtained his physics PhD. "I'm not sure I want to be called 'mafia,'" he said, "I'm not a wop."

Russo bristled, but he did so quietly. He had never publicly proclaimed his suspicions of ethnic discrimination on the part of the administration, and he was not sure how these colleagues would react to the claim. Wettermark would probably call him a wetback, or worse. But these men were his lot; they were constantly dissatisfied with anything the administration did, and they were not shy about expressing their disdain for John Steagall. If he were going to get his movement going, then they would be his allies. They were a bland lot, but so much the better in Russo's campaign to get rid of Steagall. They functioned, for the most part, under the radar; most of the other faculty considered them all harmless losers.

"I suppose I should tell you," Russo said, "before we go any further, that I wrote the flyers you all got in your mailboxes."

"Are you serious?!" Wettermark exclaimed.

"Serious as a blind man's hat band," Russo said.

"I thought so," Daniels said, "I told ..."

"Wait a minute," Katz said. " 'A blind man's hat band?' I don't get it."

"Never mind," Russo said. "Forget it."

"Well, I don't understand what you mean," Katz said petulantly.

"It's not important, Donald. Let's move on." Russo looked around the room. "What I am after is nothing less than the resignation of one John Steagall," he said.

"Are you crazy?' Wettermark blurted.

"As a blind man's hat band, I suppose," Katz said. He tossed down his drink and held up his glass. "How about another, R. D.? And this time put a little bourbon in it."

"How are we supposed to accomplish that?" Wettermark asked, getting up to fetch Katz another drink.

"We'll keep picking, picking, picking," Russo said. "We'll drive him crazy."

"Crazy as a blind man's hat band," Katz said and snorted.

"Stop saying that, Donald. This is a very serious matter."

"As serious as ..."

"Don't say it!" Russo interrupted.

"Okay," Katz said. "Sorry. You were saying?"

"We keep hitting them with these flyers, the faculty will get riled up," Russo said.

"Fat chance of that," Daniels said.

"We have *some* colleagues, Alex, who have *some* sense."

"Who?" Daniels said, looking around. "Besides us?"

"Not everybody's happy with Steagall," Russo said.

"That's true," Katz said, "but who beside us is willing to do anything?"

"I was thinking," said Russo, "of Brasfield Finch."

"What? That drunk idiot?" Wettermark asked.

"Look," Russo said, "let me lay this out for you. We keep up with the broadsides, keep stirring up the faculty. It'll take some time, sure. But eventually we want to force a no confidence vote. And we'll need someone other than one of us to make that motion in a faculty meeting. Finch is a senior professor. He's well respected ..."

"Shit," Katz said.

"Everybody knows him," Russo said.

"That's why he's not well respected," Katz said.

"So?" Russo said.

"But he drinks," Wettermark said.

"What the hell are *we* doing here tonight?" Russo asked, holding up his glass.

"You know what I mean. He's drunk in his classes, is what I hear."

"Rumors," Russo said.

"Come on, Gar. They're not just rumors."

Russo was smiling confidently. "*Rumors* for our purposes, men. As far as we are concerned, they are just rumors. We know they're true, but that only makes it easier for us to use him."

"It is my understanding that he is the one who is behind the invitation to Lenora Hart and her obscene honorarium," Katz drawled.

"All the better. A Steagall ally turned enemy."

"And how do you propose to accomplish this? In my dealings with Finch, I've been on a couple of committees with him; he is a loose cannon, apt to say anything. And do anything. He thinks of himself as a free spirit," Wettermark said.

"Isn't that convenient?" Russo said, smiling.

It was a beautiful early spring evening, and Willow and Lily walked from Comer over to the natural amphitheater in front of Flowerhill, the president's home. The students were having a sing-along, and they had both heard the music from their offices. Since it was late on a Friday, they were the only ones on the floor, and Lily had said, through Willow's open door,

"What do you suppose that is?"

"Sounds like students," Willow said. "Sometimes, when the weather turns nice, they gather at the amphitheater to sing."

"How nice," Lily said.

"Yes. One of their saner traditions. At least they probably have their clothes on."

"Would you like to walk over there?" Lily asked.

"Whatever for?"

"Well, I need a break from these papers. And it's a nice night. What do you say?"

"I don't ordinarily hang out with students," Willow said.

"Oh, come on," Lily said, "it'll be fun. Come on, loosen up a little."

"Whatever do you mean by that?"

"Just ... nothing. Have some fun, you know?"

"Fun? Listening to a bunch of beered-up adolescents cater-wauling?"

"Listen," Lily said, holding up her hand. The students were singing along with "Michael, Row the Boat Ashore."

"I really should finish going over these lecture notes," Willow said.

She was sitting at her desk, looking over her shoulder. The younger woman had obviously gone home and changed out of her "teaching clothes;" she wore a black EMORY T-shirt and kha-ki Bermuda shorts. She looked like a student herself. The shorts were tight and form-fitting, as was the shirt.

"You look kittenish this evening," Willow said.

"Pardon?"

"Pretty. You look pretty."

"Well, thank you. You look nice, too."

"Oh come now, Lily, with my dowdy dress and sensible shoes?" She'd heard a student once when she'd walked by say, "Look. Look at that old woman's sensible shoes."

Lily looked down at her own tennis shoes. They were new, very white and clean. She did not think Willow looked dowdy; she was older, more mature, but that was something Lily looked forward to being one day. Willow actually had a nice figure except for a slight bulge at the waistline. She was an attractive woman; Lily had often wondered why she was not married, or at least had a man friend. Then she would remember that of course it was because she was a scholar and had no room in her life for such frivolity. Or she could be gay. Lily had considered that possibility as well. Her gaydar let her down where Willow was concerned, though. It was difficult to tell.

Lily had had a fling in graduate school with an older woman, one of her professors. She had known immediately the first time the woman had looked at her. It was the first time she'd been with a woman, except for some fooling around when she was an un-dergraduate, and she was surprised at how hot it was. She'd been with lots of boys, and by then lots of men as well, but it was differ-ent with Dr. Carmichael. She had initiated Lily into a whole new realm of lovemaking that Lily had not even known existed. The woman had been in her late forties, Lily in her early twenties. Dr. Carmichael had been just about the age of Dr. Behn right now.

"How old are you, Willow?" she blurted, before she thought.

"Why Lily, what a thing to ask," Willow said. She laughed, to show she was not offended. "Old enough to know better," she said.

What did she mean by that? Was she reading Lily's mind? Lily laughed, too.

"I'm sorry, Willow," she said. "Sometimes I ..." She trailed off.

"That's all right, dear. I guess to you youngsters everyone over thirty is an old fart."

"Oh I didn't mean that at all. No. I don't think of you as old. Ol*der*, but not old."

"Why don't we get off that subject?" Willow asked. "It's making me uncomfortable."

"Okay. I didn't mean to ..." Willow was looking at her, not unkindly. "Why don't we walk over and listen to the music for awhile?" Lily asked.

"Lily, I ..."

"All right," Lily said. "That's okay. I just thought ..."

There was a long pause. "Well, sure," Willow said, "if you don't mind, I'd love to walk over with you."

There was a natural earthen stage in the amphitheater, and the students were sitting around on the grass. A boy with a banjo was on the stage, leading the singing. Lily thought she smelled pot in the air. Naturally. Where two or three are gathered together, she thought. She and Willow stood at the back of the crowd. A blonde girl joined the boy on stage and the two of them harmonized on "Four Strong Winds" while the crowd of students sang along. Lily thought it was like something out of an old movie. Peaceful and serene. The mellow sound of the students' voices drifted out over the campus, among the tall old oaks and up and down the brick sidewalks. It was a side of the college she'd not seen before. It was nice to be around students in their natural habitat, she thought. The song ended and the song leader announced they were taking a short break.

"Well, it's a lovely evening, isn't it?" someone said behind them, and turning Lily saw it was Wallace Jefferson, with Paulette. They were grinning broadly.

"What an occasion, eh?" Paulette said and gave a little cheerleader-like kick. They looked extremely proprietary, as though they were personally responsible for it. The dean had on jeans, his massive belly hanging out over his belt. He wore a LAKEWOOD sweatshirt. He looked as though he were playing at being a "sport." Paulette looked her usual mannish self, her tweed skirt down almost to her ankles.

"Hello, Jeffersons," Willow said. "You know Lily Putnam, of course."

"Of course, the lovely Lily," Wallace Jefferson said. He leaned forward. She thought he was going to hug her, then he seemed to think better of it. "I thought you might be with Rufus," he said.

"No," Lily said quickly.

"Rufus Doublet?" Willow asked. "Why would we be with him?"

"Well, he is your ... colleague," he said.

"We were working and we heard the music," Willow said. "Rufus hasn't stayed in his office past three o'clock in his life, and certainly not on a Friday. So, no, he is not with us."

"I see," Paulette said.

Willow looked genuinely confused. She glanced at Lily as if for an explanation. Lily shrugged. She wished the Jeffersons would move on. Their sudden appearance had cast a damper on an otherwise pleasant evening.

"How are the plans for Lenora Hart coming along?" the dean asked.

"I have no earthly idea," Willow said.

"I thought you were on the committee," he said.

"I am. But Brasfield doesn't need a committee."

"Oh, yes. I understand," Jefferson said.

"I can't wait," Paulette said, with a little clap of her hands, "I just love her book, don't you all?"

"Yes," Lily said. Willow said nothing.

"It's just amazing that John has gotten her to come," Paulette said, "you know, she rarely appears anywhere, so it's quite an honor. We should all be grateful."

"We are duly thankful, Paulette," Willow said. Willow's slightly sarcastic tone seemed to be lost on Paulette Jefferson.

"I knew you would be, Willow," the dean's wife said, "after all, her appearance will be a feather in the cap of the English Department."

"Of course," Willow said.

"I'm excited," Lily said.

"I suppose you studied her work in your graduate courses," the dean said.

"Oh, indeed," Lily said. The only mention she could remember of Hart's book in her graduate courses was in a tiresome paper given by a man in her Southern Literature seminar. His paper was entitled, "Why I like *To Lynch a Wild Duck*." She recalled the first line: "I like *To Lynch a Wild Duck* because Lenora Hart liked *To Lynch a Wild Duck*." It sounded as though he meant the act rather than the novel. It was not a very good paper. But *she* liked the novel, too. She was a sucker for novels about children, especially little girls.

"We were going to stroll down to Stache's for a drink," Wallace Jefferson said. "Why don't you join us?"

"I really should ..." Willow began.

"Oh, come on, Willow," he said. "A little drinkie-poo wouldn't hurt. They have sherry."

Willow bristled. She detested the man. "All right," she said.

"That's the spirit," Paulette said and gave her little cheerleader kick. "It's Friday night. Time for the old folks to howl."

"I suppose you're right," Willow said.

Lily gripped Willow's hand and smiled warmly at her. Willow saw that Paulette noticed the gesture and looked quickly away.

Stache's was Friday night crowded. And loud. Willow was immediately sorry she had agreed to come. This was definitely not her thing. They found a large, wobbly table in the corner. Their waiter was a boy named Randy, who was one of Willow's former students. He had a large cast on his left arm and hand.

"Good evening, Dr. Behn," he said, and nodded toward the others. "What can I getcha?"

"Heavens, Randy, what happened to your arm?" Willow asked.

"I got shot," Randy said.

"Shot?! How?"

"I was sittin in my living room and a bullet came through the window and blam, got me in the wrist."

"In your living room?" Willow asked. "Where in the world do you live?"

"Over on Salem Road," he said. "What're y'all havin? You want to see menus?"

"No, just drinks," Wallace Jefferson said. "Separate checks, please."

It was just like the man, scared he'd get stuck with someone else's drink. Like he didn't have a fat dean's salary. Willow motioned to her and Lily and ordered two Vodka and tonics. "These two," she said. She noticed that Paulette took notice of that gesture, too.

"Goodness, Willow, not sherry?" Paulette said, and she and Wallace laughed together. "Bring us two bourbons, please, with water," she said.

"Yes m'am," Randy said.

"Not draft beer?" Willow said. "I thought, dressed as you are, Wallace, that you'd want to play drinking games."

The dean chuckled good naturedly. But his face was stiff.

After Randy was gone, the dean said, "I wish students wouldn't insist on living over there. It's cheap, because it's the old black section of town."

"I can hardly hear you for this music," Willow said. "Must they play it so loud?"

"That's the way the young people like it," Paulette said, "isn't it, Lily?"

"I suppose so," Lily said, "whatever." She, too, had noticed Paulette's stern glances and was annoyed at them.

They sat listening to the music and the cacophony of voices, without trying to talk. After a few minutes Randy came back with their drinks on a tray. "I'm running two tabs," he said, "just signal me when you're ready."

"I think these will be sufficient," Willow said, but she said it to Randy's back as he was already headed back behind the bar.

"A bird can't fly on one wing," Wallace Jefferson said, holding up his glass. "Randy," he shouted, "you may as well start another round." He chuckled jovially. "Keep em comin! Keep em comin!"

"Settle down, Waldo," Paulette said.

"Why, honey, we're having a good time. This is fun!"

"I just don't think it's a terribly good idea for the dean to be getting drunk in a student hang-out."

"Who said anything about getting drunk?" the dean asked. "Just a couple of toddies."

"All right," Paulette said and laughed self-consciously.

They sipped their drinks, except for the dean, who bolted his. Willow had never seen the man quite so animated. She sensed that it was Lily's presence that caused him to act the way he was. Of course. He was attracted to the girl; he was trying to impress her. Willow smiled to herself; if so, he was going about it the wrong way. Willow had long noticed that certain types of men made total fools of themselves when around beautiful women. In her estimation, Wallace Jefferson did not have far to go to accomplish that.

"Tell us about Lenora Hart," Jefferson said.

"What about her?" Willow said.

"Share some of the plans with us," he said.

"I'm sure I am not privy to the plans," Willow said, "you need to ask Brasfield Finch or John Steagall."

"They won't tell you the plans?"

"I haven't asked," Willow said, "I don't want to know the *plans*, as you say. It is not my business."

"But surely, as an English professor," Paulette said, "you're thrilled to have a writer of such reputation visit our campus, Willow."

Willow took a sip of her drink. She was beginning to like the taste of Vodka and tonic. "Well," she said, "it would help if *To Lynch a Wild Duck* were not a children's book." Could the liquor already be going to her head?

"A *children's* book?!" Paulette exclaimed. "Whatever do you mean?"

"I remember when it first came out," Willow said, "it was marketed as a children's book."

"It won the *Pulitzer Prize!*" the dean said. "It's a beloved classic," he added.

"That it is," Willow said.

"Anyway, everyone, including members of the board of trust, is excited to have a writer of such renown lecture here. I can tell you, from talking with administrators at other schools in the state, that we are the envy of higher academe right now." Wallace Jefferson drained his drink and sat back with a self-congratulatory expression.

"I'm sure," Willow said.

Lily was watching all this with curiosity. As the decidedly junior faculty member at the table, she was hesitant to join in. She didn't want to say something out of order. Wallace Jefferson, though obviously intelligent, was a pompous ass. And his wife, who, like her husband, had a Ph.D. from the University of Georgia (she had told Lily proudly that that's how they met) was a full professor in the history department. A little nepotism? Two fat salaries. Yet Lily had been in their home; they lived like slobs.

"Well, hello," someone said. "Is this a faculty meeting? I hate to interrupt." It was a laughing Alexander Daniels. Lily did not know him well, had only met him. She was not even sure what department he was in. He was holding a long neck Corona with a slice of lime in it.

"Hello, Alex," Jefferson said coolly. "No, pure pleasure." He paused. "Join us?"

"Well, I'm with some other people," Daniels said. "Just wanted to say hello."

"Hello," Willow said dismissively. Lily cut her eyes at the older woman; she was frowning, as though she smelled something unpleasant. "Have we met?" Daniels asked; he was looking at Lily. His long dark hair curled about his shoulders, and his bushy mustache almost covered his lips. His eyes were appraising her.

"Yes, to say hello," Lily said, sticking out her hand. "Lily Putnam," she said.

"This is the lovely Lily," Wallace Jefferson said. Everything he said was with an air of possessorship. It was clear that he felt a sense of dominion over everything and everybody everywhere he was. Lily had never met a more "dean" dean.

"Nice to meet you, Miss Putnam," Daniels said, "welcome to Lakewood."

"Well, I've been here since September," Lily said, "but thanks."

"Ahhhh," he said. He continued to stare at her. Lily knew he was contemplating how difficult or easy it would be to get into her panties. Her relationships with new men always seemed to start right there. It was tiresome. It got old in a hurry. She glanced over at Willow, who had finished her drink. Her glass, with a couple of ice cubes, sat on the table in front of her. Lily signaled to Randy, who nodded.

"You're welcome to join us for a drink," Lily said to Daniels.

"I'm with some other people," Daniels said.

"So you said," Willow said.

"Another drink, Pauldo?" Jefferson asked his wife.

"Yes," she said, "one more."

"It was good to see you, Alex," Jefferson said as Daniels turned to go.

"You too," Daniels said. Over his shoulder, as he walked away, he said, "and good to meet you, Lily."

When he was gone, Willow said, "A tedious man. With, I understand, somewhat dubious morals."

"Well, Willow," Paulette said, "don't hold back. Say what you mean." She laughed gaily.

"I tire of his ego very quickly," Willow said.

"Speaking of egos," Paulette said, nodding her head, and they all looked toward the front door. Brasfield Finch had come in. He wore a blue denim work shirt, jeans and a corduroy vest. He was talking to several young people, most of whom worked at Stache's and were at one time or another Finch's writing students. Lily had heard him refer to them as his "crippled chickens."

"Look at him," Willow said, "already three sheets to the wind."

Paulette laughed. "He is an incorrigible man," she said, "but amusing."

"Let's call him over and ask him the plans for Lenora Hart," the dean said, waving.

"You'll forgive me, Wallace," Willow said, "if I wonder why the dean of the college needs to ask someone else what the 'plans' are." She was halfway through her second drink. She thought that Stache's made them strong.

"He's chairman of the committee," Jefferson said, "I understand she is a personal friend of his."

"Brasfield has friends?" Willow asked. Her tongue was loose. Maybe she should slow down on the drinks.

"That's what I hear," Jefferson said, missing her joke. Had she actually said that? Maybe not. Willow looked at Lily; the girl looked confused. Perhaps she was shocked at these senior faculty members, and the *dean*, behaving like adolescent undergraduates. Lily was really an innocent child, after all.

Brasfield Finch approached their table. "Well! Look who the cat drug in," he said. "Evening Willow. Lily. Hanging out with the enemy?"

Jefferson laughed heartily. Lily thought it was forced. "Hardly the enemy, Brasfield," he said. He chuckled.

"Last time I looked," Brass said, "the administrators were on the other side."

"Mr. Finch, it's Friday night," Paulette said, "time for a little frivolity. Not campus politics."

"You're right, Paulette," Finch said, sitting down. He waved his arm. "Randy! Scotch! On the rocks!"

"Comin right up, Dr. Finch," Randy said.

"He called you *doctor* Finch?!" Wallace Jefferson exclaimed.

"They all do," Finch said. "The older I get, the more gray in my hair, the more they call me *Dr.* Finch. I don't bother to correct them anymore."

"I'll bet," Paulette said.

Finch leaned back. "And Paulette, the older I get, the more I realize that people who have doctorates simply stayed in school too long. That's all."

"Sour grapes," Paulette said.

"That's right, *Doctor* Jefferson," Finch said.

Randy set Finch's drink in front of him. "Anybody else ready?" he asked.

"I should say not," Willow said.

"Another round, for everybody," the dean said.

"We really should go," Willow said. She looked questioningly at Lily.

"Oh, come on, Willow, where's your sporting spirit?" Jefferson said.

Willow sighed. How had she let herself be roped into this? Because, she knew, she wanted to spend some time with Lily. That's why she had agreed to walk over to the sing-along with the girl in the first place. She was really quite fond of Lily. She had grown increasingly fonder of her as the academic year had worn on. She had been wrong about her. She had known many like her, both in graduate school and in the long line of instructors and adjuncts who passed through Lakewood over the years, most of whom labored under the delusion that they were on their way to Princeton, and Lakewood was just an inconvenient stop along the way. But Lily was different. There was substance there. Willow was not yet certain that Lily was a true scholar, but there was potential.

"Why, Wallace," Willow said, "didn't you know I was the original dirt road sport?"

The dean blinked. "I'm not familiar with the term," he said.

Finch laughed loudly. "By God, Willow, that's right!" he said. "If you're not a dirt road sport, I don't know who is."

"What is a 'dirt road sport'?" Paulette asked.

"Willow!" Finch bellowed. "Willow Behn, PhD, is a dirt road sport!"

"I think we're being had, Waldo," Paulette said.

"Never mind," the dean said, "tell us, Brasfield, what are the plans for Lenora Hart?"

"She's coming, they tell me," Finch said.

"I mean, what about receptions, parties, and so forth? An opportunity to meet her and talk to her."

"Trust me, Wallace, you don't want to meet her," Finch said.

"There will be many who will want to shake this beloved writer's hand," Jefferson said.

"Why does everybody always call her 'beloved'?" Finch said.

He snorted. "You don't know her."

"I feel like I know her after reading her beautiful book," Jefferson said.

"Well, you don't," Finch said. "Hey, look at what else the cat drug in."

Rufus Doublet walked up to their table. He had on his gray tweed coat and knit tie. He was looking at Lily. "Were you at the sing-along?" he blurted.

At first Lily didn't realize he was talking to her. "For a little while," she said, "Willow and I walked over from the office."

"You told me you weren't going," he said.

"I'm sorry?" She was baffled. She had no idea what he was talking about.

"I asked you this morning if you were going, and you said no."

She vaguely remembered the brief conversation. "I think I said I didn't know anything about it," she said.

"Yes, that's what you said, and then you went."

"Of course I went. I told you, Willow and I walked over for a little while."

"And you didn't let me know," he said.

"Well," she said, bewildered, "you weren't around. It was a spur of the moment thing." He stood looking around the table. After a few moments of silence, she said, "What's on your mind, Rufus?"

That seemed to make him furious. His cheeks turned red. Abruptly he sat down at the table. "Nothing," he said. "There is nothing on my mind."

"I must say," Finch said, "that's the usual state of affairs with your mind." He laughed jovially.

"Shut up, Finch," Rufus said.

"Oh, my," Finch said, "do I detect a spurned lover?"

Willow was looking curiously at Lily. Lily shrugged. She rolled her eyes.

"You don't know what you're talking about, Brasfield," Rufus said.

"You're right, I don't," Finch said. He looked at Lily. His eyebrows were gray and bushy. "Forgive me," he said, looking around the table, "I've had a few. But what, you all say, is new about that? Brasfield Finch has had a few! Stop the presses!" He grinned. "And I think I'll have a few more," he added.

"We really should be going," Paulette said.

"Don't let me keep you," Finch said.

"And *we* should as well," Willow said. She pushed her chair back and looked at Lily, and Lily nodded. As the evening had worn on the music had gotten louder. When Willow stood, a student bumped her from behind.

"'Scuse me," the student, a girl, said.

"That's quite all right, dear," Willow said, "there's barely room to move in this place." She glanced at Lily. "Shall we?" she asked. She took the girl's arm.

The Jeffersons had risen as well. Rufus Doublet stood up; he was staring at Lily. The five of them began to move toward the front door.

"Have fun, kids," Finch said. He seemed settled in at the table, as if he would be there for some time. He gave a little wave.

Outside on the sidewalk Paulette said, "Lily, why don't you and Rufus stop by and have a nightcap with us?"

"A *nightcap*?" Willow said. "It's barely nine o'clock."

Paulette looked uneasy. Of course, Willow thought, they didn't invite *me*. Not that she cared to spend any more time with them.

"Thanks," Lily said, "but Willow promised to help me with some Romantic poems I'm doing in my sophomore survey next week."

Willow could have hugged the girl. She *was* clever and bright, to think on her feet that way. And Willow was delighted that Lily obviously preferred her company to theirs. Rufus looked cowed and hang-dog. Willow had picked up right away in Stache's that Rufus had a "thing" about Lily, though she hadn't noticed any of that dynamic around the department. She thought Rufus much preferred his older women. She was surprised at this new development; she ordinarily paid little attention to such goings on. The assignations around campus, of which she was more than aware, were of little interest to her. But she was annoyed at Rufus's behavior.

"Well, isn't that sweet of her," Paulette said icily.

"Yes," Lily said, "it is." The two women began to walk away. "Good night," Lily said.

"Good night," Wallace Jefferson called out. "Great fun tonight!"

"Good night," Willow said.

The three of them watched Willow and Lily move down the sidewalk. When they were far enough away that they couldn't hear, Paulette asked, "What's going on there?"

"Don't even ask," Rufus said.

"Listen, you two," the dean said, "I need to go by my office and make some phone calls. Why don't you go on to the house and have a few. I'll catch up."

"All right, Waldo," Paulette said sweetly.

They watched him walk away in the direction of the campus. He moved briskly, as though he were in a hurry.

"He's going to diddle his secretary," Paulette said when he was out of ear shot. "He doesn't think I know. 'Phone calls.' I guess that's what they're calling it now."

"That skinny thing?" Rufus said. "She looks like a boy."

"Wallace probably makes her lie on her stomach so he can pretend she is one," Paulette said.

"Paulette, you are one bad woman," Rufus said. They laughed gaily as they began to walk toward the Jeffersons' house. They were holding hands.

"What dreadful people," Willow said to Lily as they walked away.

"Yes, pretty much," Lily said. "But he *is* the dean."

Willow snorted. "Enough said," she said.

Someone was approaching them down the sidewalk. When he was closer Lily saw that it was Father Curbs. He stopped walking and watched them as they approached.

"Good evening, Father Curbs," Lily said.

"Well, hello," he said, "beautiful night, isn't it?"

"Where are you going, Hamner?" Willow asked sternly. Lily was shocked at her tone. Why was she speaking to the priest in this manner? "I hope you're not headed to Stache's," Willow said, "and I can tell you've been drinking."

"I can go where I want to go, Dr. Behn," the priest said. "And yes, I've been drinking. The last time I consulted the rubrics that was not a sin. We are not Baptists."

"No, we are not," Willow said. "Would you like us to walk you home?"

"Absolutely not," Curbs said, "the night is young."

"Are you or are you not going to Stache's? Is the Clara Neal closed tonight?"

"It's a little far, and I don't have a car right now, if you remember. Now if you'll excuse me," he said, brushing by them.

"Stache's is full of students," Willow said.

"So much the better," he said. He staggered on the sidewalk. "Good night, ladies," he sang.

They watched him go unsteadily down the sidewalk.

"He's drunk," Willow said. "I'll probably have to get up at three in the morning to get him out of jail."

"Oh, my," Lily said, "really?"

"It wouldn't be the first time, dear," she said.

"But he's a priest," Lily said. "He had on his clerical collar."

"He likes to go down among the sinners," Willow said. "I'm surprised he doesn't ride around town on a donkey."

They continued to walk along. "What happened to his car?" Lily asked.

"It's a long story, and I don't want to bore you with it."

They had arrived in front of Bostony house. They paused on the sidewalk. A full moon had risen and the night was temperate and pleasant. When Spring came to the Panhandle, it came in glory.

"I had fun tonight," Lily said, "in spite of ... well ..."

"You mustn't worry about those people, Lily," Willow said.

"But ... well, he *is* the dean, and Rufus is my chair. When my evaluations come up ..."

"Posh!" Willow interrupted.

"I'm on a one-year appointment, Willow. I guess I need to stay on their good side."

"Don't worry about evaluations and that nonsense. Nobody pays any attention to them."

"Huh. I wish I could believe that," Lily said.

"Trust me, Lily. You have friends."

"I do?"

"Yes, dear," Willow said. She reached out and touched the girl's arm. Lily's skin was soft and yielding. "I *could* help you with those poems," she said, "Byron? Shelley?"

"Actually," Lily said, "I'm not even on the romantics yet."

"But you'll get there," Willow said.

Lily looked at the older woman in the silver dimness from the moon. Willow's gaze was fixed on her face. Lily thought of Dr. Carmichael then, and those nights of heaving passion. Nothing since had quite matched those experiences. She had thought they were only an interlude, a phase, and she had easily slipped back into men with their sweaty clumsiness and unfeeling haste. She recalled the ease with which Dr. Carmichael had made her body sing, the fluid and smooth pleasure of it. She returned Willow's heated scrutiny.

"All right," she said, "sure." The two women walked up the steps and across the porch and into the house.

TEN

Penny Fitzgerald was a freshman from Cedar Key, Florida. She was a natural red head, and her acne had flared up on her forehead, so she was relieved to have the ski mask on. It was after midnight and she was out streaking with her boyfriend, Luther Winegrass, from Tallahassee. He was not really her boyfriend, just someone who had asked her out, and she had been thrilled because he was a member of The Masters, one of the most popular men's social clubs on campus. (Lakewood had no fraternities, so the boys had to make do with "social clubs.") She had smoked three joints and had had six snorts of vodka, and she was "feeling no pain." In fact, her sneakers felt like concrete blocks hitting the sidewalk.

"Let's go jogging," Luther had suggested, out of the blue.

"It's raining," she'd said.

"It's stopped," he'd said; he was holding the vodka bottle, and he took a slug. "Besides, if it's a little wet it won't matter if we're naked."

"Oh you bad, bad boy," she'd said. They were in her dorm room. She felt a tingling of excitement at the prospect. She had streaked once before, but not with a boy. She had streaked with another girl, her friend Melissa, whose boobs were much bigger than hers. Why not? It would be fun to streak with a boy.

"You've got ski masks, don't you?" the boy'd asked.

"Of course," she'd said.

They were jogging along the sidewalk in front of Main Hall. In the lights on the porch they could see several couples sitting, watching them go by. The spring dampness was pleasant on her bare skin. She was enjoying herself. She felt a sense of daring and freedom. It was a way of kicking sand at her parents. They would both croak if they could see her now. In all her glory.

They had turned a corner and were jogging between two tall, trimmed privet hedges along the lawns between Main and Wills, another girls' dorm. When they came to a small gap in one of the hedges, Luther said, "Wait. Let's go in here."

"What for?" she asked.

"Rest a minute," he said.

"I'm not tired," she said. "I wish you'd brought the vodka."

She giggled. She let him lead her through the passage. She felt his hand on her butt. "Bad, bad boy," she said.

Then he grabbed her. It took her a moment to understand what was going on. "You move fast for a first date," she said, laughing. His hands were all over her. "Whoa, buddy," she squealed. He was forcing her toward the grass.

"Lay down," he panted.

"It's wet!" she said.

"Fuck it," he said. He pushed her down. She felt the cold grass against her naked back. Then he was on top of her, forcing himself inside her.

"Wait a minute," she said, "you got a rubber?"

"Fuck it," he said. He was moving rapidly, mechanically. As though he were anxious to get it over with.

"Slow down," she said.

"Fuck it," he said, breathing heavily through his nose.

Then he was snorting and grunting. "Ohhh, Ohhhh, Ohhhh," he moaned.

"Don't come inside me," she said.

He was still, not moving a muscle. Heavy on top of her. "Already did," he said.

"Motherfucker," she muttered.

It was then that she heard the laughter. Masculine laughter. A couple of whoops. Luther rolled off of her. She lay there stunned, her head swimming. The little alcove was dimly lit from the lights in the windows of the dorm, and she could see the boys gathered there. His friends. The Masters. They were all grinning; they were all naked. It was like some surreal dream. The pot and the vodka steamed inside her brain. All the boys were in various stages of erection. She had never seen so many dicks at one time before.

"Look," one of them said, "the hair on her pussy's red!"

Then they were on her.

Old Officer Earl Puckett, the campus policeman, found her early the next morning. Earl was a retired Church of Christ minister who had gone into security work late in life, and he was shocked to find the naked girl in the ski mask sleeping peacefully on the grass outside the women's dorm. He had thought he had grown immune to shock, what with his several years of being a college campus policeman, but he had never expected this one.

"M'am?" he said, shaking her shoulder, careful not to touch her anywhere else.

She stirred. He could tell she was drunk. She blinked in the sunlight.

"M'am?" he said, "what happened?"

"Wha ...?" she said. She pulled the mask over her head. She sat looking around, as naked as the day she was born. Officer Puckett had seen the streaking on campus, but this was the first time he'd been this close to one.

"Where are your clothes?" he asked.

"They raped me," she said.

"Who?" he asked. He took off his blue jacket and draped it over her.

"They raped me. The Masters."

"The who?"

"The *Masters*. The Masters."

"Who is that?" he asked. "The master of what?"

"Just take me back to my dorm room, please," Penny said.

"I'm gonna have to report this," Earl said.

"Of course. You do that."

"It was a gang bang," Billy "Big Hoss" Murphy, the dean of men, was saying, "a fraternity prank."

"There are no fraternities at Lakewood," John Steagall said.

"You know what I mean, John," Murphy said.

"She says it was rape," Brandon Briggs, the college attorney, said.

Murphy snorted.

They were all sitting around the heavy mahogany table in the board room. It was a hastily called meeting.

"Any young woman," Alberta Wingate, the dean of women, said, "who runs around the campus in the middle of the night without her clothes on is asking for it."

"Now, Alberta ..." Briggs began.

"Several students on the loafing porch saw her run by. Without a stitch," Alberta said.

"Yes, I know," Briggs said.

"I knew it would come to this," John Steagall said, "when all this started I knew it would come to a bad end."

There was a brief silence. Briggs sighed. "I talked to her father. Her parents are on the way to Lakewood," he said.

"How did he sound?" Steagall asked.

"What do you mean?"

"I mean, do they sound like ... like *reasonable* people?"

"He sounded like a man who's just been told his daughter has been raped," Briggs said.

"Not rape," Murphy said. "Quit using that word." They all looked at him. "I talked to some of the guys in the Masters. Some of them admitted ... being with her. They said it was ... what's the word?"

"Consensual," Briggs said.

"Yeah. They said it was her idea."

"You shouldn't have done that, Hoss," Briggs said.

"Done what?"

"Talked to any of the subjects in a criminal investigation." Hoss snorted again. "This is serious business, folks," Briggs said, "I don't know if you realize it."

"A college boy prank," Hoss said. "Boys will be boys."

"I don't think Penny Fitzgerald agrees with that assessment," Briggs said. "Or her father, either."

"Whose side are you on?" Steagall asked.

"Side?"

"You're *our* attorney, for god's sakes."

"Yes, John, I know," Briggs said patiently. "But we can't change the facts here. She claims it was rape."

"Just because she claims it doesn't mean that it was," Alberta Wingate said.

"But the fact that it's only a claim doesn't make it go away," Briggs said.

"But we can prove she's lying," Hoss said.

"How?"

"Ask the boys. They were there, they know what happened."

"Goddamit, Hoss, do you think they're gonna admit they raped her? They're probably stupid, but not *that* stupid."

"What do you know about her parents?" John Steagall asked.

"Her father is a first generation Irishman. His father immigrated to Florida in the twenties. He is a commercial fisherman, oysters and shrimp, has a boat in Cedar Key. Penny is the first in the family to go to college. She has two younger brothers. The mother is a housewife. What more is there to know?"

"Is he likely to show up with a shotgun?" John asked. Alberta and Hoss laughed.

"Now I don't know about that," Briggs said, "but if it were me, I might."

"Good heavens, Brandon," Alberta said.

"You people can make light of this all you want, but we have a real problem here."

"Nobody is making light of it, Brandon," Steagall said.

"This is not going to be as easily swept under the rug as you might have hoped," Briggs said.

"It'll blow over," Hoss Murphy said. He smiled complacently.

Patrick Fitzgerald was a large, heavy-set man with wavy red hair sprinkled with gray. His ample belly hung out over the waist of his wrinkled khaki pants. His wife had made him wear a navy blue blazer, which he was not used to and which made him feel awkward and uncomfortable. She was a slight wisp of a woman who had worn her "Sunday best" for the occasion: a gray dress that hung mid-calf. John Steagall immediately sensed that they were intimidated by being in a college president's office, and he intended to take full advantage of his position.

"Now, let's discuss this like reasonable people," Steagall said from behind his huge desk. He had had Mrs. Hoyle adjust his desk chair so that he was sitting higher and appeared taller than he was.

"What's there to discuss?" Fitzgerald asked.

"Well, before we get down to the ... nitty gritty, so to speak, I wanted to tell you that I am arranging for your daughter Penny to meet and visit with Lenora Hart when she visits the campus this spring." He smiled warmly. That should impress the hell out of them.

"Who?" Fitzgerald said.

"Lenora Hart, the writer." Both of them looked blank. "You know, she wrote *To Lynch a Wild Duck*."

"Oh yeah, I've heard of that book," Fitzgerald said. "Didn't they make a movie out of it?"

"Yes," Steagall said quickly. "Excellent movie wasn't it?"

"I didn't see it," Fitzgerald said.

"Oh, well, next time it's on television you should catch it," Steagall said, smiling at Mrs. Fitzgerald.

"I don't have time to watch movies," Fitzgerald said, "I work for a living. What's this Lenora Hart gonna talk to my daughter about?" he asked suspiciously.

"Well ..." Steagall began. He would have to go one better. "We are giving her an honorary degree," he said. This was met with more empty stares.

Finally, Patrick said, "Penny?"

"No, no, no," Steagall said, "*Lenora Hart!*" They had not the slightest notion of what he was talking about. Honorary degrees meant nothing to them. He should have known that. He was momentarily flustered. This was not going at all the way he had expected. He took a deep breath, gathering his thoughts. He had no idea where the concept of Hart's honorary degree had come from; it was the first time he'd thought of it. He had to admit, though, that it was a pretty good idea. He cautioned himself not to get side-tracked.

He had insisted on meeting first with the parents himself, trusting in his own persuasive abilities. Now he was wondering if he should call in Brandon Briggs, who was waiting in the board room. Brandon had seemed to Steagall unnecessarily concerned about the legalities of the situation, which Steagall had been confident he could smooth over with a few carefully chosen words.

"Would you ..." he said, "would you be more comfortable with a lawyer present?"

"I'm sorry?" Fitzgerald said.

"A lawyer," Mrs. Fitzgerald said, "he said a lawyer."

"I heard what he said," Fitzgerald said. "Why do we need a fuckin lawyer? I already got a lawyer. I ain't payin for another one."

"No, no, you misunderstand," Steagall said. "The college retains a lawyer. There may be legal considerations ..." He trailed off.

"You're goddam right. She was raped, and we want compensation."

"You want ... what?" Steagall sputtered. That was quick. This was moving too fast for him. He hit the buzzer on his desk and after a few seconds Eloise Hoyle stuck her head in the door. "Send Brandon Briggs in," he said.

"Yes, sir," she said.

They sat in silence for a few minutes. Steagall adjusted the French cuffs under the sleeves of his blue serge suit.

Mrs. Hoyle came back in. "Dr. Steagall," she said, "there is a reporter from the *Tallahassee Tribune* in the outer office."

"Not now, Mrs. Hoyle!" Steagall blurted. "Tell them to go away."

"Yes sir," she said, and darted out.

Through the open door, John could hear Briggs talking to the reporter. "I'll let you know when we have a statement," he said, and he came in and closed the door behind him.

"What is that about?" Steagall asked him. Briggs ignored Steagall and approached the girl's parents. He stuck out his hand. "Brandon Briggs," he said. They shook his hand without standing or uttering a word.

"I asked you a question," Steagall said.

Briggs sat down and crossed his legs. "We've had an incident on campus, John, that is unfortunately newsworthy. They want a story."

"A story?!"

"Yes."

"Well, don't tell them anything," Steagall said.

"We have to tell them *something*, John," Briggs said.

"Let me talk to em," Fitzgerald said, "I'll tell em a thing or two."

"You can't do that," Steagall said.

"You tellin me I can't say what I want to say?" Fitzgerald said. He looked angry now. His cheeks glowed red. His fists were clenched on the knees of his khaki pants.

"I'm sorry, I ..." John sputtered. "Please calm down, Mr. Fitzgerald."

"You tellin me to calm down, when my daughter has been raped, President Steagall? Fuck you," he said.

"There is no cause for vulgarity, Mr. Fitzgerald," Steagall said.

"Let's everybody just slow down here," Briggs said.

"Listen to the man," Mrs. Fitzgerald said. "He's a lawyer," she added.

"That's right, Mrs. Fitzgerald," Briggs said. "This is a situation that should be approached with caution."

"What *situation*?" Fitzgerald asked angrily. "Since I been in this office nobody has mentioned the word 'rape' but me. Bottom line, what are you assholes gonna do about it?"

Mrs. Hoyle stuck her head in the door again. "Dr. Steagall, I hate to interrupt," she said, "but the remote truck from WX-AL-TV in Tallahassee is outside."

"Why are you telling me that?" Steagall barked. "Tell them

to go away." He was becoming increasingly more agitated. He felt his control slipping rapidly from his grasp. "What do these people want?" he said, to no one in particular.

To Fitzgerald, the president looked like a little blonde midget sitting behind his enormous desk. He thought these college folks were trying to pull a fast one on him. But they were not as smart as they thought they were. They spent their time shuffling papers and living high off their fat salaries from his own tax money. But they were a bunch of weasels. Bunch of wimpy folks who didn't know how to wipe their own asses. They had no idea who they were dealing with.

"Where's the boy?" Fitzgerald asked.

"Who?" Steagall said.

"The boy that raped my Penny, that's who. I want to see this asshole. Tell him a thing or two."

"He will be dealt with," Briggs said.

"I want to 'deal' with him myself," Fitzgerald said. He rapped his hammy fist into his knee.

"There will be no violence," Steagall said.

"What the fuck?" Fitzgerald said. "There's already been violence. My innocent daughter has been *raped*!"

"All right," Briggs said, "all right." This was going to be a long meeting, Briggs thought.

Brasfield Finch watched Lily Putnam walking into the side entrance to Comer Hall, carrying her green book bag. She had on a tight white micro mini-skirt that barely covered her goodies. Finch timed his own walking so that he'd be behind her as she walked up the steps to the second floor, where their offices were. She was halfway up when he reached the stairs and he got a good look. He could clearly see her golden orbs wriggling beneath the skirt. The girl either wore no panties or had on a thong, either of which was a delightful proposition.

When he got to the second floor he saw that her door was still open. "Good morning, Lily," he said through the door.

"Oh," she said, "mornin, Brass. I didn't hear you come up."

She was perched on her chair, her book bag on her desk. Her legs looked especially long this morning. Her hair was slightly ruffled from the early breezes.

"I was sneaking," he said, "to try to get a look."

"Oh, you," she said and laughed.

"How are you?" he asked. She nodded and smiled. He came into her office and closed the door. The expression on her face was a mixture of alarm and curiosity. "Did you hear about the rape?" he said, his voice low, barely more than a whisper.

"*Rape*?!" she said. "What? Where?"

"On campus, last night," he said.

"Here? At Lakewood?"

"Yeah. Quiet little Lakewood. A student."

"Who?"

"A freshman. I believe her name is Fitzgerald," he said.

"*Fitzgerald*?" she exclaimed. She rustled in her book bag and came out with her grade book. She flipped it open, ran her finger down the list of students in one of her classes. "*Penelope* Fitzgerald?" she asked.

"That sounds about right," Finch said.

"She's in my class. Do you suppose it could be her?"

"Well, I wouldn't imagine there to be that many Fitzgeralds in the freshman class," he said.

"Penelope Fitzgerald," she said again, "mousy little red head with pimples. Never says anything. What happened?"

"The scuttlebutt is that it was a gang rape," he said.

"How do you know this? I mean, is it common knowledge?"

"Not yet," he said.

"Who told you about it?"

"I have my spies," he said.

"What do you mean, 'not yet?' " she asked.

"It hasn't hit the news yet, but it will."

"Oh, my," she said. "Is she ... I mean is she all right?"

"I understand that she's ok. Not physically harmed. She was examined by old Palmer, but her parents want her seen by a real doctor."

Dr. Palmer was the campus doctor. His office was in Wexler Hall, across campus. "Dr. Palmer's not a real doctor?" she asked.

"He used to be," Finch said, "but he's three days older than God and doesn't exactly have his senses about him. And he drinks. Which endears him to me, though he is a bourbon man."

"Well, I'm glad to hear that," Lily said.

"That he's a bourbon man?"

"No! That she's ok."

"Yes, that's the good thing," he said. He stood looking out

her window, at the sunlight playing on the new leaves of the live oak outside. He wore a green corduroy jacket that had seen better days, a Dickies work shirt and jeans. The jacket had brown suede elbow patches; the one on the left arm was ripped from the fabric and hung flapping. His beard was tied at the bottom with an old black shoelace. He shook his head. "I would have thought," he said, "that with as much sex as there is on this campus, rape would not be necessary."

"Rape has nothing to do with sex, Brass," she said, "rape is about power and control."

"I agree," he said, "men are pigs."

"This coming from a man?"

"A man who's lived long enough to know that men are pigs." She was looking at him queerly. "Oh, I know I'm a pig, too," he said, "all men are, present company not excluded."

"You have remarkable self-knowledge, Brass," she said. She laughed.

"I am just free from delusion, my dear," he said.

"Who was the boy? The rapist?"

"There were several. The only one I know is a boy named Luther Winegrass. The reason he's been identified is that she knew him, she was dating him. They all wore ski masks."

"Ski masks? They were streaking?"

"Apparently."

"My God, a gang streak," she said. "What's this campus coming to?" She giggled.

"I'll bet John Steagall's ass is tight on this one," Finch said. "Wait till it hits the news. There'll be a story on WXAL, on the five o'clock news. Steagall will shit his little junior size pants."

"I thought the streaking had died down," Lily said.

"It had. Until this. According to the skivvy, some students saw them streak by in front of Main Hall around midnight. They didn't know who they were, of course, or claimed they didn't. Then old Puckett found the Fitzgerald girl naked on the lawn the next morning, and she told him she'd been raped. Old Puckett went ape-shit. That's what I hear."

"There is no reason to get the police involved in this," Steagall was saying. His voice was getting hoarse.

"The police already are involved," Fitzgerald said. "It was the campus police who found her."

"Reverend Puckett is not the police," Steagall said, "he is campus security. We'd prefer to keep all this in house."

"In house? What the hell you mean by that?"

"Mr. Fitzgerald, the reputation of our institution is at stake. What with all the streaking last semester, that got out, got to be common knowledge around the state, and it hurt us. The applications for next year are already down. Parents are hesitant to send their children to a school with streaking. So we want to keep this as quiet as possible."

"This? You mean the rape of my daughter? Quiet?!" Mrs. Fitzgerald blurted. She had not said much up to now.

"Your daughter was streaking, Mrs. Fitzgerald," Steagall said.

"John," Briggs said, holding up his hand. "Please. Watch what you say."

"Well, she was," Steagall said.

"What's streaking?" she asked.

"Running around the campus buck naked," Steagall said.

"My daughter wouldn't do that," Fitzgerald said.

"She did. We have witnesses. The dean of women, Miss Wingate, has observed that any girl who does that is asking for what she got."

"John!" Briggs said.

"Are you lookin to get your ass sued?" Fitzgerald said. "I put in a call to Mike Shenarrah, the guy that advertises on the television, and he said he would take my case free and would only collect his fee when we won."

"He'll not win," Briggs said.

"Think not?" Fitzgerald said. "Game on, then." He stood up stiffly. He smoothed his wrinkled khakis. He grabbed his wife's arm and yanked. "Come on, Ethel," he said. They started to the door.

"I did not dismiss you," Steagall said haughtily.

"Fuck you," Fitzgerald said, going out the door.

"Well, you certainly made a mess of that one," Briggs said when they were gone.

"*I* did?! While you sat over there with your finger up your butt?!"

"We don't want them bringing suit, John, even if this Shenarrah is an ambulance chaser. The resulting publicity ... It would be better to settle."

"Why should *we* settle?" Steagall said. "The Winegrass boy is the one who raped her, not us."

"*In loco parentis,* John."

"Bull frocky," said Steagall.

"There is a law in this state that institutions of higher learning are legally responsible for the health and well-being of their students when they are on the campus."

"I don't need you to remind me about the laws of Florida, Brandon," Steagall said.

"What do you pay me for, then?" Briggs asked.

"We pay you to get us out of messes like this. Now, start doing your job. Get this over with, ASAP. Okay?"

"Okay," Briggs said.

ELEVEN

FIRST STREAKING, AND NOW RAPE!!!!!!, screamed the headline of the latest broadside. WHEN WILL WE DO SOMETHING ABOUT THE LACK OF LEADERSHIP ON THIS CAMPUS??????? It went on, but John Steagall could not bring himself to read any more. He could not imagine the person who hated him this much. What was his motivation? To stir up trouble, John thought, as though he didn't already have enough. He had a pretty good idea who was behind it, but he had no proof. It was that pool of negative ferment over in Harmon Hall, he was just about sure of it. He was tempted to fire every one of them, show them who was boss.

"Dr. Jefferson is here," Eloise Hoyle said, sticking her head through the door.

"Tell him to come in," Steagall said. When his dean was in the office and settled in a visitor's chair, Steagall said, pointing to the paper on his desk, "You've seen the latest Bolshevik propaganda, I suppose."

"Yes," Wallace Jefferson said, "they were all over Ferguson Hall this morning." He wore a blue pin stripe suit almost exactly like Steagall's.

"What shall we do about this, Wallace?" Steagall asked. "It's getting out of hand."

"Yes, it is," the dean said.

"Find out who's behind this, Wallace, and get on it immediately."

"Yes, sir," the dean said. He settled back in the chair with the air that he was in no hurry to do anything much. "But that's not why I asked you over this morning," Steagall said. "I have a proposition. I want to give Lenora Hart an honorary Doctor of Letters degree."

"Sounds like a good idea," Jefferson said. "But we'll have to sell the faculty on it."

"Why? What do they have to do with it?"

Jefferson sighed. "I remind you, John, that honorary degrees are granted by the *faculty* of the college. In the past they've been a little ... uh ... reticent about giving them. They cling to that privilege as though it were the only power they have left." He laughed jovially.

"Maybe it is," Steagall said, joining him in his laughter.

"At most other colleges and universities the board and the administration are free to hand honorary degrees out to whoever might benefit the college, wealthy donors or influential politicians and such. At Lakewood, it's the faculty. I've always thought the practice was relatively quaint."

"But surely they wouldn't object to granting one to a beloved writer like Lenora Hart. She's a Florida institution. And a Pulitzer winner."

"Of course you are right. But you can never predict what faculty might do. Our faculty can be a bit ... uh ... unstable."

"Hah! Tell me something I don't already know," Steagall said. He sat contemplating the leaflet on his desk. "You don't suppose Brasfield Finch has anything to do with this," he said, pointing again.

"I wouldn't be surprised," the dean said. "He's a general, all-around trouble maker."

"He has let it be known that he is not pleased with having Miss Hart to the campus. Some sort of personal vendetta, I suppose," Steagall said.

"Jealousy, probably," Jefferson said. "His books have sold a fraction of what Hart's has."

"If even that much," Steagall said and chuckled. "Tiresome stuff, his novels. I can't read them."

"I don't even try," the dean said. "Paulette read one of them, the historical one. She said it was amateurish but passable."

"Yes, well, anyway, we know he writes. And somebody has written this drivel. I'm beginning to think it has something to do with Lenora Hart's visit."

"Really? I don't think so, John."

"What is it about, then?"

The dean sat up in the chair. He straightened his pants and grunted; they were too tight in the crotch. "I think it's about the streaking," Jefferson said, "the general decline in discipline on the campus. They equate it with a decline in morality. Remember the rape, John."

"What makes them think I am responsible for that?" Steagall said. "I can't control these heathen students. What kind of leadership are these people looking for?"

"What people?"

"The people behind all this. And you know who they are as well as I do, Wallace. All you have to do is identify them and then prove it!"

"I have my ideas, yes," Jefferson said. "And what they say in these broadsides, John, is just smoke and mirrors. What they are after is your job."

"Why?! What have I done to them?"

"They just don't like you, don't like the way you've governed," the dean said. "They want to see you resign."

"How the hell do you know this?" Steagall asked indignantly.

"Because they say so, right there," Jefferson said; it was his turn to point to the paper on the desk. "Not in so many words, maybe. But the handwriting on the wall is clear. There is an element of unrest on this campus that wants you gone, John."

"What do we do about it?" Steagall said, his face turning pink. His blonde hair bristled. "I'm going to fire every damn one of them," he said. "You just find out who they are. Give me a list!"

"Unfortunately, we can't do that," the dean said, "though it is a consummation devoutly to be wished."

"What?"

"Never mind."

"If Brasfield Finch is behind this, I'll have his head," Steagall said.

"I'm afraid he has tenure. But, ummm, maybe I *can* find out if he has had a hand in any of this, John," Jefferson said.

"How?"

"I have an idea. Why don't I let you know what I find out?"

"All right," Steagall said.

After the dean was gone Steagall sat fuming behind his desk. He stared at the ferns under the windows that Eloise watered every morning. The day ahead of him was empty and forbidding. He had little to do but sit and worry about the insurrection on his campus. He didn't think his dean had offered sufficient support. Of course, he now thought, and why didn't I think of this before? Of course, the fat slob wants my job!

Alicia Martin, Dean Jefferson's secretary, called Lily's office and informed her that the dean would like to see her in his office at four o'clock that afternoon. It was getting close to spring evaluation time, and Lily wondered if her summons had anything to do with that. She had not discussed her next year's contract with anyone other than Willow, who had simply said, "Don't worry dear, these things have a way of taking care of themselves." Lily was not so sure of that.

When Lily arrived, she was asked by Alicia to wait in the outer office until the dean was finished with a phone call. Lily was suspicious of that, but she didn't let it bother her. She had learned, in both graduate school and in her almost completed first year on the faculty at Lakewood, that administrators often pretended to have pressing business that made them feel important. Their usual method of ending a conversation was, "Well, I must run. I have a meeting." They apparently didn't think you would respect them if they didn't have a meeting to go to or didn't keep you waiting. They were worse than doctors.

Alicia Martin was an extremely thin woman with frizzy dark hair. She had once been a social work major at Lakewood and had been Wallace Jefferson's student assistant when he was a professor in the history department. She had dropped out of school to marry a local mechanic, had been divorced, and had come back and gotten the job as the dean's secretary. When she and the dean began sleeping together, he had raised her salary and given her a new title: Executive Assistant to the Dean of the College, much to the displeasure of Eloise Hoyle, who remained only secretary to the president, even though she was sleeping with John W. Steagall, III. Mrs. Hoyle felt that, given the circumstances, she should be awarded a promotion, too. But the president was not forthcoming with one. She suspected that Alicia Martin did things with the dean that other women, especially his fruffy wife, wouldn't do.

Finally, Lily was ushered into the dean's office.

"Well, the lovely Lily," he said, smiling broadly. Lily noted that he waited until his secretary had gone out and closed the door before he moved to hug her. He pressed her boobs against his belly. She waited for him to pat her ass, but he didn't. She would let him if he tried; she was not sure how far she would go to get that renewed contract, but she knew that a little goose on the ass was not even close to a deal breaker. "Won't you sit down," he said rather formally.

He was in his shirt sleeves, and there were circles of sweat under his arms. His suit coat was hanging on the back of the door. He wore a wide, red and blue diagonally striped tie. She crossed her legs, tugging at her miniskirt, and she saw his eyes go to her legs. He sat down behind his desk.

"How have you been, lovely lady?" he asked, smiling warmly. "I haven't seen you since that night at Stache's. Fun evening that was, eh?"

"Yes, sir," she said.

"Please, not sir. It makes me feel old. Just Dr. Jefferson will do."

"Yes, Dr. Jefferson," she said, smiling as well. You *are* old, she thought. "I never know whether to call you 'Dean Jefferson,' or mister, or what. This is all still new to me, how to address a dean and a president, you know?"

"You can call me Wally," he said.

"Wally?"

"That's what my fraternity brothers called me when I was an undergraduate," he said and chortled. "You remind me of my undergraduate days."

There was a long silence. "Yes," she said, "well ..."

He shifted in his chair and seemed to tug at his pants leg. "I mean, I dated many a lovely lassie like you in those days," he said. I'll bet, she thought. "Ahh, yes, those were the days."

"I'll bet," she said, "fun days, huh?"

"Oh, yes. Oh, yes." He settled back and stared at her. "Tell me, Lily, what is it you want?"

"Sir?" she said.

"I mean, how do you want your life to go? If you could tell me what you'd be doing, say, five years from now, what would it be?"

"I'll be teaching, I guess," she said. "I haven't given it too much thought."

"I mean, if you could write your own ticket. I want you to describe for me the job you'd hope to have five, maybe ten, years from now. Assuming, of course, that you'd be here at Lakewood. That's the only way I could have a hand in making your wishes come true."

"Well," she said. She paused. Was he saying that she *would* be at Lakewood? "Well, I guess five years from now I'd like to be an assistant professor. And ten years on down the road I'd like to be an associate teaching modern American fiction."

He was looking at her peculiarly. "You have very simple desires, Lily," he said.

"Yes sir, I guess so," she said. "I mean, what more is there?"

"No marriage? Children?"

"I thought you meant just my appointment here at the college.

But yeah, if it happens, it happens. I don't much care."

He put his index finger beside his nose as if he were deep in thought. Then he said,

"We've missed you at church, Lily."

"Pardon?" she said. He was jumping around so much he was difficult to follow.

"Father Curbs was asking about you last Sunday," he said, "where, oh where, is the lovely Lily, he said."

I'm *sure* that's *exactly* what he said, she thought. "Oh," she said, "I've been pretty busy. With my dissertation," she added.

"Oh yes, about the colored lady writer," he said. He smiled. "You see, Lily, I'm very interested in what my faculty is doing. I keep up with their, uh, interests and such. I'm happy that you're making progress with your dissertation. I want you to get that degree."

"Yes ..." She almost said "sir." "I'm moving right along." The truth was that she had written not one word since September; she had so many papers to grade that she didn't have time for much else. But she wasn't about to tell him that.

He looked at his wristwatch. "It's after five in Miami," he said, "would you care for a little toddy for the body?" He snickered.

"Sir?" she said, genuinely puzzled.

He opened a drawer and pulled out a bottle of Pappy Van Winkle and two tumblers. "A cocktail? A drink? An aperitif? I usually have a little libation after a long day. Join me!"

"Well ... okay," she said.

He poured them each three fingers of whiskey. He settled back and took a drink. "I love me some sippin whiskey at the end of the day, don't you?"

"Oh, yes," she said. She didn't ordinarily take her liquor neat, but she had to admit that this was some smooth stuff. Where in the world was this interview going? She had no idea. The Pappy Van Winkle was already relaxing her. She took another heady swig.

He stood up and came around and stood leaning back with his butt propped on the desk, holding his drink. His belly pressed against his belt in front. He tilted his face and grinned down at her.

"You are so beautiful, my dear," he said.

"Well," she said, "thank you." The look on his face made her uneasy. She knew where this was going. All men were the same. She glanced at the closed door, wondering if Alicia Martin was still at her desk. "Wally," she said, "I don't think ..."

"Nonsense!" he said genially. He seemed buoyant and sportive. "Nonsense! Drink up!" He tossed down his whiskey and poured himself another. She wondered if he'd been nipping on the bottle all afternoon. Maybe Brasfield Finch was not the only daytime imbiber on campus.

"You *know* how I feel about you," he uttered suddenly.

"No, I ..." She steadied herself with another hefty sip. Was this it? Was this the moment of truth? Did her entire future at Lakewood hang in the balance? "What ... what are you saying, Dr. Jefferson?" she whispered.

"I love you, Lily!" he said. "I want to divorce my wife and marry you!"

"Are ... are you serious?" she stammered. She was stunned by his intensity. She needed to buy time. The man was insane. She had a sudden impulse to break and run, but she was frozen in the chair. He was red in the face; droplets of sweat laced his forehead. Maybe this was some elaborate prank and he was putting her on. But no, he looked deadly serious. For the first time fear crept into her mind. Was this man about to rape her? Was an epidemic of rape running rampant on the campus? Should she call out to Alicia Martin?

He guffawed. "Oh, Lily, Lily, you should see the look on your face," he said. He kept laughing. He began to march in place, raising his knees as high as he could get them. Then he ponderously marched back and forth in front of the desk. His belly and his jowls shook. "Look at me," he said, "I'm a Clydesdale! This is a new dance I've invented, 'the Clydesdale!'"

The man really *was* deranged. Lily laughed a forced laugh. Oh, well. "Go, Wally," she said weakly.

Then he stopped and grabbed her, pulling her up. Before she knew what was happening he was kissing her. He shoved his meaty tongue into her mouth. She smelled his sweat and his deodorant. She pushed at his fleshy shoulders. When she could get her mouth away from his she said, "Whoa, buddy."

"Oh, Lily, Lily," he panted. His bulbous belly pushed against her. She could feel his erection against her leg. He was really a big man and she felt overwhelmed and smothered. And he was about as sexy as a dead octopus. His breath smelled of whiskey and tic-tacs. She struggled against him. She decided in the moment that there were some things that even she would not do, even if it meant jeopardizing her job.

"Dr. Jefferson!" she said, "slow down. What are you doing?"

"What do you think I'm doing?" he said breathily.

"What would your wife think?"

"My wife? To hell with her." He held her tighter. "I want you," he said. "I ache for you. I hunger for you."

"Please," she said.

As suddenly as he had started, he stopped grabbing at her and sat back down behind his desk. He poured himself another drink. He nodded. "Lily," he said calmly, as though nothing that had transpired had occurred, "I called you over this afternoon to ask a favor of you."

"Anything," she said. "Well, *most* anything." She stirred nervously in the uncomfortable chair. She had no idea what was coming, and she feared the worst. She was anxious to get out of this man's office. She didn't know if she had blown her chances at a job next year or not. But if she could do him a favor, she would, short of blowing *him*. The very thought of his porcine penis in her mouth turned her stomach.

"Lily," he said, seeming to savor saying her name, "as you know, Lenora Hart is coming to the campus this spring."

"Yes," she said.

"And I'm sure you're also aware of these annoying leaflets that are being distributed around the campus."

"Yes," she said, "I've seen them."

"Needless to say, certain higher ups in the administration, myself included, including the board of trust, are very concerned about the origin of these dastardly and cowardly anonymous missals. Well, and this is just between the two of us, mind you, there is a theory that Brasfield Finch is behind these things."

"Mr. Finch?" she said.

"Yes. He has let it be known that he is not entirely enamored of Miss Hart's visit, and, well, you see what I am driving at. Since you and Mr. Finch are colleagues in the English department, I am hoping that I might enlist you to be my agent over there, to, well, sort of keep an eye out, so to speak. There are those who think that Brasfield Finch is out to sabotage her appearance here, for his own reasons, I'm sure, of which I am not aware. I am assigning you to his committee so you can keep an eye on him. Will you do that for me?"

"I'm already *on* the committee," she said, "Brass ... uh ... Mr. Finch asked me to serve on it. I'm happy to do as much service as

I can. Evaluations coming up, you know?" Why had she said that?

"Good," he said, "service is very important, especially to junior members of the faculty, those looking for tenure and promotion and uh ..." he paused, "and those looking for a contract renewal for the next year." He winked at her.

"Yes," she said. "Wally," she added.

"I thought he was going to rape me," she said to Brasfield Finch in his office back at Comer.

"Must be something in the water here at Lakewood," he said. He was leaning back in his swivel chair, his boots propped on an open drawer in his desk. The top of his desk was piled high with manuscripts.

"Lots of writing going on," she said, nodding to the stack.

"Ha," he said, "diarrhea of the mind. Why did you think he was going to rape you? Other than the fact that he was in the room with you."

"He came on to me pretty much. He's a hard one to figure." He did not reply. The bottom of his beard was tied today with a length of pink yarn. "Anyway, he wants me to keep an eye on you."

"Keep an eye on *me*?"

"He wanted to put me on the Lenora Hart committee. I told him I was already *on* the committee. He said the suits think you're going to try to sabotage her appearance. Oh, and they think you're the one sending out these silly broadsides."

"They think *I* would write such callow crap?" he said. "Oh, good grief, their idiocy is beyond belief."

"I'm beginning to agree with you," she said.

"What happens to men's brains when they become administrators? Over the years I've known some perfectly normal people who, when they rise to the administrative level, become monsters. Lily, my dear, don't *ever* become a dean."

"I won't. Are they all like that?"

"You ask *me*? Is there something wrong with your own powers of observation?"

She laughed. "Well, I haven't been around as long as you have."

"True. You are young and fresh. And innocent."

"Not so innocent," she said.

"Trust me, Lily, you are truly innocent! In all the ways that matter."

"If you say so."

"I *do* say so. So tell me, what did you tell Fatso Jefferson?"

"I let him think I'd be his spy. But I wouldn't tell him anything you didn't want me to tell him."

"Good," Finch said.

Willow ran into Bob Lallo in the Caf. Willow liked to eat lunch in the Caf on Thursdays when they served grilled chicken; they gave large portions and she could take half of her lunch home for supper. She did not really enjoy eating lunch there, since the place was full of noisy students and she often got stuck with other faculty members she ordinarily would not have joined for a meal. One such was Bob Lallo. Lallo taught in the biology department, and his wife Lillian taught in the business department; she was also chair of the faculty council.

"Well, hello, Willow," he said when she sat down. He was picking at his salad. His collar seemed much too large for his thin neck. His tie was a pale blue polyester. "Big doins for the English department, huh?"

"It seems, Bob, that we've had this conversation before," Willow said.

"Lillian tells me that you are on the committee for the big event," he said.

"Unfortunately, yes," she said.

"Are you excited?"

"Hardly." She chewed her chicken.

Fred C. Dobbs sat down with them. "Is it true that we're paying this writer fifty thousand dollars?" he asked. He had two huge chicken breasts on his plate, with an enormous pile of rice. His red suspenders strained against his belly. He held his plate out to them. "Look, it's Jayne Mansfield!"

Willow cringed. If she hadn't had a mouthful of chicken she would have snorted.

"Well, are we paying her that much?" he said.

"I have no idea," she said.

"But you're on the committee," Lallo said.

"I heard we're giving her an honorary degree," Dobbs said. "No way!"

"Whattaya mean, no way?" Lallo asked. "Lillian said ..." he

began.

"I don't give a shit what Lillian says," Dobbs said, "we ain't givin this woman any honorary degree."

"It's not up to you, Fred," Lallo said.

"The hell it ain't," Dobbs said.

Willow was wishing she'd sat with a bunch of chattering, giggling sophomore girls. This was onerous and tedious. She should have invited Lily to accompany her to lunch, but then she really *would* have had a crowd of slobbering men around the table.

"Please, gentlemen, it's lunchtime," Willow said.

"This faculty still has some integrity," Dobbs said, "we don't hand em out to any hack that comes along."

"*Hack?!*" Lallo exclaimed. "She's a Pulitzer winner. And a beloved American writer."

"All the same," Dobbs said.

"Are you saying that we shouldn't give a degree to *any* writer, Fred?"

"Maybe that's exactly what I'm sayin, Bob," he said.

"Well, I never ..."

"Eat your salad, Bob," Willow said, "and shut up." Lallo quaked and shook like a puppy. Willow thought surely he would demand that she stop speaking to him in that manner, but he didn't. He ate his salad obediently. Why were there always only men eating in the Caf? Willow would not have been happy eating with a bunch of women, either. One should always dine alone, she thought. Dr. Dobbs let out a belly laugh. "Na, na, nannie, nannie," he said to his colleague, "she got *you* told." Oh what fun the boys must have in the biology department, she thought.

They ate for awhile in silence. Then Dobbs said, "I heard they're settlin with that girl that got raped for two hundred thousand dollars. Is that right, Bob?"

"I don't know," Lallo said.

"You mean the faculty council ain't even been consulted on that?"

"I am not on the faculty council," Lallo said.

"But Lillian is chairman of it," Dobbs said.

"I am not privy to everything the council does," Lallo said huffily.

Dobbs chewed and swallowed a mouthful of grilled chicken. Willow expected him to belch. Instead, he said, "That was some expensive pussy, wasn't it?"

Willow put her fork down beside her plate. "Dr. Dobbs," she said, "please save your vulgarity for your buddies on the golf course."

"I'm sorry Willow," he said, "did I offend your delicate sensibilities?" He chortled.

"Yes, you most assuredly did," she said. "I don't like that word."

"What? Pussy?"

"You enjoy saying that word, don't you, Fred," she said.

"You don't enjoy hearin it, but you like munchin it," Dobbs said.

Willow stood up. There was a half-eaten chicken breast left on her plate. She took it and flung it in Dobbs's face.

"Hey!" he exclaimed, rearing back, his chair legs scraping on the tile floor. He wiped at his grease streaked face.

"You are a pathetic, fat fool, Dobbs," she said. Students at surrounding tables had stopped their incessant talking and were staring at them. "An ignorant scientist. May you rot in your own lab," she said.

She walked away. She had not saved the half of her chicken breast for her supper, but she felt it had served a better purpose.

Brasfield Finch was in his office, and Willow stopped in his doorway. The scent of whiskey was so strong she coughed.

"What can I do you for, Willow?" he said.

"Have you heard that they've settled with the Fitzgerald girl?"

"With the who?" he said.

"The girl who was raped," she said impatiently.

"Oh," he said, "no, I haven't heard anything like that. Have they?"

"I just heard a rumor in the Caf that they had settled a substantial sum of money on her."

"Well, good for her if they did," he said. "Who told you that?"

"The honorable Fred C. Dobbs," she said.

"Oh, then it's likely bullshit," he said.

She turned to go. "Will you let me know if you learn anything?" she asked.

"Of course. But I'm always the last to know anything around here."

"Oh?" she said. "You with your 'spies?'"

"What do you know about my spies?" he said.

"I know considerably more than you think I do, Mr. Finch," she said, and moved away from his door.

Lily was in her office with her door open. She was hunched over her desk. "Good afternoon, Lily," Willow said.

"Oh," Lily said, looking up. "Willow! Come in, give me a break from these papers."

"All right," Willow said, sitting down. "How are you, dear?"

"I'm fine," the girl said. She had on a tiny green miniskirt that barely covered her thighs. Her blouse revealed the beginning swellings of her breasts. Once, early on, Willow had said to the girl, in the role, she supposed, of her "mentor," "Lily, don't you think the way you dress will drive the young men in your class wild?" "That's the idea, isn't it?" Lily had said.

"I just walked over from the Caf," Willow said, "it's a beautiful day outside."

"You couldn't prove it by me," Lily said, and nodded toward the desk and its pile of composition papers.

"You work too hard, dear, you should get out, enjoy the spring."

"Ha, I wish," the girl said.

"Lily, are you happy here?" the older woman asked, and Lily felt a flicker of alarm; then she realized she was flashing back to her episode with Dean Jefferson. Willow's tone had reminded her too much of the dean's.

"Why, yes," Lily said, "why do you ask?"

"Because I want to see you happy."

"I'm happy, I guess. I haven't had too much time to think much about it."

"Do you know what happiness is, Lily?" the older woman asked.

Lily thought for a moment. She shook her head. Then she said, "No."

"I thought not," Willow said.

They sat in a heavy silence for a few moments. They could hear students laughing and talking on the brick sidewalks outside. Willow looked at the older woman, at her dowdy dress and sturdy shoes. Willow could be attractive if she let herself be. Maybe Lily should be *her* mentor instead of the other way around. But it wasn't that way; Willow was Lily's mentor.

"Well," Lily finally said, "aren't you going to tell me what happiness is?"

"I wish I could," Willow said, "but I don't know myself."

"You don't ... know?"

"No. I was hoping maybe you could tell me."

The sounds of the students faded as they made their way on down the walk. Then Willow laughed, and Lily laughed, too.

"Maybe happiness is having nothing left to lose," Willow said.

"You've been listening to 'Me and Bobby McGee,'" Lily said.

"To what?"

"Never mind." Lily sat looking at the older woman. That will be me twenty-five years from now, Lily thought. The idea was not entirely unpleasant. One could do worse than be Willow Behn.

TWELVE

A chubby girl named Beth Carlton was reading her story in Finch's workshop. She was animated, "acting" the story. It was an overlong story about a little girl and her cat named Snowball. At the end of the story, Snowball died. Miss Carlton was visibly moved by her own story. Finch let the concluding words settle. He paused, letting the silence lengthen. Then:

"Who's first?" he said.

The other overweight girl in the class raised her hand. Her name was Maude Pearson. "I thought it was beautiful," she said. "I got choked up. I actually had tears in my eyes."

"You did?" said Finch. "I find that remarkable."

"You didn't like it," said Beth Carlton. She looked angry.

"It's not so much a question of 'like,' Miss Carlton," Finch said. "The real question is, is it a good story? What are the elements that make a story good? And what are the elements that make a story bad?"

"Are you saying that my story is bad?"

"No. I'm not making a judgment on it at all. At this point." He looked at Maude Pearson. "Miss Pearson, why don't you tell us why you think the story—what is the title? 'I Love Snowball,' yes—is beautiful?"

"I just thought it was," Maude said, "you don't always have to have a reason."

"Oh, yes, you do," Finch said, "if we are ever going to understand how a story works, we must consider the 'reasons' we respond to it the way we do. This is a workshop, not an admiration society."

"Well," Louis Bradford said, "I liked the way she developed the character of the little girl. I mean, I *believed* her when she told us how much she loved her pussy cat."

"*Pussy* cat," Finch said, "interesting choice of words, Mr. Bradford." There were muffled chuckles around the table. Beth Carlton looked annoyed. "Let's talk about the techniques Miss Carlton uses to develop the character—what is her name? Mary?—in the story. What is the main conflict in the story?"

Silence. "Miss Gener?" he said.

"Well, she loves the cat and it dies," Miranda Gener said.

"That's just it," Finch said, "she *tells* us that she loves her pussy, but she doesn't really *show* us, does she? And how do you, as a writer, show that? You put your character in a situation where the character must *act*, you dramatize the situation, and the reader responds to the character's *actions*. What does Mary do to dramatize the way she loves her pussy?"

"Stop using that word," Beth Carlton said.

"What word is that?" Finch said.

"You know."

"Oh. Pussy. Used to name an animal, Miss Carlton, a pussy cat. Nothing more than that. Get your mind out of the gutter."

"*My* mind's not in the gutter!" Miss Carlton replied.

"Oh, yes, I remember when you introduced yourself to the workshop you said your father was a Baptist minister. So your mind is definitely not in the gutter. Forgive me."

"Cut her some slack," Gerald Grimes said.

"Oh, ho, the brave Mr. Grimes to the rescue again," Finch said.

"Why do you have to be so sarcastic?" Grimes said. "Everything you say is sarcastic!"

"Really?" Finch said. "My, my. But back to the story at hand. What sort of conflict does Mary go through to arrive at the epiphany that she loves her pussy?"

"I didn't go through any kind of conflict to know I love Snowball," Miss Carlton said.

"*You?* I thought her name was Mary."

"It's about me and my cat," she said.

"So it's autobiographical? It's not really about Mary at all but about Beth?"

"Yes."

"Why, then, didn't you write it as a personal essay rather than fiction? What's the point?"

"The point is, I wanted to make it a story."

"For this workshop?"

"Of course, for this class."

"So, what you are saying is, why the hell would I write a story if not for this class? To fulfill an assignment?" Finch said.

"I didn't say that," she said.

"Okay. You didn't say *exactly* that. Granted. By the way, I'm sorry for your loss."

"Pardon me?"

"Snowball."

"Oh, Snowball didn't die. I just let him die in the story."

Finch feigned shock. "You mean you killed your pussy off for effect?"

Beth Carlton narrowed her eyes at him. "Exactly," she said, "I wanted it to be sentimental."

"Well, you certainly succeeded," Finch said. "Your story is exceedingly sappy and sentimental. It drips with phony sentiment. There is nothing wrong with honest sentiment, Miss Carlton, but it must be *earned* sentiment."

"I don't know what you mean," she said.

"I'm sure you don't. That's only about the two thousandth time I've said it since this workshop began. Re-write your story, Miss Carlton, and give us some conflict and resolution. Don't just tell us, but show us. Then we, the readers, will love your pussy, too, so much we'll want to kiss it."

There was a burst of laughter around the table. One of the boys made smacking noises with his lips.

"Now Mr. Martin, control yourself," Finch said.

Two days later, on Friday afternoon, Brasfield Finch received a call from Alicia Martin, Dean Jefferson's assistant, summoning him to the dean's office for a conference with Beth Carlton and her parents.

Her father was a stern-faced, bald headed man in a shiny brown suit. Her mother was a head taller than her father, dressed in a wildly flowered, calf-length dress, and she wore a little straw pill box hat. When Finch entered the room, they blanched at his appearance. They looked back and forth from Dean Jefferson, in his pressed gray pinstriped suit, to Finch, in his boots and jeans. His shaggy, unkempt beard was tied with a bright green shoelace.

"Why, he dresses like a field hand," Mrs. Carlton said incredulously, as if her worst fears were exceeded.

"Come in, Mr. Finch," Jefferson said, assuming his most serious demeanor. "This is Mr. and Mrs. Foster Carlton—excuse me, *Reverend* and Mrs. Carlton—and you know, of course, their daughter, Beth."

Beth was sitting next to them, a scowl on her face. She was staring at Finch with a look that said, you're about to get it, buster!

"Yes, of course," Finch said, sitting down.

156

"This is Brasfield Finch, our writer in residence here at Lake-wood," the dean said.

"I won't say we're pleased to meet you, Mr. Finch," Mr. Carl-ton said. He was glowering.

"What can I do for you this afternoon?" Finch said calmly.

The dean cleared his throat. "We are here, Mr. Finch, on a matter of grave concern. The Carltons are upset over some extremely inappropriate comments you made to their daughter in your writing workshop."

"Oh?" Finch said. "What was that?"

"You told my daughter, in front of the whole class, that you wanted to kiss her private, most intimate parts," Mr. Carlton said.

"I did not," Finch said. "I said no such thing."

"Wait just a minute now," the dean said, "let me conduct this interview. Mr. Carlton, what you describe is an *alleged* comment. Mr. Finch says he did not ..."

"You calling my daughter a liar?" the man heatedly asked the dean.

"Oh, no, not me," the dean said, "Mr. Finch is calling your daughter a liar."

Finch looked at the dean. His bulbous self was perched behind his desk like a stuffed sack of potatoes. There was a self-righteous smirk on his face. Finch thought: *the bastard is going to throw me under the bus.* "Let's get one thing straight," Finch said. "I never said what she apparently told you I said. Now, she may say that it's my word against hers, but it's not. Call the whole goddam class in here. They'll tell you I never said that."

"There is no cause to use the Lord's name in vain, Mr. Finch," Mr. Carlton said.

"There is plenty of cause," Finch said.

"There is never any cause to ..." Mr. Carlton began.

"Moving along here," the dean interrupted. "Now, Beth, tell me, did Mr. Finch say that to you? That he wanted to kiss your ... private parts?"

"Not in so many words," Beth said. "But he used the word 'pussy.'"

Mrs. Chaplain gasped. "Beth!" she blurted.

"He used that word in class?" Dean Jefferson asked her. He fixed his gaze on Finch.

Finch sighed. He shrugged. "She wrote a short story about her pussy cat. I used it in that context."

"In referring to a feline animal?" the dean asked.

"Yes." *Maybe he wasn't going to toss him after all.*

"Well, that's a whole another matter," Jefferson said.

"Wait a minute, now!" the reverend said irately. "This man ..."

The dean held out his hand, palm toward them. "Just hold on. I am conducting this interview, and it will not degenerate to angry ..."

"The only degenerate here is that feller there," Reverend Carlton said, pointing to Finch.

"Please, Mr. Carlton, let's remain civil," the dean said.

"Civil?! How am I gonna remain civil when you people let perverts like him run loose in this college? What kind of place is this, anyhow?"

"If there has been an ... error in judgment, or a misunderstanding," the dean said, "you can be sure it'll be corrected, Mr. Carlton."

"An error in judgment? Ha!" said Mrs. Carlton. It was the first time she had spoken. Her eyes were flashing with fury. "That man is a Sodomite, to suggest something like that to my daughter. She is a Christian, God-fearing girl!"

"No doubt," Wallace said. "Mr. Finch? What do you have to say for yourself?"

"I already said it," Finch said. "I never said anything like that to Miss Carlton. We were discussing her story, which she, herself, maintained was based on her pussy cat Snowball ..."

Mrs. Carlton blurted, "Snowball?! You dare bring that innocent little kitty into this?"

"*I* didn't bring Snowball into anything, Mrs. Carlton, your daughter did. I've never seen Snowball in my life, and I must say, after reading Miss Carlton's story, I *still* have not seen her. Or it. Whatever. I was merely pointing out to her ..."

"But you used the word ... 'pussy,' " Mr. Carlton said, whispering the word.

"Yes, I did. Have you never used the word 'pussy,' Mr. Carlton?"

"Not to mean ... *that,* no."

"Mean what?" Finch asked.

"A woman's privates, Mr. Finch," Mrs. Carlton said.

"But," Finch said, "I never used it in that context. No. I have never in my life used it in that context." They were staring at him, their mouths agape, as though they had encountered something they never in their wildest dreams expected to confront. Finch knew they had no idea what to make of him. "So, if there's nothing else, I really must get back to my office."

The reverend was staring at him, his eyes narrow slits. "You're one of them secular humorists, ain't you?" he said.

Finch looked at the dean, who looked down at his desk. After a minute, Finch said, "I think you mean secular *humanist*, and yes, I am one, a proud card-carrying one."

"And you sit right there and admit it," Mr. Carlton said with a look of disgust. "I can't believe, Dr. Jefferson, that you let these Godless people run around on your campus just like they was good Americans like everybody else. And you put em out there to teach our youth. Shame on you, Dean."

"Yes, well ..." Dean Jefferson said. Finch studied the dean's face, and saw no trace of amusement there. It was all Finch could do to keep from laughing out loud. These were preposterous people. "Well, Mr. Finch," the dean said, "perhaps now would be a good time for you to apologize."

"To *what*?"

"To apologize to these good people."

"Apologize for what? I don't have anything to apologize for." The dean nodded to him, urging him. His face was pained. Finch knew he wanted to order him to apologize, but he couldn't. "You look constipated, Wallace," Finch said.

"What!? What did you say?" the dean exclaimed.

"Never mind," Finch said.

The three Carltons were watching them as if they were an exhibit in a side show. Wallace Jefferson's face was florid. His thick fingers gripped a pen on his desk. Finally Mr. Carlton said:

"Ain't you gonna apologize?"

"No," Finch said, "of course not."

"Just say you're sorry, you were wrong, and we'll go," Mr. Carlton said.

Finch stood up. "I'll save you the trouble, Mr. Carlton, I'll go myself," he said. He started for the door.

"Brasfield!" the dean said.

"Yes, Dr. Jefferson?" Finch asked.

The dean said nothing. He sat very still. His jaw was clenched, making his jowls swell.

"It's been fun, guys," Finch said, "but I really must go. I bid you good afternoon." And he was out the door.

On her way home from Lucky's Market, Lily stopped by Stache's for an afternoon drink. Her waiter was Randy; he no longer had the cast, but his arm and wrist were wrapped with gauze. "The usual, Miss Putnam?" he asked, and she nodded. He made Lily feel as if she belonged, that she had found a home. He brought her her vodka and tonic, with a garnish of lime. He smiled at her when he set it on the table. She sipped. She suspected that Randy gave her more than the usual pour, and she was grateful. He seemed to enjoy looking at her when she was in there. Another conquest, she supposed. She couldn't go anywhere without men constantly sneaking looks at her, and she might as well take advantage of it.

She was looking forward to a long, quiet evening. She was mercifully between sets of papers and she had her preparations for the next week all done. She relaxed, allowing the vodka to flow gently through her brain and body. This was more like she had imagined her new life as a college teacher to be, allowing her busy day of classes to pass calmly through the afternoon toward an evening of reading, reading for pleasure and not for her preparations. She was re-reading her favorite novel, Faulkner's *Absalom, Absalom.* It was hard for her not to keep thinking of Faulkner's influence on Morrison, but she had already made notes on that. That was scholarship. Now she was just *reading.*

She looked up and saw J. J. Underwood coming across the room toward her. J. J. was the director of the college theater, a tall, gaunt man with a shock of blonde hair that fell across his forehead. His face was angular; he had what Lily would have called a theatrical nose, remembering old pictures of John Barrymore. His wife, Tulah, also taught in the theater department. She was an actress. She had once told Lily, "Actually, my name is Tallulah, but since I'm an actress, I thought that was a bit much. So it's Tulah." She was red headed and a little on the heavy side. The students called them J. J. and Tulah Underwear. They were in their mid-forties.

J. J. was ostentatiously mannered. Lily thought him prissy, without being effeminate.

"May I join you for a brief moment, Miss Putnam?" he said, stopping at her table.

"Please," she said, "and it's Lily."

"The loveliest flower of the valley," he said. He sat down and crossed his long legs.

"Would you like a drink or something?" Lily asked. "I could order it for you."

"No thank you, darling," he said, "I have rehearsals this evening. Grueling. Oh, dear, I shouldn't have said that."

"Why?"

"Because I'm about to ask you something."

"What?"

"I should have prepared you. I hate to just spring it on you. Oh, drat, you'll say no!"

"What?"

"Well ..." He leaned forward, looking into her eyes. "Please don't say no."

"Tell me what you're going to ask me," Lily said, "and I guess I'll say either yes or no." She smiled. She fluttered her eyes.

"I am casting *Cat On a Hot Tin Roof* for the mainstage spring production, and I'd like you to read for Maggie. Please say yes."

"Oh, goodness. I've never acted before," she said. "I ... I don't think I could remember my lines."

"Nonsense," he said.

Randy was suddenly standing by the table. He looked at J. J. "Can I get you anything?" he said.

"A glass of your house white, Randy," J. J. said. "I can never resist drinking with a beautiful woman."

"You good?" Randy asked Lily.

"Bring me another one," she said.

When he was gone, J. J. said, "Randy was in *Twelfth Night* last spring. He's quite the actor, that boy."

"Randy?" Lily said. She was surprised. Shakespeare?

"Oh, yes. Well, it was a small part, hardly more than a walk on. I don't suppose you could say Randy did a whole lot of acting, really. But he had a presence. It's a comedy."

"I know," Lily said, "I taught the play at Emory." She had not been to any plays on campus. Even when she was an undergraduate, she had had little patience with student theatricals. They always seemed to her pompous, taking themselves far too seriously.

"You were on the faculty at Emory?" he asked.

"Teaching assistant," Lily said. She smiled. "English survey."

"Oh," he said, "yes."

Randy brought his wine. "Thank you so much, my good

man," he said. When Randy had gone back behind the bar, he said, "You simply *must* read for Maggie! You'd be perfect."

"Well ..." she said. She was flattered and tempted. "I don't know if I have the time. You know, papers to grade, and my dissertation and all. I really shouldn't."

"Never say 'shouldn't,' sweet lady," he said.

"You know," she said, "it's a *student* production. I'd be older than everybody else in the play."

"Not *that* much older, Lily. You look like a student."

"Still ..." She paused. "I don't know."

She had visions of one of her sophomore boys in a fake, gray beard playing Big Daddy. She shuddered.

"Come on. At least consider it." He watched her take a sip of her drink. Her face was perfection. And that body! In a slip! He would make sure it was a skimpy one. "*Read* for me, Lily. What's the harm?"

"The harm is you might give me the role and I'd be committed to weeks of rehearsal, that's the harm. I'm just not prepared to do that at this point, J. J." She didn't think she wanted to spend that much time with students, especially drama majors; those in her classes seemed tiresome. They were overly dramatic, always "on stage." She and Willow had observed groups of them in Stache's, and they were loud and self-centered, as though they were the only ones in the room. "Lord deliver me from amateur actors," Willow had said on one such evening. "I long ago ceased going to plays on campus. I always found them tedious and annoying." Willow's opinions mattered to Lily. "I don't think I can do it," Lily said.

"I tell you what. I can take Maggie's audition monologue home and you can come over and have a drink with us, and read. In the privacy of our apartment. What do you say?"

"Gosh, J. J., you're being really persuasive. But I don't know."

"We've got vodka. Come on! Five o'clock?"

"Well ..." she said. She wasn't going to do the part, but it might be fun to read for it. She didn't suppose there would be anything wrong with that. She was adamant that she did not want to be in a play, and she planned to be firm about it. "All right," she said, "I'll be there."

The Underwoods lived in a big old green shingled house that had been split into two apartments. It was just adjacent to the campus. There were air conditioning units in most of the windows, and the Underwoods' apartment had a small screen porch. There were lamps already lit in the living room and Lily could see them glowing through the drapes as she went up the walk. She had decided she would have a drink—or two—and read the monologue and then politely decline the invitation to be in the play. She realized she might be getting ahead of herself; her reading might be lousy and they wouldn't want her, which would be just as well. She'd never done anything like this before and didn't know what to expect.

Tulah Underwood came to the door in an emerald green dress with a cape. She appeared to be in some sort of costume.

"Come in, Lily, darling," she said. She was smoking a cigarette, not, Lily was relieved to see, with a cigarette holder. She led Lily into the living room. "Please sit," she said. "J. J. says you like vodka and tonic."

"If you're having one," Lily said.

"Not a vodka tonic, I'm afraid. We always have gin martinis, straight up, very dry. Would you like one of those?"

"Vodka and tonic will be fine," Lily said. She did like martinis, but she figured she'd better stick with her drink. She didn't want to get carried away and commit to something she'd regret.

When she came back in with their drinks, she sat down across from Lily. She sipped her martini, holding her cigarette between her second and third finger in an affected way. She blew a cloud of smoke toward the ceiling.

"J. J. tells me you're interested in reading for Maggie," she said. "He wanted me to do the part, of course, but I'm just a little too old for it. The boy playing Brick is a sophomore, eighteen years old. I would feel like his fucking mother!"

"Oh, I'll bet you'd be good," Lily said. Or his fucking *grand*-mother.

"I may yet play Big Mama, but to tell you the truth I'm not to the point of accepting character roles. I'm up for the lead in *Bus Stop* at Theater Guild of Tallahassee. Besides, the boy playing Big Daddy is a senior but he looks about twelve years old."

"I was afraid of that," Lily said.

"Oh, you'll be fine. You look like a child yourself."

Lily didn't quite know how to take that. She was certain the woman was being catty, but if she was she was a good actress. Just then J. J. Underwood came bustling in. Lily was astonished that he had on a paisley smoking jacket with velvet lapels and an ascot tie. Were these people expecting other guests? Or what?

"Ahh, yes, very dry," he said, sipping the martini that Tulah had made for him. He sat down on the sofa next to his wife. "You, Lily," he said, "are a vision of loveliness. You are my Maggie!"

"I haven't even read for it yet," Lily said.

"In good time," he said.

"I think she might be a little young for the part, J. J.," Tulah said. "How old *are* you, darling?"

"I'm twenty-six," Lily said. "Actually, I was thinking I might be a little *old* for the part. I wouldn't want to be playing with a sophomore Brick. I teach sophomores every day."

"Don't we all?!" Tulah exclaimed.

"I mean ... well, this is awkward," Lily said.

"Let me freshen your drink," J. J. said. He disappeared into the kitchen.

"Relax, dear," Tulah said, "I can see you are nervous."

"It's just that I'm not used to situations like this. I've never auditioned before."

"Would you prefer the casting couch?" Tulah asked.

"Pardon?" Lily was not sure she had heard her correctly.

"Oh, ha, ha, ha, ha," she said, "you must forgive me, I'm afraid this martini has gone straight to my head. Ha, ha, ha, ha."

"I thought you said ..."

"Your ears deceive you, darling," Tulah said. "Whatever you thought I said, I didn't say it."

This was getting weirder and weirder. Lily took a good, strong slug of her drink, which finished it off.

"Ice for the lamps of China!" J. J. said, re-entering the room with her fresh drink. "What's that from? What's that from? Quickly, quickly." He snapped his fingers at them. "Come on, you know," he said.

"*The Cherry Orchard*," Tulah guessed.

"Don't be stupid," he said, "Lily?"

"I don't have any idea," Lily said.

"*Who's Afraid of Virginia Woolf?!* You knew that, Tulah."

"No, I didn't know that," Tulah said, pouting.

Lily sipped her drink. It was mostly vodka. She set it on the coffee table in front of her.

"Well, let's see," said J. J., "has everyone relaxed themselves well enough? Shall we proceed?" He opened a brief case sitting on the floor and took out a single sheet of paper. "This is an audition text, Lily. Now, I must tell you before we begin that you have a very nice and delightful Southern accent."

"I was born and raised in the deep South," Lily said.

"But you will have to make it more Southern in your reading," J. J. said.

"More Southern?"

"Yes. You'll have to lay on a thicker accent."

"But you just said I already have an accent."

"But it's not enough. Thicker, Lily, thicker. It's a stage convention. We know that Southerners on the stage don't talk like Southerners, they talk like the people putting on the plays *think* Southerners talk. Audiences expect that. So lay it on thick! Moonlight and molasses, honey!"

"I don't know," Lily said.

"Trust me," he said. "We'll work on it. Don't worry about it right now. Just give it a try."

"Okay," Lily said.

"Why don't you stand?" he said, handing her the page. "Read over this. Remember, a master wrote those words. A true master." Lily read through the page. "Ready?" he said.

"I guess," she said.

"Now, I'll set it up for you, and Tulah will read Brick's line, which'll be the cue for your monologue. All right?"

Tulah crowded up next to Lily so they could look on the page together. She smelled of cigarette smoke and gin, and a cloying rose perfume.

"Okay, I'll read Maggie's line to Brick, then Tulah will give you your cue. Ready?" He read in a syrupy drawl: " 'Brick, y'know I've been so God damn disgustingly poor all my life—that's the truth, Brick.' "

Tulah read in the same saccharine way: " 'I'm not sayin it ain't.' "

Lily began to read. " 'Always had to suck up to people I couldn't stand because they had money and I was poor as Job's turkey.' "

"Thicker, Lily, thicker," J. J. said. Tulah was breathing through her nose next to her face. Lily tried to put it on a little bit, but she did not feel it.

" 'That's how it feels to be as poor as Job's turkey and have to suck up to relatives that you hated because they had money and all you had was a bunch of hand-me-down clothes and a few old moldy three per cent government bonds.'" Lily continued reading and finally lowered the page.

"Oh, Maggie," Tulah said, and kissed Lily square on the lips. Her tongue darted around. Lily struggled back away from her.

"What are you doing!" Lily blurted.

"That was excellent!" J. J. said.

"I just got so carried away as Brick," Tulah replied to Lily. "Your reading was so convincing. I couldn't help myself."

Lily remembered then a story Willow had told her, about a visiting gay playwright and the party at the Underwoods that turned into an orgy. Lily was not averse to the prospect of orgies, but she was very particular as to *who* the people she might orgy with might be. And the Underwoods were not her idea of desirable orgy partners.

"I really think I'd better be going," Lily said.

"But wait, don't you want to hear my notes?" J. J. said.

"Notes?" Lily asked.

"On your reading. It was superb, Lily, you are a natural. You'll need to work on your accent, of course. Tulah and I are good voice coaches. Oh, Lily, you are my Maggie!"

He swept her into his arms. She quickly turned her cheek and he kissed her there. He gripped her around the hips. She felt three hands on her butt and knew that Tulah had joined the embrace. She wriggled away, both of them clinging to her. "Stop it. Stop it right now," she said.

"But you are our Maggie," J. J. said.

"I'm not your anything," Lily said.

THIRTEEN

"Fifty thousand dollars!" Fred C. Dobbs was saying. The men were again sitting around in R. D. Wettermark's Auburn decorated den. They were Russo, Daniels, Wettermark and Katz. This evening they had been joined by Dobbs.

"I don't think it's *that* much, Fred," Garcia Russo said.

"Well, however much it is, is too much," Katz said.

"And the rumor that they've settled with the rape girl for a hundred thou is just that, a rumor," Russo said.

"I heard *two* hundred thou," Dobbs said.

"Well," Russo said, "we need to keep our eye on the prize and not get sidetracked by all these rumors. We've got plenty to get him on. He's a dead man. However they manage to resolve and spin this rape thing is not going to go well with him. Steagall will take the fall!"

"Here, here," Katz said, raising his glass. "Hit me again, R. D."

"In my newest editorial, which will hit the campus tomorrow, I'm drawing a direct line of cause and effect between the streaking epidemic—that Steagall was too weak to control—and the rape of an innocent girl," Russo went on. "I will make it clear that the reign of terror on this campus must be laid directly at Steagall's feet!"

" 'Reign of terror!' That's a good one," Daniels said. "Do you really say that?"

"You're goddam right," Russo said. "I'm not gonna start pulling punches now."

"No, you don't want to do that," Wettermark said, handing Katz his fresh drink. "Anybody else?" They all raised their empty glasses. Wettermark sighed and shook his head; he began to gather their glasses and take them to his bar against the wall, a chest high shelf with a "War Eagle" sign hanging over it. These men were fast depleting R. D.'s supply of Early Times. Next time they'd meet at someone else's house!

"Now," Russo said, "Eloise Hoyle has slipped me a tip. Steagall is calling a general faculty meeting for next week."

"Really?" Daniels said, "so the son-of-a-bitch can stand up there and suck on his breath mints and bullshit us for an hour?"

"According to Eloise, the agenda is to give this Lenora Hart an honorary degree. The faculty has to vote on it," Russo said, "if it were left up to the little saxophone playing dwarf, he would just award her one and be done with it. But he can't do that." They all chuckled.

"It'll be a cold day in hell before I vote to give that bitch a degree," Dobbs said.

"Me, either," Katz said.

"I tried to pump that wimp Bob Lallo for some information from the faculty council," Dobbs said, "but he's so pussy whipped he wouldn't tell me anything."

"Is that what's wrong with him?" Katz said.

"Does Lillian even *have* a pussy?" Wettermark asked and they all convulsed with laughter.

"Let's stay on task, here," Russo said, giggling.

"Awww, Gar, a little levity never hurt anybody," Dobbs said. Russo leaned back in Wettermark's leather recliner. He was wondering if it had been a mistake to invite Dobbs. He knew Dobbs shared his contempt for anything administrative. So when he'd run into him in the hall in Harmon, he'd invited him to tonight's meeting. "We call ourselves 'the Harmon Hellions,'" he'd said. Now he was having second thoughts. Fred C. Dobbs had a way of taking over any discussion he was a part of. Russo had been told that he did it in departmental meetings, and Russo had observed him in action in Arts and Sciences and general faculty meetings. Russo was in charge of this effort, and he was not about to allow any competition for the position of leadership. After all, he was responsible for starting the broadsides. (There had been some co-py-cat material distributed that was not of his authorship, but he didn't mind that. He considered it collateral wreckage.)

"Maybe we should reconsider being so opposed to this woman's honorary degree," Wettermark said.

"What?!" Russo said.

R. D. shifted on the hard seat. He was a little resentful that he had to sit on a dining room chair brought in rather than in one of the plush chairs of his man-cave, which had all been claimed by the other men. "After all," he said, "everybody loves that book of hers. Maybe we should be careful here."

"What do *you* think of it, R. D.?" Russo said.

"Me?" R. D. looked around. "Well, I haven't read it. I don't read fiction. That's just made up shit."

"There you go, then," Katz said. "That settles it."

"Wait a minute, now," Wettermark said, "if we're going in to try to get them to vote no-confidence on the guy, and also to vote against this popular woman writer all at the same time, that might be a bit much. We need to choose our battles."

"R. D. might be right," Daniels said. "It's gonna be hard enough to get this faculty to agree on *anything.*"

"But we're against anything that little nerd is for," Russo said. "We have to stand firm. With my editorials, I have them primed and ready. Everybody hates that bastard's guts by now."

"I wouldn't be too sure," Dobbs said.

"What's your problem, Fred?" Russo said. He was getting increasingly more annoyed with the man.

"Problem? I don't have a problem, except I'm not as sure as you are that everybody is going to jump on this no-confidence bandwagon. What if the vote goes the other way?"

"It won't," Russo said. He thought for a moment. "Okay, maybe you're right, R. D. How's this? We just raise objections to Hart's degree, just to let Steagall know he's got opposition, and let the rest of the faculty know as well. Then we let it go. He wins on that one. And then we wham him on the no-confidence vote."

"How do you know we'll vote in that order?" Katz asked.

"Because, dummy, *I'll* be the one making the motion for no-confidence. I'll time it right. I plan to be fully in charge of that meeting."

"All right!" Katz said, "that sounds like a plan. Let's have another drink!"

Willow asked Lily if she would like to go with her to the AAUW book club meeting that night. "Brasfield Finch is the special guest. They're discussing his novel, *The Fox and The Pheasant,*" she said.

"I thought his books were out of print," Lily said.

"Oh, there're plenty of copies around," Willow said. "Doodles usually has some. They have a section on Lakewood authors."

"Wow," Lily said, "how many 'Lakewood authors' are there?"

"Well, there's Brasfield Finch, of course, and Lucy Willard's History of Florida text book. That woman has made a fortune on that book. Hamilton Douglas, over in physics, has a tome on 'black holes,' whatever they are, something to do with the space continuum, you probably know about that. His book is about 900 pages long and costs $90, so nobody ever buys it. Much less reads it. And the president has a book he wrote, *The History of The Wilton Bible Baptist Church,* on the shelf."

"President Steagall is a Baptist?"

"Oh, no. He just wrote the book for them."

"Oh," Lily said.

"Anything for a publication, huh?" Willow said. She chuckled. "Anyway, I thought you might enjoy it, though the women are all considerably older than you are."

"I don't know," Lily said. Since she had been fifteen years old and had fully filled out, she had been wary of older women, most of whom treated her with suspicion, if not downright disdain. That's one reason she was so grateful for Willow's friendship. It was especially difficult in a professional setting to be young and pretty, where older women seemed to resent the very sight of her. It was not at all unusual for her to enter a room and all the other women in there to fall silent and pretend to ignore her. She was used to that. She wasn't sure she was ready to run that gauntlet at an AAUW meeting.

"Oh, come on," Willow said, "you will have met most of the women there. Paulette Jefferson will be there ... you know her from church."

"Yes," Lily said. That's what she was afraid of. Paulette had been decidedly cool to her the last couple of times she'd seen her at church, after that night at Stache's. Lily had not been invited back to the Jeffersons for drinks or B for Bottecelli, for which she was thankful, but worried. Rufus Doublet was also noticeably distant and unfriendly to her, and she was concerned that she'd made powerful enemies at the worst possible time. She was just a klutz, who was not going to get along wherever she was. She sighed. They were sitting in Willow's office; her window was open and what were probably the last cool breezes of the spring were wafting through.

"Actually," Willow said, "I think discussing Mr. Finch's book is just an excuse to get him there. I suspect they just want to pump him about Lenora Hart. They've already discussed his book with him, both of them, years ago. Nobody liked his first one; it was too dirty. Filthy."

"Surely, Brass ... uh ... Mr. Finch knows they're just curious about Hart."

"Of course. He doesn't care. He just wants to be lionized. He

170

loves it. He enjoys knowing famous people. I suppose it makes him think he's famous himself." She punctuated that with an abrupt laugh.

"Well ..." Lily said.

"It's in the Comer Commons," Willow said, "we can walk up there together."

"All right," Lily said.

The women were sitting around on sofas and easy chairs in the Commons. Most of them were holding cups and saucers and munching on brownies. Brasfield Finch was nowhere in sight. When Willow ushered Lily in she said, "You all know Lily Putnam. She's visiting with us tonight."

There were several mumbled hellos and nods. For the most part the women didn't look her in the eye.

A squatty, dumpy woman in a loud purple caftan, vaguely familiar, scuttled across the room to Lily. "Hello, dear," she said, holding out her hand, "I'm Nelle Steagall, the president's wife." She giggled self-consciously. "I'm the one responsible for all the day lilies," she said.

"Oh, yes, beautiful," Lily said. Lily had heard about the woman's obsession with day lilies. The president's wife had planted them in profusion all around Flowerhill and all over town, seemingly in every vacant patch of dirt. "I think Lakewood should be designated the day lily capital of the world," Lily said, smiling.

"Oh, it already has been, dear," Nelle Steagall said, "not the *world*, maybe, but Florida, by *Southern Living* magazine!"

"Really?" Lily said, "how nice." The woman drifted away, her caftan swaying.

Willow was greeting some of the other members. There was an empty cushion on a sofa, so Lily sat down between two other women. The one on the right smiled. "Welcome," she said, "I'm Libby Russo."

"Nice to meet you," Lily said, "Lily Putnam."

"And that," Libby Russo said, pointing across Lily, "is Lillian Lallo."

"Oh, yes. Pleased," Lily said. "You're chair of the faculty council."

"So they tell me," Lillian Lallo said. She was a harsh looking little woman with thin lips and faded red hair. She sniffed, staring across the room. Her legs were very thin and bony. We will never be friends, Lily thought, we will never even be civil to each other. Lillian Lallo would not even look at Lily. All right. Lily would not say another word to her.

She turned to the woman on her right. "So," she said, "how do you like *The Fox and The Pheasant*, Mrs. Russo?"

"The what?" the woman said.

"Mr. Finch's novel," Lily said.

"Oh, that," she said. She leaned toward Lily and whispered. "To tell you the truth, I haven't read it. I tried to read the first one and was horrified. Terrible. Not scriptural at all."

"Not what?" Lily asked, genuinely puzzled.

"It's ungodly. Immoral. It should be banned."

"Really?" Lily asked.

"Really," the woman said.

Lily looked around the room. She was hoping she wouldn't encounter Tulla Underwood there; the woman was not present. But still, this was going to be a long evening. She wished Brasfield Finch would show up and liven things up a bit. She spotted Paulette Jefferson across from her. Willow had told her that Paulette was president of the local chapter. Naturally. Even just standing as she was, talking with another woman, Paulette looked proprietary, as she always did. Lily recognized the woman Paulette was talking to as Joanne Katz, whose husband taught in the math department. She knew who Joanne Katz was because she made and sold earrings at the local arts festival down in the park. Lily had bought a pair from her. Little dangling polished stones. She saw Eleanor Bufkin and Katherine Klinger talking together in the corner. Lily's eyes ranged around the room. Most of the women were familiar to her but it was difficult to come up with their names. She saw Joan Hudson, the artist, who was a friend of Willow's, and Sylvia Wettermark, a woman she'd chatted with while shopping in Lucky's. All the women seemed engaged in serious conversations. She felt like a total outsider. It was not the first time Lily had felt lonely and isolated in a crowd, especially since she'd been at Lakewood. She sat quietly observing the scene. Why was it so hard for her to join in their gabbing discourse? She was bored by it all. And the women made her nervous. She remembered the old clichéd remedy for nervousness when talking to a crowd: to imagine your audience naked. She amused herself by examining the women to determine which ones of them—if any—had ever given blow jobs. She was just about ready to visualize Paulette Jefferson and Rufus Doublet together when the room fell silent.

Brasfield Finch had arrived. He wore his usual jeans, denim work shirt and boots, and this evening he had on a pinstripe vest from an old suit. The vest hung open on each side of his bushy beard, which was tied at the bottom with a length of white cotton cord. The contrast between his appearance and the muted, conservative dress of the AAUP women was striking. Finch stood in the doorway, looking around. Lily thought he looked alarmed, as if he were about to break and run.

"Come in, Mr. Finch," Paulette Jefferson said loudly, "have a brownie."

"No thanks," Finch said.

"Well," Paulette said gaily, "our guest of honor has arrived! Everyone finish up your brownies and coffee and we'll get the meeting started."

There was a rustling and clinking as coffee cups and saucers were put away, and everyone sat. Paulette ushered Finch to the front of the room, where there was a desk and a chair.

"Now," Paulette Jefferson said, "we all already know Brasfield Finch, our esteemed writer-in-residence. But what all of you might not know is that his first novel, *Coming of Age at ...*" She paused and looked at Finch.

"South Beach," he said.

"*Coming of Age at South Beach*, of course," she said, smiling, "was nominated for the Pulitzer Prize!"

There were several affirmative nods and some mumbling. Mrs. Russo, next to Lily, snorted loudly through her nose.

"Many are called, but few are chosen," Finch said.

Mrs. Russo snorted again. Lily looked at Brass, whose jaw was clenched. He looked angry. Lily wished she was not seated next Mrs. Russo.

"Lenora Hart *won* it," Mrs. Russo whispered in Lily's ear. Her breath was hot and smelled of coffee.

"Yes, she did," Finch said. "I heard that, Libby. Lenora Hart *won* it. We all know that."

Lily felt the woman squirming on the couch.

"Let's move along," Paulette said. "Mr. Finch asked that the format be question and answer, so that what he talks about will be what you're interested in hearing."

Willow thought: and that way he doesn't have to prepare any

remarks.

"We've all read *The Fox and the Pheasant*," Professor Jefferson went on. "And I know Mr. Finch will be happy to answer any questions about *Coming of Age* ..." She paused and looked at Brasfield.

"At South Beach!" he said impatiently.

"*At South Beach*, too," she said. "So who has the first question?"

A slim, buck-toothed woman raised her hand.

"Yes, Suzanne?" Paulette said.

"I'm Suzanne Daniels," the woman said, "and ..."

"I know who you are," Finch interrupted. "What's your question?"

"Well, it's a long book," she said, and there were several appreciative titters. "How long did it take you to write it?"

"Two or three years," Finch said. "Next question."

A chubby woman in a boldly flowered dress that made her look even more chubby raised her hand.

"Yes, Mrs. Dobbs," Paulette said, "go ahead."

"Mr. Finch," she said, "do you outline your books? Do you map them out before you write them?"

"No," Finch said. "I rarely know where I'm going from one page to the next. From one *paragraph* to the next!" He snickered.

"You mean," Mrs. Dobbs said, "you don't even know how a book is going to *end*?"

"No," he said, "I don't know how it's going to end until I get there." There was a thick silence in the room. "That's the reason one writes novels, Mrs. Dobbs, to find out what's going to happen in them." This was met with more silence.

"Sort of like automatic writing?" Willow Behn asked.

"Yes. Sort of. Thank you, Willow, for clearing that up for the ladies." There was stirring, legs crossing and uncrossing. Whispers and sighs. "You know what 'automatic writing' is, don't you, ladies? *God* tells me what to write. I'm just like his number two pencil, I just write what he tells me to. He doesn't really tell me what comes next, just what to put down at the moment. And he never, *ever*, tells me what it means. So don't bother to ask me that."

"You mean you don't even know what your writing *means*?" Nelle Steagall asked.

"Of course not. Do you?"

"I should say not," the president's wife said.

"Did you mean to say," Lillian Lallo said next Lily, "that you write with a pencil?"

"No, I did not," Finch said. "I write on a typewriter."

"Pat Conroy writes with a pencil, I understand," another woman said.

"Pat Conroy can write with whatever he pleases," Finch said. "You know, of course, that Renoir painted with his penis."

There were gasps of shock.

"That's an urban legend," Joan Hudson said. "He did no such thing."

"We'll never know, will we?" Finch said. "The next time you look at his painting of that little girl, think about that."

"That's *ghastly*, Mr. Finch," Nelle Steagall said.

"I think Mr. Finch must have written *his* first novel with his own ding-dong," Libby Russo said. There were murmurs of agreement.

"Let's change the subject, please," Paulette Jefferson said.

"Yes, please," Brasfield Finch said.

"Well, *you* got us off on that distasteful subject, Mr. Finch," the president's wife said.

"Next question," Finch said.

"*When* do you write?" asked the buck-toothed woman. "I find the early mornings so quiet and peaceful. Is that when you write?"

"No," he said, "I sleep late. Dr. Doublet is gracious enough to give me my writing workshops in the afternoons. Most of my writing is done between the hours of midnight and four a. m., after I've had enough Scotch to prime my pump."

"You don't mean that you *drink* when you write this stuff," the president's wife said. There were more titters.

"Yes m'am," Finch said, "you don't think I'd write this *stuff* sober, do you?"

There was cordial laughter. They think he's kidding, thought Lily. More likely, they don't know what the hell to think. Maybe they are just being polite, except for Nelle Steagall, who was scowling. Willow had brayed, a kind of yelp, at what Finch had said. Lily inspected the president's wife, her disapproving demeanor, and she wondered briefly if Brass might be flirting with trouble with the administration before she remembered the open contempt he had shown the little man that day in the president's office. Brass has balls of brass, she thought. She laughed aloud. Libby Russo sneered at her.

"This man is a disgrace to this institution," Mrs. Russo said to Lily. "He is not funny."

"Oh yes he is," Lily said, "he's very funny."

Libby Russo snorted. "Brasfield Finch is one of Steagall's toadies," she said.

"He is?" That was certainly news to Lily. That Brass was anyone's toady was patently absurd. Much less President Steagall's. "I think you're mistaken," she said to the woman.

"What do you know?" the woman said. "You haven't been here long enough to know anything. And you look like you don't have a brain in your head."

Lily was taken aback. Where was this woman coming from? She seemed unduly angry; at Lily? She was likely one of those dowdy women who became incensed just looking at Lily. Lily looked away. Better to let it pass. She glanced over at Brass; he seemed to be enjoying himself immensely. Did Lily really want to spend the rest of her professional life in Lakewood? There were other jobs. With her credentials—as incomplete as they were— Lily would have little trouble getting interviews. She dreaded the prospect of starting the process all over again. It was so time consuming and energy draining. But she was not a slave to these people, even if she'd let herself play that role. Who was she kidding? That's exactly what she was.

"You don't understand what goes on on this campus," the woman said. "Changes are coming," she added ominously. Was she referring to the series of balmy, immature throwaways that kept appearing in everyone's mailbox? Threatening some kind of "revolution?" Lily thought the leaflets were childish. If that's what she was alluding to, Libby Russo took them very seriously.

"Any more questions?" Finch asked.

"How well do you know Lenora Hart?" Joanne Katz asked. Here it comes, thought Lily.

"What does that have to do with *The Fox and the Pheasant?*" Finch said.

"Well, everybody's curious about her," Mrs. Katz said. "I understand that you know her personally."

"One of the very few who does, yes," Finch said. "But she's coming to Lakewood. You can ask *her* anything you want to know. She won't answer, of course."

"I wouldn't be too sure of that," Libby Russo said.

"What's that, Libby?"

"That she's even coming." Murmurs went around the room.

Finch chuckled. "You're absolutely right. I wouldn't be at all surprised if she stood us up."

"She wouldn't dare!" Nelle Steagall said.

"She doesn't care about you, Mrs. Steagall," Finch said, "she doesn't care about *anybody.*"

"Come now, Brasfield," Paulette Jefferson said, "she would have to be a wonderful person to have written such a warm hearted book."

"Well, she's not," Finch said.

"So I have heard you say," Paulette said. "I guess we'll find out for ourselves."

"Yes, you will."

"Sour grapes," Suzanne Daniels said.

"No, not at all," Finch said. "All you ladies want is some gossip. You want me to tell you some 'inside dope' on Lenora Hart. Well, I don't know any. You would have to ask some of her girlfriends in New York."

"*Girl* friends?" Paulette asked. "Whatever do you mean?"

"You know very well what I mean, Paulette," Finch said.

"What does he mean?" Sylvia Wettermark asked.

"That she has girlfriends?" Mrs. Lallo said.

"What you are suggesting is outrageous, Mr. Finch," Nelle Steagall said.

"What is he suggesting?" Sylvia Wettermark asked. There was more murmuring around the room. Lily sat looking around. Was Brass intimating that Lenora Hart was a dyke? If so, things were getting more interesting. Most of the women appeared not to know what he was talking about, if that *was* what he was talking about. Sometimes with Brass it was hard to know.

"I've got time for one more question," Finch said.

"All right," the woman in the flowered dress, Mrs. Dobbs, said. "Did Lenora Hart name the father of the little girl in her novel 'Finch' because of you?"

"Me?" Finch said. "No, *his* name is *Perecles* Finch. Pure coincidence, I'm sure."

"But ..." the woman sputtered.

"Thank you all for asking me here," Finch interrupted her. "It's been great fun." He stood up.

"Thank you so very much for coming, Mr. Finch," Paulette Jefferson said. She began to clap her hands, which resulted in a round of tepid applause. Lily looked over at Willow. The older woman was smiling. She winked at Lily.

FOURTEEN

Willow and Lily walked down to the faculty meeting together. It was being held in the large auditorium/classroom on the ground floor of Comer Hall. There was considerable buzz around the campus about the meeting, since it was the first one of the year, coming as it did well toward the end of the spring semester. They had heard that they would be told the details of Lenora Hart's visit, which was imminent. "Surely the plans have all already been made, at this late date," Willow said as they walked, "we will merely be 'informed.' That's what our faculty meetings are, dear, just venues for dispensing information."

"I heard that we're giving her an honorary degree," Lily said.

"Yes, I heard that, too. I suppose we'll be 'informed' about that as well."

"The faculty will have no input?" Lily asked. This was all still very new to her. All that she knew about what went on in this part of the academic world was what little she had gleaned from talking with younger faculty members when she was in graduate school at Emory.

Willow chuckled. "There is no faculty governance on this campus," she said.

"But we have the faculty council," Lily said.

"Ha," Willow said. "The faculty council is simply an extension of Steagall's office."

"Oh," Lily said.

The auditorium was filling up. She and Willow found seats toward the back. "In case we have to beat a hasty retreat," Willow said.

Lily watched John W. Steagall, III, and Dean Jefferson come in and stride down the center aisle to the front. Both men wore identical blue serge suits, except that Wallace Jefferson's looked like an outsized tent and the president's as if he might have bought it in the junior department at J. C. Penny's. They each wore a bright red tie; Lily had heard them called "power ties." Lily was becoming increasingly more amused at men and their adornments. Jefferson and Steagall strutted as though they were very pleased with their appearance. They made it obvious that they felt quite superior to everyone else in the room, which continued to fill up. They conferred, whispering together in a self-important manner, making it a point to ignore the gathering crowd.

Mrs. Hoyle came in with her stenographer's pad and took her place on the podium. The two men sat as well, surveying the room with wide smiles, nodding to individuals. When the last stragglers had come in from the hallway and noisily taken their seats, Dean Jefferson stood up.

"I call this meeting of the faculty of Lakewood College to order," he said, in stentorian tones. "I'd like to welcome you all, especially our newest faculty members, whom you all met at the new-faculty reception at Flowerhill last September. I won't call you by name, but would you all stand?" Lily stood up, along with several others scattered around the auditorium. There was languid and spiritless applause. Wallace Jefferson looked directly at her and smiled broadly. Lily was afraid he was going to say something about the "Lovely Lily," but he didn't. When the clapping died down he went on: "We have several items on the agenda this morning, so let's get started. First ..."

He was interrupted by a loud, harsh voice. "When do we get to make a motion?!" Garcia Russo shouted.

"In good time, Dr. Russo," Dean Jefferson said. "I'd like to ask President Steagall to come forward and share with you the plans for our visit from Lenora Hart."

"That's what I wanted to make my motion about," Russo shouted.

"Excuse me?" Dean Jefferson said.

"How much are we paying this woman?" Russo asked.

"You are out of order, Dr. Russo," Jefferson said.

"*I'm* out of order? Come on, Jefferson, what are we paying her?"

"The Foundation!" Steagall said, stepping forward. "All the money is coming from the foundation."

"What difference does that make?" Russo said. "Money is money. Come on. Fifty thousand, or what?"

"Miss Hart is a very famous writer," Steagall said, "any amount would be ..."

"Come on! How much?" Russo said.

"Twenty-five thousand," Steagall blurted. A buzz went around the room. "But it's from the foundation. Not a penny from operating expenses."

"Aha!" Russo said.

"Are you satisfied, Dr. Russo?" Dean Jefferson said. His face had turned crimson.

"May I make a motion?" Russo asked.

"No, you may not!" Jefferson said, raising his voice. "And sit down, please."

Russo sat down. He was grinning. Lily saw that he was sitting with a group of men, all of whom were grinning at each other. "They seem quite pleased," Lily whispered to Willow, "what's going on?"

Willow shook her head and pressed her finger against her lips.

"Can we please move on?" Jefferson barked. "We have pressing business here this morning." Russo laughed loudly. "Dr. Russo," the dean said, "if you can't comport yourself, I shall have you ushered out!"

"Oh, yeah? You and whose army?" Russo sneered. Jefferson stood there, his jaw working. Beads of perspiration popped out on his forehead. "All right, all right, I'll be quiet," Russo said, "but I got a motion—maybe a couple of motions—to make. And it's my right to make em."

The dean took a deep breath. He paused a moment. "Of course. Of course it is. In due course."

President Steagall stepped up to the podium. His hands were shaking as he rested them on the lectern. He smacked his lips. Lily thought he was sucking on something. Maybe a breath mint? He cleared his throat. "If I may proceed," he said. "As you all know, the honored and revered writer, Lenora Hart, who has been called Florida's, and indeed, America's, greatest treasure, has agreed to be our speaker for our annual Seniors' Day convocation, one of our most cherished traditions here at Lakewood, when we award our seniors their caps and gowns. There will follow a reception for her in the basketball arena, open to the public. Everyone will be allowed to meet and greet her, and she has agreed to sign copies of *To Lynch a Wild Duck.*" Lily heard a loud snort to her right, and she looked down the row and saw a pair of jeaned legs sticking into the aisle; she recognized the scuffed boots as belonging to Brasfield Finch. "Prior to the convocation, there will be a private reception for her at Flowerhill, with invited faculty guests and members of the board of trustees. We had hoped to have a gala dinner the night before, but Miss Hart regretfully was otherwise engaged." Lily heard Brass snort again. She looked at Willow; the older woman looked amused. She again pressed her finger against her lips. "Are there any questions?" Steagall said.

"Yes!" Russo shouted. "Who are these 'invited' guests?"

"Mrs. Hoyle will mail out invitations," Steagall said.

"Who determines who gets these? You?"

"They will be carefully chosen, Dr. Russo, rest assured," Dean Jefferson interjected.

"I'll just bet!" Russo said.

"I want on that list," a man next to Russo said. Lily thought he was Donald Katz, from the math department.

"Make a note of that, Mrs. Hoyle," Jefferson said.

"Me, too," another man in the group shouted. There were mumbles and babbles around the room. Shifting and loud whispers.

"People! People!" Dean Jefferson said, holding up his hands. "This is not the place for this. Everyone who wants to be invited should send a memo to Mrs. Hoyle. Okay?"

"Get ready, Olive," someone shouted, "you're gonna be swamped!" Lily looked around and saw it was J. J. Underwood.

"All right! Please, let's have some order here," Dean Jefferson said. "We know that everyone wants to meet Miss Hart, and we'll try to accommodate everyone. But we don't want to overwhelm the woman."

"For twenty-five thousand dollars, she can afford to be overwhelmed," Fred C. Dobbs said loudly. There was much laughter. When it died down, Dobbs went on: "What does she need the money for anyway? She's already a millionaire. She ought to donate it back to Lakewood."

"We'll discuss that with her," Steagall said.

"Yeah, yeah," Dobbs said.

"I want to remind everyone that the occasion will be an academic procession with full regalia," Dean Jefferson said. "Dr. Trilling will send out a memo about the order of procession and so forth." Uh-oh. Lily would have to rent the regalia. Another expense. But she had to admit it was exciting, her first academic procession as a faculty member. Maybe one rental would do for both Senior day and graduation. She hoped so. Lily's mind wandered. Sometimes she wondered just what she was doing here at Lakewood. She knew she hadn't given it a great deal of thought, had just been grateful to have an offer. There were others in her class who had been struggling just to get an interview. And here the completion of her first full teaching year was fast approaching, with evaluations coming up. She had dreaded the evaluations all year long, but now, somehow, they didn't seem all that important. Sometimes she wished she was religious, so she could believe that the Lord would provide. Something, somehow, would provide, she was sure.

Lily's consciousness popped back into the faculty meeting. "Yes, Dr. Jefferson?" Dean Jefferson was saying, and Lily was momentarily confused until Paulette Jefferson said,

"Thank you, Dean Jefferson." She was standing. "I move that the faculty of Lakewood College grant Lenora Hart an honorary Doctor of Letters degree on the occasion of her address to the senior class."

"I second," a voice down front said.

"Wait a minute!" Russo said. "You're out of order, Mrs. Steagall. You're not a faculty member!"

Mrs. Steagall stood up. "I am first lady," she said, "I have a vote."

"You do not!" Russo said.

"All right, all right!" Willow said. She was standing now, too. "*I* second. Now let's move to discussion." She sat down. She still looked amused.

"Dr. Behn is a certified member of the faculty, wouldn't you agree, Dr. Russo?" Dean Jefferson said sarcastically. "It has been moved and seconded. Is there discussion?"

"Yes, you better believe it," Russo said. "In the first place, this woman has no connection to Lakewood College. She lives way down in Naples, and she graduated from the University of Florida. To my knowledge, she has never set foot on this campus. She is just coming to say a few words for a fat check, and you want to give her an honorary degree! Ridiculous."

"Thank you, Dr. Russo," Dean Jefferson said. "Other discussion?"

"In my many years here," Lucy Willard said, standing up, "we have granted very few honorary degrees. We have always prided ourselves on the fact that granting one really means something."

"Are you saying that giving one to Lenora Hart means nothing?" Paulette Jefferson said. "I am appalled."

"No, I'm not saying that at all," Lucy Willard said. "I'm merely pointing out that ..."

"Lenora Hart is one of the most beloved, most respected, writers in America," Paulette Jefferson interrupted her. "Her novel is taught in schools all over the country, and she is our own, right here in Florida. We should do everything we can to show our appreciation of her. How can anyone ..."

"Nobody is saying she is not a great writer, Dr. Jefferson," Lucy said.

"Well, what *are* you saying, then?"

"I'm simply suggesting ..."

"What does she need a doctorate for?" Fred Dobbs asked. "She's an old lady."

"Oh, good heavens, Fred," Paulette said, "go back to school!"

"The dean's wife has got her panties in a wad," Dobbs said.

"There is no need for this level of discourse," Dean Jefferson said, "Let's keep this on an acceptable, professional level, please."

"I call for the question," a quavering, slim voice said.

"What's that, Dr. Lallo?" Dean Jefferson said to Bob Lallo.

"I said," Lallo said, a little louder, "I call for the question."

"No! The discussion's not over yet," Garcia Russo said.

"He calls for the question!" Dean Jefferson said. "All in favor say 'Aye.'"

There were several scattered 'Ayes' around the room.

"The 'Ayes' have it," said Wallace Jefferson. "Now, all in favor ..."

"Wait a minute!" shouted Russo.

"All in favor of granting Lenora Hart an honorary Doctor of Letters raise your right hand ..."

"I demand a secret ballot!" Russo said.

"Oh, good heavens, Dr. Russo, must we?" the dean said. He sighed and nodded to Mrs. Hoyle. "Eloise," he said, "prepare the ballots and distribute them, please." She began tearing the pages of her stenographer's pad into smaller sections, and John Steagall rushed over to help her.

Lily sneaked a look as Willow marked her ballot. 'YES' Willow wrote, so Lily wrote the same and folded the small slip of paper and passed it down to the end of the row, where Lillian Lallo was waiting to gather them. She watched as Brasfield Finch wrote a large "NO" on his page and handed it to Lillian without folding it.

"Should I sign my name?" Finch asked her, chuckling.

"That won't be necessary, Mr. Finch," the woman said, her thin lips tight.

Dean Jefferson, Mrs. Hoyle, and President Steagall counted the votes down front. "All right, we have the results," Jefferson said. " 'Ayes' - 88, 'No' - 42." A hum of whispering rumbled across the room.

"*42* Nos?!" someone said. It was J. J. Underwood again.

"So it's settled," Jefferson said. "We award the degree. I thank the faculty for your diligent—"

"I demand to count the votes!" Russo shouted.

"Recount!" Donald Katz echoed.

"—for your diligent deliberation," Jefferson went on. "Now, that concludes our business for this morning ..."

"I said I have a motion!" Russo said.

Jefferson sighed. He rolled his eyes. "All right, Dr. Russo, what is your motion?"

Russo stood up. "I move," he said, "that we as a faculty hold a confidence vote on President Steagall."

There was a stunned silence.

"Are you joking, Dr. Russo?" Jefferson asked. He paused. "No, I *know* you are not joking. But you are out of order. The very idea ..."

"Why am I out of order? I have a right to make a motion if I want to."

Jefferson looked at Steagall, then back out at the faculty. He shrugged. "I suppose you do, Dr. Russo, but to call for a confidence vote like this, out of the blue, is absurd."

"I second the motion," Fred C. Dobbs said.

"Call for discussion," R. D. Wettermark said.

"I think Dean Jefferson is losing control of the meeting," Lily whispered to Willow.

"No kidding?" Willow said.

Russo was on his feet again. "May I speak?" he asked.

"Would it do any good if I said no?" Dean Jefferson said.

"I urge the faculty to vote no-confidence in John W. Steagall, III," Russo said. "The man has allowed this institution to flounder with no leadership. First there was the shameful streaking, naked men and women running rampant over the campus, and the administration was powerless to do anything about it. And look at the result, the rape of an innocent little girl! Paying this speaker for senior day such an obscene sum is just the tip of the iceberg. It is a fact that the college has settled with the family of Penny Fitzgerald for *five hundred thousand dollars!*" There were gasps of shock and disbelief. "This is money that could be used for faculty salaries, for library books, for research funds and so forth," Russo went on, "and yet it is thrown away because of the immorality that Steagall has allowed to reign on this campus!"

"Aha!" Willow whispered to Lily, "I knew he was the one."

"The one what?" Lily whispered back.

"Shhhhh," Willow said, again putting her finger against her lips.

"This man has defiled the very office of president!" Russo continued. As he spoke Lily inspected the two men and the woman down front. Mrs. Hoyle had put her stenographer's pad down in her lap and sat with a flabbergasted look on her bony face. Steagall looked even shorter; he seemed to shrink even as Russo continued his diatribe. Dean Jefferson's face was flame-red, and his jaw worked as if he were aching to respond but couldn't find the words. Lily thought she detected circles of sweat that were beginning to show under the arms of his suit. His eyes flashed with intense fury. Then Russo had finished his speech.

"Yes, Dr. Doublet," Dean Jefferson said, his voice tight. It was up an octave from his usual tone.

Lily looked around and saw Rufus Doublet standing, in his olive green tweed jacket. His tasteful knit tie was, as usual, just so.

"First of all," Doublet said, "I am astonished at this development. Dr. Steagall is the finest president this institution has ever had. He has been the victim of a mean-spirited and vicious distribution of malicious misinformation that is shameful, if not criminal. I know for a fact that the settlement that was reached with Miss Fitzgerald's family was not nearly that much!"

"How much was it, then?" Fred C. Dobbs shouted.

There was a hushed, expectant noiselessness in the auditorium. Wallace Jefferson looked at Steagall, who appeared frightened and panicked. The little man unbuttoned and then buttoned his suit jacket. Willow leaned over and whispered to Lily, "All my life I have heard the expression he didn't know whether to shit or go blind, and now I know what it means." Lily giggled and Willow pressed her hand on her arm.

Dean Jefferson stepped back up behind the podium. "We ... we are ... we are not at liberty, *legally*, to disclose the amount of the settlement," he said.

Silence. Then Katherine Klinger, the Chaucer lady, said, "Was it bigger than a bread box?" It seemed to break the tension and there was general laughter. Lily sensed that nobody but Garcia Russo and his band of malcontents cared very much how big the settlement was. Lily was relieved to know that the poor girl had gotten *something*. If it could be believed that it was true that there was even a settlement. Lily was beginning to think that she could believe very little she heard on this campus.

"I move for adjournment," Lillian Lallo said down front. She was standing facing the faculty and she looked as though she were ready to fight anyone who might disagree with her.

"Wait a minute!" Russo said. "You're out of order."

"I second," Paulette Jefferson said.

"There's a motion on the floor!" said J. J. Underwood from the back of the room. "Robert's Rules of Order say that—"

"Fuck Robert," Dean Jefferson said. "All in favor? The ayes have it," he said without waiting for anyone to say anything, "this meeting is adjourned!"

FIFTEEN

Brasfield Finch stuck his head in her office door and asked Lily if she'd like to ride over to Tallahassee with him that evening.

"Well, maybe," she said, "what for?"

"To see Lenora Hart, of course," he said.

"What? Lenora Hart?"

Finch came in and closed the door. It was the day before Senior Day, when Lenora Hart was to be on campus.

"Lenora Hart's in Tallahassee?" Lily asked.

"Yes. She's at the Wynfrey Hotel. It's the closest four-star hotel to Lakewood. She wouldn't stay on campus."

"How do you know she's there now?"

"Because I talked to her on the phone," Finch said. "She's holed up over there with a few bottles of Jack Daniels, and she said to come on over."

"She invited *me*?" Lily asked.

"She said if I had plans to bring plans. Since I don't, would you like to be my plans?"

"Well hell *yeah*!" Lily said.

Finch had an old battered sixty-eight Mustang, mustard brown in color. When Lily paused and looked at it, he said, "It gets me there." Lily had gone home to her apartment and fussed in her closet, trying to decide what to wear. She had decided on a plain black mini dress and heels, though she knew—and it turned out she was right—Brasfield Finch would have on his usual jeans and corduroy vest. He headed the Mustang east on I-10.

"I guess that's what you'll wear under your academic gown tomorrow," she said when they were underway.

"Oh, no," he said, "I go naked under my gown."

"You're *lyin*!" she said, giggling and poking him on the arm.

"I'm serious," he said, "I'll flash you tomorrow on the steps of Ferguson." Ferguson was the hall with the large auditorium where most convocations were held. It also housed the offices of the dean of the college and the deans of men and women.

"I wouldn't be surprised," she said, "I'll look forward to that."

"You just want to get another look at my manly member," he said.

"Not a bad idea," she said, "if my memory serves me correctly. Pretty impressive."

The rode along for a while, the only sounds the hum of the tires on the asphalt.

"Brass," Lily said, "why didn't we ever get back together?"

"Oh, I figured you were busy with the younger guys."

"*What* younger guys?" she said. She chortled.

"Didn't Rufus Doublet give you a rush?"

"He's a pervert. He only likes older women. *Old* women!"

"He may be a pervert, but he can probably still fuck," Finch said.

"I wouldn't count on it," she said.

"Oh," he said, "please spare me the details."

"Okay," she said. She paused for a minute. "Dr. Steagall said that day that Lenora Hart had a previous engagement the night before her speech."

"Yes," Finch said, "me."

"But ..." She paused. "But I thought you didn't like her very much."

"I *don't* like her very much. She's a pluperfect bitch, but she's an old friend of mine."

"An old lover of yours, you mean."

"Oh, now, Lily, you know I don't kiss and tell."

The Interstate was as straight and flat as an airport runway. The sun was setting behind them, reflecting golden on the sand and the scrubby live oaks that lined the road. There was practically nothing between Lakewood and Tallahassee; Lily thought it must be like driving across the surface of the moon. Finch fished around under the seat and came out with a bottle of Chivas Regal. He handed it to Lily, and she took a robust swig. Then Finch turned the bottle up and gulped. They passed it back and forth for a couple of miles.

"What about Owen?" Finch asked.

"Owen *Fielder*?" she said, "good god!" Owen Fielder was the other new instructor in the English department. "I went out with Owen once. *Once!* He didn't drink, took me to a pizza place and then rode me around in that little MG of his. I think he thought I'd be impressed out of my mind. Then he took me back to his apartment and spent the evening showing me pictures of girls, yearbook beauties from last year, that he'd dated. He had put a little X in the corner of the pictures of the ones he'd been out with. I couldn't believe it. I got out of there as fast as I could."

"No luck there, huh?"

"No, not by a loooong shot!"

"What about students?" Finch asked.

Lily cut her eyes at Brass; he was focused on the highway ahead. Could he know about David Godby?

"I don't have tenure," she said.

"Tenure doesn't make a whole hell of a lot of difference when it comes to fucking students," he said.

"What about you?" she asked.

"Oh, I've been known to partake. Specially when I was younger. Some of them are so delicious it's hard to resist."

"I know what you mean," she said, thinking of David. He had dropped her class, probably at the insistence of his girlfriend, and she had seen very little of him after that. She had heard that, after the spring baseball season began in February, he had been kicked off the team for violating training rules and had left school. Sad. Such beautiful junk. It was probably for the best, though, that it had worked out like it had. Even though she was tempted from time to time when boys came by her office with their tongues hanging out she had decided that, if just for this first year, until she got her contract at least, she would steer clear of student involvement.

"Doesn't hurt to look," Finch said.

"Yeah," she said, "but it makes it hard." She paused. "They are so ... so there for the taking."

"Tell me about it," he said.

They were now on the outskirts of Tallahassee and the traffic had picked up. Finch drove fast and he didn't slow down at all in the city congestion. Lily reached up for the "oh-shit" bar but the old Mustang didn't have one. She decided to trust that Brass knew what he was doing. The car rumbled and rolled as it switched lanes back and forth rapidly, causing a cacophonous chorus of car horns behind them.

"Maybe you should slow down," Lily finally said.

"Why?" Finch said. "I'm in a hurry." He leaned on his own horn. "Out of the way, motherfucker!" he yelled.

The car in front of them moved over into the right lane and Finch whizzed by them. "Eat my dust, motherfucker!" he yelled.

"Do you always drive like this?" Lily asked.

"Like what?" Finch said. "If you don't run over them, they'll run over *you!*"

"You'd be right at home driving in Atlanta," Lily said. She held on to the cushion of the worn leather seat with both hands. Finch suddenly darted into an exit lane. He came to a screeching halt at a red light at the foot of the ramp.

"The Wynfrey is right up here," he said, indicating to their left. As they sat waiting for the light, Finch took another long drag from the bottle. He handed it to Lily. "You better fortify yourself," he said.

They parked in the garage underneath the hotel. They took an express elevator to the twenty first floor. "She's in 2112," Finch said. "It's the presidential suite. She would settle for nothing less."

"How'd she rate that?" Lily asked.

"Lenora Hart gets what she wants," Finch said.

Once on the floor they could hear loud country music, thumping guitars and ringing banjos, coming from an open doorway.

"That must be 2112," Finch said, and they headed toward it.

Lily sniffed the air. There was a strong odor of tobacco smoke that seemed to be coming from the room. "The sign on the elevator said this is a non-smoking floor," Lily said.

"Ha!" Finch said.

They entered the suite. The smoke in the room was so thick that it stung Lily's eyes. And the room was dim, only one table lamp glowing. The bluegrass music assaulted her ears. She blinked, her eyes adjusting to the dark. There was a man in what looked like some sort of uniform sitting on the sofa with a glass of clear liquid. Standing against floor to ceiling drapes against the wall to the right was a woman. Lily felt a jolt of excitement. This must be Lenora Hart!

The woman was shorter than Lily, and she was plump, generous in size. Actually she was rotund. She wore a gray tweed skirt that seemed to hang crooked from her ample waist and a wrinkled white blouse that was not tucked in. Wisps of thin grayish hair crowned her spherical head. Her face was round and flat. From the corner of her mouth jutted a large cigar, obviously the source of the acrid smoke.

"Well," Lenora Hart said, looking at Brasfield Finch. Then she looked at Lily. "Tell me, dearie, how *is* this fucker?"

"M'am?" Lily said.

"I'm not your school teacher, girl," she said.

"He's ... he's fine, I guess," Lily said.

"Sit down and have a drink," Lenora Hart said, "your choice. I ordered up everything, even some Flanagan single malt for Brass. One thousand and eight dollars a bottle! Compliments of Lakewood College."

"You shouldn't have," Brass said and laughed vigorously.

"What'll it be, dearie?' she asked Lily. "Move over, Frank," she said to the man on the sofa, "where's your goddam manners?" She sat on the sofa and patted the cushion next to her. Lily sat down. "Get your squeeze a drink, Brass," she said. "I guess she *is* your squeeze."

"So to speak," Finch said. He began pouring himself a Scotch and Lily a Jack Daniels. "I suppose you could say that she *was* my squeeze, once upon a time." He handed Lily her drink. "Lenora, this is Lily Putnam," he said, "she's a great admirer of your one little novel."

"Nice to meet you, dearie," Lenora Hart said. "She's a bit young for you, isn't she, Brass?"

"Ask *her*," Finch said.

"Oh ho, ho, ho," Hart said, "Same old Finch!"

Finch stuck his hand out to the man at the end of the sofa. "Brasfield Finch," he said. "Are you in the military?"

"Frank Wembley," the man said.

"He's my *limo driver*," Lenora Hart said. "He picked me up at the airport and we've gotten to be best friends. Have another drink, Frank. He likes tequila, neat."

Frank stood up. His blue uniform was wrinkled. He began pouring his drink.

"While you're up," Finch said, "turn that goddam music down, will you?"

Frank obediently walked over to the large radio perched on a credenza against the wall and turned the knob. "Not *too* much," Lenora Hart said, "Brass never could stand good music."

"Good music?" Finch said, "this is hillbilly shit."

"This is good bluegrass, you ignorant hack," Hart said.

"Who are you calling a hack?" Finch said.

Hart looked at Lily. "Brass has never gotten over the fact that my book sold zillions of copies—and is still selling them—while his didn't do diddly squat. So he thinks I'm a hack." She stared at Lily, puffing on her cigar. There was an uncomfortable pause.

"Yes m'am," Lily said to fill the silence.

"Yes *m'am?*" Hart said. "You mean you agree with him?"

"No, no, I didn't say that!" Lily said.

"Okay. But if I thought you did, I'd knock that silly little butch head of yours off. I like your haircut, by the way. Do you get it cut at your local barber shop?"

"No, I ..."

"Let her alone, Lenora," Finch said.

"Excuse me," Lily said, standing, "I need to visit the ladies room."

"Right through there, Butch," Hart said, motioning.

When Lily had gone, Lenora Hart said, "That, Brass, is a delicious little morsel."

"You should see her naked," Finch said.

"I intend to," Hart said. She pulled her cigar from her mouth and blew a thick cloud of gray smoke.

"That stinks," Finch said, "where do you buy those things, Wal-Mart?"

"These are imported Cuban cigars," she said. "Two hundred dollars a box."

"They smell like they were rolled in a Cuban manure factory."

"Would you care for one?" she asked. "You used to smoke an occasional cigar, I remember. Then you took up a pipe. I thought you felt that made you look writerly."

"I *am* writerly, Lenora. I'm a *real* writer," he said.

"Except that you don't write," she said.

"How the hell do you know?"

"You haven't published anything in years," she said and snorted.

"Neither have you. Nothing after that one little children's book."

"I don't need to," she said. "*To Lynch a Wild Duck* sold six million copies last year, worldwide. Why should I write another book? I have all the Cuban cigars and Jack Daniels I want. Which reminds me," she said, holding up her empty glass, "fill me up, Frank."

Frank hopped up to fetch her another drink.

"You've got this guy well trained," Finch said, "when did he pick you up at the airport?"

"This morning," Hart said. She grinned around her cigar. "We christened the presidential bed at eleven thirty-five."

"Fast mover, Lenora," Finch said, "but then you always were."

Lily came back into the room. "All refreshed now, dearie?" Lenora said, "everything come out all right?"

"Yes," Lily said shortly and sat back down.

"Did I hurt the little girl's feelings?" Lenora said. "Oh, my, you must forgive an old lush."

"All right," Lily said.

"Did I hurt her feelings?" Lenora asked Finch in a mincing voice.

"I asked you to leave her alone," Finch said, "she's my date. My *plans.*"

"Not for long, she isn't," Lenora Hart said. She covered Lily's hand with her own. "You're a fetching child, Lily," she said. "Do you like older women?"

"I don't know what you mean," Lily said. She glanced at Finch, sitting holding his glass of expensive Scotch. She was grateful to Brass for saying she was his date. Was Miss Hart coming on to her right in front of Brass and her ... boyfriend, or whoever he was? Her limo driver? Frank? He was sitting across from them, contentedly sipping his tequila, seemingly paying little attention to their conversation. She moved her hand from under Hart's. She took a long swig of her drink. She didn't want to offend this famous writer, though Lenora Hart was not behaving as Lily had expected a famous writer to behave. Maybe she should just play along. Lily fluttered her eyes. "I like you okay, if that's what you mean," she said.

"She plays the coquette, eh, Brass?" Hart said.

"She doesn't *play* it, she *is* it."

"Hey," Lily said, "I'm sitting right here."

"Oh, you most certainly are," Hart said, staring at Lily's legs in the mini dress.

"We're really going to have to be going," Lily said. "I have to get up early in the morning."

"Oh, no, you don't," Hart said. "Frank, get them another drink."

Frank stood up and ambled unevenly to the bar in the corner. He poured them each a generous drink. He gave them to Lily and Finch.

"Hey, shit-face, you forgot me," Hart said, holding up her glass. "Hit me again."

They sipped their drinks for a few minutes.

"Well, it's been fun," Finch said, "but we really ..."

"Don't give me that crap," Hart said, "the evening's young."

"Don't forget, Lenora, that you have a speech to give tomorrow," Finch said.

"Speech? What speech?"

"At Lakewood College, remember?" Finch said. "You're getting an honorary degree, though for the life of me I can't figure out why."

"Because everybody loves me," Hart said. "Everybody loves my book!"

"As P. T. Barnum was said to have said," Finch said, "'never overestimate the taste of the American people.'"

"Come again?" Hart asked.

"Never mind, Lenora, you're drunk. You need to get to bed."

"Wait a minute, wait a minute," she said. "I've got something I want to show you."

She began to get unsteadily to her feet.

"What?" Finch asked impatiently.

"Just hold your horses. There. Sit tight. You want Frank to freshen your drinks?"

"We're fine, thanks," Lily said.

Lenora Hart weaved to the bedroom door. "Frank, come in here and help me," she said. They disappeared into the bedroom.

Lily and Finch sat sipping their drinks. "What do you suppose she wants to show us?" Lily asked.

"God only knows," Finch said.

"I'm getting drunk," Lily said. "I *am* drunk."

"Ain't we all?" Finch said. "Let the party begin."

"Do you think you can drive home?"

"Oh, hell yeah. I drive better drunk than I do sober."

Lily recalled the chaotic drive into the city. She was glad that she was good and drunk, too, and grateful that the interstate back to Lakewood was as straight as a plumb-line.

"Ta-da!" Lenora's voice rang out from the bedroom. "Drum roll, please," she said, as she stepped back into the room. She had changed into a floor length, shiny gold lamme evening gown with a plunging neckline that revealed an ample portion of her pendulous breasts. There were ruffles on the shoulders and at the hem. The cigar protruding from her lips was even more ludicrous in the dress. She held her hands out to the side and bowed low, displaying even more of her cleavage.

Lily and Finch sat in stunned silence. Then, Finch said,

"Very nice, Lenora."

She glared at them, chewing on the cigar. "You don't like it," she said.

"Oh, no," Finch said, "it's very ... attractive. Isn't it, Lily?"

"If you say so," said Lily.

"I think it's just right for the occasion," Hart said.

"Occasion?"

"My speech! My honorary degree, dumb-ass."

"Well," Finch said, "you'll have on a gown."

"A what?"

"An academic gown, Lenora."

"No, I won't. I'll have on this dress."

"It'll be covered by the gown, but then there's the reception." Finch chuckled. This would be good.

"I'm not wearing any goddam gown," Hart said. "And I'm not attending any fucking reception!"

Finch laughed out loud then. He chortled. "You'll just have to take that up with John W. Steagall, III," he said. Then he guffawed. He couldn't stop laughing. When he paused for breath, he said, "It's a damn fine dress, Lenora!" His laughter bubbled over. "A damn fine dress!"

"*You* like it, don't you, dearie?" Hart said to Lily. She sat down next to the girl, her dress rustling around her. She patted Lily's bare knee. Then she caressed it. Lily shifted away, uncrossing then re-crossing her legs.

"We really should ..." Lily began.

"Brass," Hart said, "you're not taking this delectable morsel away from me!"

"I'm afraid you'll have to make do with Frank tonight, Lenora," Finch said.

"Why, you impotent hack!" Lenora said

"He's not impotent," Lily said.

"You would know, wouldn't you, dearie?"

"I didn't mean *that*," Lily said, "and I don't think you did, either."

"No, I was referring to the fact that he hasn't published anything in years."

"But he's *writing*. I read some chapters of his new novel."

"He showed them to you, huh?" Hart said. "So he could get into those sweet panties of yours."

"He didn't have to go to that much trouble to get there," Lily said.

This seemed to make Lenora Hart very angry. She yanked her cigar from her mouth and blew a puff of smoke at Lily. Lily coughed and waved her hand in front of her face.

"You are a very crude woman, Miss Hart," Lily said.

"Frank! Throw these people out!" Hart yelled.

They all looked over at Frank, who was sleeping peacefully in an easy chair.

"I think we can show ourselves out, Lenora," Finch said, "but thanks, anyway."

SIXTEEN

Lily woke up the next morning with a hangover. She made coffee and ate a bagel with cream cheese. She sat at the little table in her kitchen, looking out into the enclosed back yard of the apartment building. She let the events of the previous evening, some of which were blurry, drift through her mind. It had been quite an experience. Never would she have expected Lenora Hart, the author of *To Lynch a Wild Duck*, one of the most beloved books in American literature, to be quite like she was. Just as you couldn't judge a book by its cover, you couldn't judge an author by her book, she thought.

It was a beautiful spring day, perfect for an academic procession, and, in spite of her disappointment with Lenora Hart and with her own hangover, Lily was still excited about her first one. A first year of teaching was a year of firsts. It was as though she were constantly losing her virginity, over and over again. She chuckled. As she sipped her coffee, she thought back over the year, from the day she had first stepped foot on the campus to last night, which seemed a culmination of sorts.

During the previous week she had passed out the forms for student evaluations in all her classes. Back in her office after she had collected them, she nervously looked through them. The students gave her a number, five being excellent and one being poor. She had mostly threes, with a few fours, one five, and two ones. She was annoyed at the ones. She didn't understand the numbering system, which seemed to her intentionally vague.

Rufus Doublet had explained it to her: "When you turn them in, we'll average your numbers. Then we'll give you a departmental number, and as it goes up the ladder, the dean will give you a number and finally the president's office. All the numbers will be averaged to get your final evaluation number. And that, together with our subjective comments, of course, will determine whether or not you get a contract for next year. Simple, eh?"

"But what 'number' will I have to have to be reappointed?" she asked.

"Well," he said, "it varies. We look at each case on its own merits. We don't like to pin down an explicit number. We can't say exactly." He smiled at her across his desk. "Don't worry about it.

It just happens."

"But, it ..." She paused. She didn't want to say out loud what she was thinking. Which was: what is the point? Why go through all the motions of getting students to evaluate you when they were simply going to give you the 'number' they thought you should have? "I guess, what I was going to say," she said, "is it would help if I had some guidelines, you know, what I should aim for, all that."

"Just do your best job, Lily, and let us take care of that," Doublet said.

She began to look through the students' anonymous comments. The first one made her smile. "Ms. Putnam made me think," it said, "she made all that dumb literature make sense." Her eyes widened at the next. "I would like to fuck her till her hair falls out," it said. They got worse. "I'd give her an A if she sucked my dick." The next one—she thought she recognized the handwriting of a tall, scholarship volleyball player—said, "I want to lick her pussy and have her lick mine, and we will live happily ever after." Is this what these students, with their vacant, passive faces, had been sitting there thinking while she blabbered on about Wordsworth? There were a few other nice ones: "Good job, teach!" and "She really cares about us." But the majority of them were obscene. What in the world will Doublet, Dean Jefferson and President Steagall think when they read them? She was sunk.

"Oh, don't pay any attention to those things," Brasfield Finch said when she went to his office on the verge of tears. "Nobody reads them. They don't care about what students say. Hell, they don't care about *students*!"

"But ..."

"There's nothing you can do, Lily. They've got you by the balls."

"But *you've* got tenure," she said, "you got promoted."

"There you go," Finch said. "If *I* can get the stamp of approval of the administration, *anybody* can."

"I don't know," Lily said.

"Trust me. Anybody who looks like you ..."

"Ha," Lily said, "women hate me!"

"But those ass-holes are men," he said.

"Well ..." she said, "are you sure?"

Finch snickered. "No," he said, "are you?"

As she sat there looking out into the back yard, she wished she still smoked. A cigarette would be nice with her coffee. The morning sunlight sparkled over the shiny leaves of the tangle of live oaks against the back fence. She thought of the day David Godby had slipped up the back outside stairs to her apartment. She wondered where he was, what he was doing. He was stupid, but one hell of a lay. And a pretty good baseball player, as she recalled.

Her eyes wandered into the living room, where she could see her rented academic gown with its blue and gold hood hanging on the back of the door. She had ordered a tam rather than a mortar board; she felt that it looked better, and she wanted to look her best. Her coffee cup was empty. Her morning leisure time was over. She'd better get moving. This was a big day.

The dignitaries—those who would be on the dais—began to gather in President Steagall's suite of offices to gown. Eloise Hoyle was there to assist, as was Nelle Steagall. Some members of the board of trust trickled in. Father Hamner Curbs was to give the invocation and he had arrived in his priestly garb.

Dean Wallace Jefferson came bustling in. His gown billowed; there was enough material in it to make a mainsail. His red and black doctoral hood was lined in white fur and covered his entire back.

"Where is she?" he asked when he entered. Paulette Jefferson was with him, a wide expectant grin on her face. She wore an identical hood to her husband's.

"She isn't here yet," Nelle Steagall said.

"This is absurd!" Jefferson said.

"Yes, it is!" Nelle Steagall said.

The pre-convocation reception at Flowerhill had been cancelled at the last minute. President Steagall had invited Lenora Hart to come an hour early so they could spend some quiet time together before the reception. He had arranged with the Caf to have sweet rolls and coffee. When Hart had not showed up, he phoned the hotel. When he finally got through to her, she informed him that she had not agreed to any reception before the speech.

"I'm not dressed," she'd said. "It's too goddam early. I ... Tell him, Frank."

"Hello?" a male voice said.

"Who *is* this?" John Steagall said.

"Frank."

"Frank *who*?"

There was a click and the phone was hung up. When Steagall called back he was told by the front desk that Miss Hart was not receiving any more calls. He was incensed. The very idea of treating a college president that way!

"She'll be here," Nelle Steagall said to the Jeffersons, "we sent her explicit instructions to come to John's office to gown before her speech. She said she'd be here. But she told John this morning that she'd never agreed to a reception beforehand. There must have been a misunderstanding, because we understood ..."

"Yes, Nelle, settle down," Wallace Jefferson said.

"But the members of the board, other guests ... we have had to tell them ... oh, it is an embarrassment, I tell you."

"Of course it is," Paulette Jefferson said, "you poor dear. It must have been a misunderstanding, crossed wires, somehow. We'll survive. You mustn't worry about it."

"How can I not worry about it? We had the wine all chilled!" Nelle Steagall said, wringing her hands.

"The important thing is she is here now," Dean Jefferson said, "isn't that her?" He nodded toward the door.

A woman in a bright, shiny gold evening dress had come in, accompanied by a beefy man in a dark gray uniform.

"Where in the world did she get that hideous dress?" Paulette Jefferson asked.

Nelle Steagall headed straight toward her, holding out her hand. "Is this Miss Hart?" she asked cheerfully.

"Well," the woman said grumpily, "this is one of them."

"Welcome ... welcome to Lakewood," Nelle said, stuttering slightly, "I'm Nelle Steagall, President Steagall's wife."

"I'm sorry for you," Lenora Hart said.

Mrs. Steagall stood there puzzled. She looked around to see if anyone had overheard the exchange. "Come with me," she said, taking Lenora Hart's arm, "I want to introduce you around."

"Must you?" Hart said.

"Oh, everyone is *dying* to meet you, Miss Hart. It's not every day that we have a writer of such renown here at the college."

"Save it for the introduction," Hart said.

"Oh, dear, I didn't mean I was going to introduce you at the convocation. That honor goes to this distinguished gentleman here. I think you know Brasfield Finch, our writer in residence, don't you?"

Finch was standing against the wall. He had on a wrinkled,

stained gown, ancient in appearance. His mortar board was cocked on his head at a jaunty angle. His beard was hanging outside his gown and tied at the bottom with a bright, electric pink string.

"Yes, I know the old fart," Hart said.

As they moved on to the next person, Nelle Steagall questioned her own hearing. Had Lenora Hart said what she thought she had said? Surely not. Nelle must have misheard her. They approached a tall, Lincolnesque gentleman in a seersucker suit with old acne scars on his cheeks.

"And this is Matthew Switt, the chairman of our board of trust," Nelle said.

"Charmed," the man said, holding out his hand.

Hart slapped his hand. "What's happenin, Matty?" she said.

Moving on, Nelle whispered to Lenora, "I didn't know you knew Matthew."

"I never saw him before in my life," Hart said.

"Oh," Nelle said. She seemed confused, then she brightened. "While you're here, I want to show you my day lilies."

"Your what?"

"Day lilies! I'll bet you didn't know that Lakewood had been designated the Day Lily capital of Florida!"

"No, I didn't know that," Hart said. "if you pay attention, you learn something new every day. Frank?" she barked. The man in the uniform walked up carrying a small valise. "A little Jack, Frank," she said. Frank produced a bottle of Jack Daniels and a shot glass from the leather case. He poured a shot for Lenora, which she tossed back.

Nelle Steagall looked on aghast. "I ... I ..." she blabbered.

"Oh, I'm sorry," Hart said, "my manners. Would you like one too, Mrs. ... what did you say your name was?"

"Steagall," Nelle said, "I am the first lady. And I certainly do not want one. It's a bit early in the day for hard liquor."

"Never too early, and never too late, huh Steagall?"

"It's Nelle. Nelle Steagall."

"Whoa, Nellie," Hart said.

Dr. Steagall walked up. He stuck out his hand. "Miss Hart! I am delighted to meet you at last. I am John W. Steagall, III."

"You must be the first man," Hart said.

"Pardon?"

Lenora Hart snapped her fingers at Frank. He opened the valise and poured Lenora another drink. John Steagall and his wife watched her sip from the shot glass, then throw the remainder against the back of her throat. "Ahhhh," she said. "Are you sure you won't join me? This is Frank, my bodyguard, by the way."

"Ahh, yes, *Frank*," Steagall said. He stood as straight and as tall as his five foot three inches would allow him. He would not be intimidated by some famous writer's bodyguard, by damn. "*Enchanté*, Mr. Frank," he said.

Frank just looked at him with a vacuous stare.

"We really need to proceed with the robing," Eloise Hoyle said brightly. "Miss Hart, I am so pleased to meet you. I *love* your book. It has meant so much to me and ..."

"And who are you?" Hart interrupted.

"I am Eloise Hoyle, Executive Assistant to the President," she said. "Miss Hart, your gown doesn't have a hood. We'll present you with a Lakewood hood when we give you the degree." She had a gown on a hanger.

"I'm not wearing that thing," Hart said.

"But ... but this is an academic occasion," Steagall said. "Everyone will be gowned."

"Everyone but me," Hart said, "end of discussion."

"But what will you wear?" Steagall asked.

"What's wrong with this dress?"

"It's an absolutely stunning dress," Nelle Steagall said, "but it's an *evening* dress. Inappropriate for a morning ceremony."

"Jesus, is it still morning?" Hart asked.

"Day time, then, day time," Steagall said in a pleading tone.

"I said 'end of discussion,' " she said. She fumbled in the folds of her dress and came out with a half smoked cigar, which she stuck between her lips and chomped with her teeth. Everyone in the office was abashed. The Steagalls were mortified. There was a long, dumbfounded silence in the room, broken only by Brasfield Finch's burst of delighted laughter.

Dr. Rock Trilling lined up the procession on the quad. He had a stiff military bearing and carried a heavy bronze mace. The seniors were first, most of the boys lined up in jackets and ties, the girls in Sunday dresses, all holding their folded gowns and caps in front of them. They were followed by the faculty, beginning with the full professors on down to the instructors at the very end. That's where, according to the memo she had received from Dr. Rock, Lily would be.

Lily and Willow walked over to the quad from Comer Hall.

Willow joined the senior professors at the head of the line and gave a wave to Lily, who continued on across the clipped grass to the clump of awkward looking instructors bringing up the rear. They were, for the most part, fidgety and timorous. According to the chart that accompanied the memo, Lily was next to Owen Fielder, who was already there. He made a point of ignoring Lily when she walked up. "Jerk," Lily said under her breath, making Owen glance over at her and then look quickly away.

There were buses lining the street between the quad and Woodfin Hall, disgorging hundreds, maybe thousands, of noisy school children. "They'll never get all those kids into Ferguson," someone said. Someone else said, "What'll they do, turn em away?" "Jesus Christ!" said the first. Their teachers were lining them up as if they were going to march right into the auditorium, which was likely already full of parents and townspeople. Most of the students were holding paperback copies of *To Lynch a Wild Duck.* There were buses still arriving, maneuvering for parking spaces; old Officer Puckett was frantically trying to keep some order.

"Everybody wants to see the great Lenora Hart," Owen Fielder said. "They want to touch the hem of her garment. Ha, ha, ha."

Lily saw the dais party emerging from Peterson Hall. Her eye was immediately caught by Lenora Hart's golden dress, vivid and shimmering in the sunlight. It made a stark contrast to the black gowns of the others, even though most of the doctoral gowns were bedecked with colorful stripes of fake fur. They all looked like pruning pea-fowl. The school kids began crowding onto the campus, pointing at the procession and laughing; most of them had probably never seen grown men and women decked out like this. The dais group fell in behind Dr. Rock and his mace and made its way to the very front of the procession. Lily smiled, wondering what might have transpired in the president's office when Lenora Hart refused to wear a gown. She saw Hamner Curbs, swaying along with his signature swagger, and she could see Brass in the bunch, slouching along with his mortar board crooked on the back of his head, his tassel hanging down his back like a ponytail. His very air radiated contempt for the tradition of the march, but Lily was still excited. As the line began to move, she was thrilled to be a part of this culture and heritage that dated back to Mediaeval times, and she wasn't going to let Brass or anyone else spoil her enthusiasm for the adventure.

When they caught sight of Lenora Hart, small factions of the crowd of students began to surge forward. "Hey, Miss Hart!" they were yelling. "Miss Hart!" The dais party kept going, the teachers struggling desperately to keep the huge crowd of students back.

The procession wound up the steps of Ferguson Hall and inside. As Lily neared the doors to Ferguson, she could hear the strains of the gigantic organ mounted on the wall of the auditorium. "Pomp and Circumstance," of course. The organ was played by a woman from the department of music, Betty Lou Larkin, who was fond of joking that she had "the biggest organ in all of Florida!" which never failed to elicit knowing chuckles. Lily followed the line as it moved through the lobby and into the auditorium, whereupon the music swelled mightily.

Down front, the members of the dais party were standing in front of their chairs on the stage, smiling out at the packed auditorium. The notes of the famous walking march blasted around the huge room, ricocheting off the high, rounded ceiling. Behind the dais was a towering, outsized replica of the Lakewood College seal, featuring a lamp of learning with the institution's Latin motto mounted above it: *SAPIENTIA*. Lenora Hart, in her gold rag of a dress, stood next to President Steagall, weaving slightly as if in time to the music. She *was* swaying to the music, Lily realized. And she was holding a small leather satchel that Lily had not noticed her carrying on the quad. This should be good, Lily thought. She had a pretty good idea what was in the satchel.

The march was over, and Betty Lou Larkin launched suddenly into "The Star Spangled Banner," startling everyone. There were some attempts in the audience to sing along, but Betty Lou played it so rapidly it was impossible. After that, the *Alma Mater*, which was played in a calmer, more reverent tone. The seniors gave it a game try, but it was obvious that few of them knew the words. They managed mostly to just hum along.

As the final notes died away and President Steagall approached the lectern with its smaller version of the seal, a cacophonous babble of voices and squeals and giggling sounded from the lobby of the building. The doors, which apparently were locked, rattled in their frames. President Steagall's tassel hung in his face and he frowned and pushed it aside with his fingers. He removed his hat and cleared his throat. "You may be seated," he said. He glared at the back of the auditorium. He then welcomed everyone, commenting to the seniors and their parents that this was their day, when they would be awarded their caps and gowns and be accepted into the sacred fold of academe. He then briefly introduced everyone on the dais.

"Ladies and gentlemen," he went on, "students and distinguished faculty, we are pleased to have with us today one of America's most treasured and cherished writers. The beloved Lenora Hart has graciously consented to speak to our seniors and to us, to give us inspired and inspiring words, such as we find in her remarkable novel, *To Lynch a Wild Duck*, that has made Florida famous around the world. But first, Father Hamner Curbs will lead us in a prayer to the Almighty."

Father Curbs swaggered unevenly forward. He wore a gigantic gold cross on his chest, hanging from a gold chain around his neck. His wispy curly blonde hair was matted from his cap. "The Lord be with you," he said abruptly, and there were a few scattered and muffled "And also with you's" around the auditorium. Dean Wallace punctuated the responses with a loud "And with thy spirit!" that he bellowed from the dais. He glared around as though he were personally annoyed that most of the people in attendance were ignorant of the proper response. Father Curbs looked back at him in surprise, then turned back around and began his prayer. Lily thought he was slurring his words; she had heard a rumor that he was on his way to a drying out place for priests in Miami.

When Father Curbs said the Amen and returned to his seat, the clamor and commotion continued in the lobby. It sounded like bedlam was ensuing. President Steagall came back to the podium and began the ceremony of awarding the academic regalia to the seniors. There was a brief speech by a member of the board of trust, who told the seniors that very soon they would be "commencing" their lives. Then there was much rustling around and quite a few giggles as the students donned their gowns and caps. Lily, who was seated in the very rear of the faculty section, strained to see what was going on down front. They had not had such a tradition at Birmingham-Southern when she had graduated. She didn't know many of the seniors, but there was still something impressive and exhilarating about it, and she wanted to take it all in.

Next, Dr. Steagall was introducing Dean Wallace Jefferson, who would introduce Lakewood's own writer in residence, Brasfield Finch, who would in turn introduce Lenora Hart. Dean Jefferson came bounding to the podium, his voluminous robe heaving about him. He looked like an enormous bird that might take flight.

Lily could tell he eagerly relished his chance at the microphone. He, too, glared at the racket coming from the lobby, then welcomed everyone again. He talked about Lakewood's honored tradition of robing its seniors; he made a few remarks to them, stretching his comments out as lengthily as he could. He then got around to introducing Brasfield Finch. "Our own writer in residence," he said, "who has written some of the greatest novels in American literature." Lily was stunned and shocked at the declaration, but pleased for Brass, until she immediately realized the insincerity of the dean's words. She was certain they made Brass furious. She sneaked a look at him; he was sagging in his chair and seemed to be asleep. She took in Lenora Hart, too, and watched as the woman took a bottle out of the small satchel and poured herself a drink of whiskey, which she proceeded to drink right there on the stage in front of everybody. Even from this distance Lily could see that Dr. Steagall's jaw was tightly clenched and his face was deep red.

When the dean finished his introduction, Finch shuffled to the lectern. Lily could see his jeans and boots sticking out below his gown. Finch slumped over the podium. The din of the pandemonium in the lobby continued. "Can't somebody do something about those infernal barbarians?!" he said into the microphone, eliciting howls of laughter from the audience. There was a loud bang, as of a body hurled against one of the doors, followed by a shrieking teacher's voice: "Stop it!" There was more hilarity, especially among the seniors.

President Steagall came forward and stood next to Finch. "Excuse me, Mr. Finch," he said, and leaned in to the microphone. "Mr. Murphy? Mr. Murphy?" he said. Billy "Big Hoss" Murphy, the dean of men, stood up down front. "Mr. Murphy, will you go out and ... see what you can do?"

"Will do, boss," Murphy said. He headed up the aisle with a fixed, determined demeanor. When he passed Lily, who was seated on the aisle, she could hear the breath whistling in his nostrils like an old bull. The door was opened and then slammed shut with a clanging boom.

"We may now proceed," Dr. Steagall said, nodding to Finch. He returned and took his seat next to Lenora Hart, who had poured herself another glass of whiskey. Steagall could feel his pulse raging in his ears; his blood pressure must be over the mountain. He had never in his life expected such indignity as this. He tried to take a deep breath; the packed auditorium swam before his eyes. Finch began to speak, but Steagall could hear only the ruckus ensuing beyond the doors. He had had Eloise Hoyle send letters to all the high schools and Jr. High schools in the area, inviting them to come and bring students to meet Lenora Hart. She must have sent them to every school in the *state*! They had sent *bus-loads* of students, which Lakewood College was not at all prepared to accommodate. He wished he had instructed "Big Hoss" to herd them on to the gym. He shuddered. *That* could be a disaster. The caf was setting up tables of snacks and punch for the reception, along with a table where Lenora Hart could sit to autograph copies of her novel. Doodles Bookstore had ordered two hundred copies. God, this is a total catastrophe.

"... never expected in my wildest dreams that I would be called upon to introduce Lenora Hart ..." Finch was saying. Steagall crossed his fingers. Finch wouldn't! Oh, yes he would! Steagall knew he should have known better, but when the governor had declined, he had asked Brasfield to introduce her, never even imagining that the man would do other than the gentlemanly thing. After all, Finch was their writer in residence, and he should be expected to show the common courtesy of one writer to another, even though he had acted so ugly about Miss Hart in Steagall's office. He wouldn't dare choose this occasion to utter those distasteful, nasty words again. Steagall should have known better.

"She is a charlatan, a phony," Finch said.

"Here! Here!" Hart said next to Steagall. She was holding up her glass in a toast to the audience. A ripple of murmuring spread over the crowd. There was a rustling of uneasiness.

"I said many years ago," Finch went on, "in an essay in *The Sewanee Review*, that her novel was juvenile pabulum, and I stand with that assessment today."

"What the hell?!' someone shouted. It was one of the seniors' fathers. There was a clamor of agreement around the auditorium. "Who *is* this guy?!" another shouted.

Finch continued. "The shallowness of Lenora Hart's one single novel is surpassed only by the ignorance of her many admirers, who wouldn't know a good novel if it jumped up and bit them on the ass."

There was a chorus of boos.

"That is *enough!*" Dean Wallace said, leaping to his feet.

"So I give you," Finch said, with a wave of his arm, "Miss Lenora Hart, America's sweetheart, America's most beloved writer."

Lenora Hart!"

There was a burst of wild applause. Miss Hart moved unsteadily forward. There was a series of shrill wolf whistles. (Ironic, Lily surmised.) Hart slammed her glass down on the podium, which the mic picked up and amplified like a cannon shot. People were on their feet, still applauding. There were more whistles. Some of the seniors threw their mortar boards into the air. John Steagall was annoyed by this gesture and made a mental note to remind the seniors that they were fiscally responsible for their garb.

When the applause died down, Lenora Hart looked back at Finch, who had resumed his seat. "Thank you, son of a bitch!" she said. She turned back toward her audience. "Very nice," she said, "wasn't that a nice introduction?" There was a shrill feedback sound from the speaker system. Hart slapped the mic. "What's wrong with this fucking thing?" she said. There were guffaws from the seniors. Dean Wallace came forward and adjusted the mic for her.

"That just goes to show you," Hart said, "that you can't believe one damn thing your fancy pants English professors tell you. They probably told you that Shakespeare was a queer, didn't they?" There were gasps from parents and knowing chuckles from the seniors. "They'll fill your head with a lot of liberal crap," she said. "Most of the professors on this campus don't know their asses from a hole in the ground! Especially those so-called *English* professors with their asinine essays in *The Sewanee Review* that nobody ever reads but other so-called English professors. *Billions* of people, I mean *billions*, have read *To Lynch a Wild Duck*, and loved it, and most of them never even heard of the fucking *Sewanee Review!*" Lily wished that she was sitting next to Willow, so they could exchange glances. She could imagine what Brass would say about all this. He was still slouched in his chair, his eyes closed. Dean Wallace and President Steagall were squirming in their chairs with mystified looks on their faces. Willow would say they looked as though they didn't know whether to shit or go blind. Lily chuckled to herself. Most of the instructors around her were listening with rapt attention.

"I have to talk loud to be heard over those unruly brats," Hart was saying, her mouth close to the mic. The uproar in the lobby grew more deafening. The students had started up a chant: "We want Hart! We want Hart!" "Who *are* those little shits?" Lenora Hart asked.

"They are your *admirers*," shouted Finch.

There was another loud bang on the doors. Lenora Hart threw her arms into the air. "I don't know what they want," she growled, "I don't sign books. If I signed that many books, my hand would fall off."

She began to rummage in the leather case, causing the lectern to wobble and screech on the floor. "What's wrong with this fucking thing?" she said, yanking at the podium. She pulled the bottle of Jack Daniels out of the satchel and held it up to the spotlights over the stage; she peered through the bottle at the lights. "Only half full," she said. "Frank! We need another bottle!"

"Yes m'am!" Frank stood up down front. He moved quickly up the aisle.

"In the meantime," she said, "no use wasting time." She turned the bottle up and gurgled a long drink. "Ahhh," she said, shaking her head and smacking her lips. "That puts hair on your fucking chest!" There was laughter from the seniors, a generous bubbling of merriment that warred with the grumbling and growling from the rest of the audience. As she attempted to cram the bottle back into the case she lost her balance and grabbed the shaky lectern, which teetered for a moment at the edge of the stage before it went crashing into the orchestra pit. The mic was still attached, and there was a hugely magnified clattering on the concrete floor of the pit.

Dr. Steagall and Dean Jefferson both leapt to their feet.

There were two sets of double doors at the back of the hall and Dr. Steagall could see them shaking in their hinges. Just as he was about to turn to Wallace Jefferson and observe to him that he thought the doors might give, they swung open. Standing in one was Officer Puckett; in the other was "Big Hoss" Murphy. Both men held their arms out to the side in a vain attempt to block the entrance. Streaming around them were students, all with copies of *To Lynch A Wild Duck*. "We can't hold em out!" Officer Puckett shouted above the din. The students flowed down the aisles, babbling and squealing and giggling.

"What the fuck!" Lenora Hart said loudly.

Dr. Steagall was horrified and panicked at this development. "Do something, Wallace," he said to the dean.

"What the hell can I do?" Jefferson said. He tried to fix a grin on his face. "Smile, John," he said, "these are prospective students."

"God help us," Steagall said.

The first of the students had reached the stairs up to the stage. Several senior boys had taken it upon themselves to help and they were in the aisles, in their new graduation gowns, pushing and shoving the high school students.

The students were fighting back; several burly football types were throwing punches.

The senior boys' black gowns flapped around them in the melee.

There were screams and shrill laughter from the girls.

"Jesus H. Christ!" Steagall said.

"Tell me about it," said Hamner Curbs from the other side of Dean Wallace.

A number of parents and townspeople—and others who had journeyed to see Lenora Hart—joined the high school students in storming toward the stage. Most of them had copies of *To Lynch A Wild Duck*. A teacher, a tall middle aged woman in a brown suit, led the charge up the steps.

"Block those people!" Lenora Hart shouted. She then backed away toward the rest of the dais party. "Frank!" she said. Frank ran up the steps to the stage, pushing students aside as he came. He stopped at her side. He assumed a defensive posture, his burly arms out to his sides. He held an unopened bottle of whiskey, which he wielded by its neck like a billy club.

"They just want to see Miss Hart," the teacher said, "and get her to sign their books." The students were bunching up behind her. They were staring around her at Lenora Hart, their eyes wide.

"Not a fucking chance," Hart said.

The people and students who had backed up in the aisles began to chant again. "We want Hart, we want Hart!"

"Get off my stage!" John Steagall said to the teacher.

"John ..." Dean Wallace cautioned.

"I said, get off my stage!" Steagall said again.

"Well, I never," the woman said, "we came all the way from Cottondale!"

"Where is Murphy? Where is Puckett?" Steagall pled.

At that point Dr. Rock Trilling stepped forward. "You heard the man!" he said.

"No, we're not moving until we talk to Miss Hart," the woman said. She planted herself defiantly on the stage.

"I said MOVE!" Trilling said. When the woman didn't budge

he loosed the mace from his arms and, gripping it, swung it like a baseball bat. It missed the woman and slipped from his fingers and went wheeling into the orchestra pit after the crushed podium, where it clanged loudly on the concrete floor. It must have landed near the still-live mic. There were screams of alarm all around.

"What are you *doing*?!" screeched Dr. Steagall. "What has got into you?!"

"Just doing my job," Dr. Rock said.

By then "Big Hoss" Murphy and Officer Puckett had arrived on the stage. They, together with Dr. Rock, formed a wall, behind which the others moved quickly into the wings. Lenora Hart looked shaken, Dr. Steagall was wringing his hands and Dean Wallace was snorting through his nose. Brasfield Finch convulsed with laughter. He howled. He snatched the bottle from Frank's hands.

"Hey!" Frank said.

"You owe me a drink, Lenora," Finch said. He turned up the bottle and drank, his Adam's apple bobbing up and down so that his beard wiggled. He wiped his mouth with the sleeve of his gown.

"You won't be able to see the stain with all the others," Lenora said.

"Don't worry about it," Finch said, and, shaking the bottle, sloshed whiskey down the front of her dress, making several dark stains on the gold lamme.

"Hey!" Frank said again.

Finch handed him the bottle. He turned and walked calmly down the steps and out the back stage door. He walked across the grass to the front of the library, then went up the steps and inside. The large front reading room was almost deserted. He went up the stairs to the second floor, where the fiction section was. It was mercifully quiet and peaceful as he walked between the shelves of books. Finch found a carrel in a corner and went in and pulled the curtain. It was dark inside, but he did not turn on the lamp. He relaxed in the reading chair and took a few deep breaths. He was wishing that he'd gone by his office and retrieved his trusty bottle of Chivas Regal. The fact that he didn't have it was the only thing that prevented this from being a perfect afternoon.

SEVENTEEN

Lily was surprised to get a letter from the president's office not only offering her a contract for next year but promoting her to Assistant Professor and placing her on a tenure track. She received a raise of $4,000 a year. She sat at her desk, conflicting emotions floating through her brain. She was not sure at all that she wanted to stay in such an insane place.

On the previous day Lily had participated in graduation ceremonies, which were peacefully calm. All her grades were in and the academic year was wrapped up. The letter from the president, on its lavender paper with the *Sapientia* seal, seemed hot to her touch. She dropped the letter on a pile of blue exam books she had not bothered to read; she had simply looked at the chain of grades after a student's name in her book, quickly averaged them in her head, and given that as the final grade. It seemed unlikely that the final exam would alter that assessment, so why go to the trouble? She was learning.

When she had come in to the quiet and otherwise deserted building she had noticed that Willow was in her office. She walked across the hall and told the older woman about her appointment and raise.

"I told you not to worry, didn't I?" Willow said. She gave Lily a little half hug. "These things generally have a way of working themselves out," she said.

"But … but," Lily said, "what did I do to warrant this? I mean, I've not published anything or stuff like that. I mean, I didn't *apply* for it or anything."

"You're not complaining, are you?" Willow said. "Come, come, Lily, don't look a gift horse, as they say."

"I guess I'm just suspicious. I don't trust those people. I mean, it's like it came out of the blue."

"It did, dearie. That's the way things happen in academe."

"They do? After all that complicated process and—I don't mind admitting to you, Willow—my evaluations were not all that great and I was just worried that I'd get renewed for another year."

"You were competent, Lily. You kept your nose clean."

"Well, *moderately* so, I guess," Lily said.

Willow looked at her out of the corners of her eyes and actually blushed. "You needn't worry, Lily," Willow said.

"I'm not worried." Lily shook her head. "It's been quite a year," she said.

"Just another year, dearie. They all run together after a while."

Lily took note of the fact that, even though the summer break had started, Willow was working. She had lecture notes and several textbooks scattered on her desk.

"What are you going to do this summer?" Lily asked, anticipating the answer would simply be "work."

"I'm going to England for a month," Willow said, "to do some research and some traveling."

"With a friend?" Lily asked.

"Mercy no," Willow said, "alone and happy. I'll be working on my Georges Sand book. I suppose you'll be working on your Morrison book."

"Hardly 'book,'" Lily said.

"You never know. You are a bright young woman, Lily. I have no doubt it'll be an excellent dissertation, and chances are someone will want to publish it."

"I doubt it," Lily said.

"Don't put yourself down. *I* believe in you, Lily."

"Even if no one else does?"

"Oh, bosh. I didn't mean that at all. The administration of Lakewood College obviously believes in you, don't they?"

"I don't know. They all seem out to lunch."

"That they do, dearie, but even a blind squirrel finds an occasional acorn. They've done a good thing in promoting you, even if they don't know it themselves. If you keep at this long enough, you'll learn to laugh at them like I do. It's the only way to deal with administrators."

"That's the thing," Lily said, "I don't know if I want to 'keep at it.'"

"You mean you're considering not coming back?"

"I don't know. I'm just having second thoughts. I don't know if this is what I want to do with the rest of my life."

"Well, dear, give it another year. If you're not dedicated to being a scholar, then you probably shouldn't be here. But give yourself time to find out."

It was a temperate early summer day, and Lily decided to walk to Brasfield Finch's apartment. She strolled across the campus and down the tree shaded street; the afternoon was warm but the heat of the season had not yet settled in.

She rang the doorbell to Brass's condo. He came to the door dressed in a pair of baggy khaki shorts and a sleeveless black T shirt.

"You're not in uniform!" she said.

"No," he said, "these are my summer writing clothes."

"Where's your hog?" she asked.

"My what?"

"Your motorcycle," she said, "your muscle shirt."

"Oh, is that what this is? I'm just going for comfort. Florida summers are quite hot."

"Yes, I know," she said, coming on into the living room. The air was cooled and comfortable. "This is a nice place, Brass," she said, "thanks for having me over." She could see his balcony through the sliding glass doors and beyond that the thick green tangle of live oaks and palmettos and Florida grass.

"The pleasure is mine, dear," he said. "What will you have to drink?"

"I think I'll have a vodka martini, if you have the fixins," she said.

"Who are you talking to? Of course I have the 'fixins,' as you put it in your charming Alabama drawl, I always have the 'fixins.' I'll join you."

"I didn't think you were a martini man," she said.

"Like Will Rogers, I never met a drink I didn't like," he said. "I keep my vodka and my vermouth in the refrigerator, so I don't have to use ice. Nothing worse than a watery martini."

"But you always drink Scotch," she said.

"Yes, that is my drug of choice," he said, "however, I love a good martini when I have the time to mix one. Or, in this case, two. But we won't stop with one apiece."

"Of course not."

He made the martinis in a small glass pitcher with a glass stirrer. "Dry? And dirty?" he asked.

"Yes, on both counts."

When they had their drinks they went out to the balcony. The sun was behind them and it was shady and pleasant. They sat looking out over the verdant and lush Apalachicola River basin. The air was sweet and fresh.

214

"You ever see alligators?" she asked.

"All the time," he said.

She relaxed against the cushions, stretching her legs out. She was wearing shorts; if they sat there long enough, she might get some sun on her legs. She sighed contentedly.

"I love Florida," she said, "I may never leave."

"Oh, you'll leave, Lily," he said, "you'll keep going."

"What an odd thing to say," she said. "I was just telling Willow that I might not make teaching my life's work."

"I suspected as much," he said. "You are too fine a person for such drudgery."

Just then a large seabird—she thought it was a pelican, but she wasn't sure—circled out over the thicket and settled in at the edge of a small stream. They watched it in silence for a few moments.

"He's a long way from home," Lily said. "Lost in a strange land."

"He is," Finch said, "but he'll make do."

She looked at Finch. He sat sprawled in the chair, his winter-white legs splayed in front of him. He wore frayed canvas shoes instead of his boots, and his graying beard was tied with an old strip of typewriter ribbon. He looked back at her, his eyebrows bushy and his eyes twinkling.

"You are one hell of a woman, Lily," he said.

"Thanks, Brass," she said.

THE END

photo: Loretta Cobb

William Cobb was for thirteen years Writer-in-Residence at The University of Montevallo before he retired to write full time. He has published eight critically acclaimed novels: *Coming of Age at the Y, The Hermit King, A Walk Through Fire, Harry Reunited, A Spring of Souls, The Last Queen of the Gypsies, A Time To Reap, Wings of Morning*, and collections of short stories, including *Somewhere In All This Green,* which won the Alabama Library Association Fiction Book of the Year Award in 2000. Cobb has also written for the stage; three of his plays, *Sunday's Child, A Place of Springs,* and *Early Rains* were produced Off-Broadway in New York. He has held writing fellowships from The National Endowment for the Arts and the Alabama State Council on the Arts. He lives in Alabama with his wife, Loretta, a short story writer and novelist.